The Sound of Sleighbells

More Christmas romance from Janet Dailey

Published by Kensington Publishing Corp.

JANET DAILEY

The Sound of Sleighbells

ZEBRA BOOKS
Kensington Publishing Corp.
www.kensingtonbooks.com

ZEBRA BOOKS are published by

Kensington Publishing Corp.
900 Third Avenue
New York, NY 10022

All Kensington titles, imprints, and distributed lines are available at special quantity discounts for bulk purchases for sales promotion, premiums, fund-raising, and educational or institutional use.

Special book excerpts or customized printings can also be created to fit specific needs. For details, write or phone the office of the Kensington Sales Manager: Kensington Publishing Corp., 900 Third Avenue, New York, NY 10022. Attn. Sales Department. Phone: 1-800-221-2647.

Zebra and the Z logo Reg. U.S. Pat. & TM Off.

First Kensington Books hardcover printing: July 2023
First Kensington Books trade paper printing: October 2023
First Zebra Books mass market printing: September 2024

ISBN-13: 978-1-4201-5109-1
ISBN-13: 978-1-4201-5113-8 (eBook)

10 9 8 7 6 5 4 3 2 1

Printed in the United States of America

With many thanks to Elizabeth Lane for
introducing me to Branding Iron!

Chapter One

Branding Iron, Texas
November 1998

"Mommy, when is Daddy coming home? Will he be here for Christmas?"

As she tended the bacon on the stove, Ruth McCoy felt the words tear at her heart—not for herself but for her four-year-old daughter, who couldn't understand what her father had done or why he was gone.

Nearly a year had passed since Ed's abuse had turned deadly dangerous. He'd gone to prison, and Ruth had filed for divorce. He would never harm his family again. But little Tammy had been too young to understand. She was still too young.

"When is he coming home, Mommy?" Tammy tugged at Ruth's shirttail.

"He isn't coming home, silly. He's in jail!" Six-year-old Janeen strutted into the kitchen, dressed in her Saturday play clothes. "He did something bad, and he's never coming home again!"

"No! Don't say that!" Tammy burst into tears. Sobbing, she ran out of the kitchen.

"Janeen, you know it hurts your sister's feelings when you talk like that," Ruth scolded gently.

"Then why does she keep asking? She knows it's true."

Ruth sighed as she turned the bacon in the big cast-iron skillet. Ed had never abused his daughters, and they hadn't been there on the day he was arrested. Each of the girls had her own way of dealing with the loss of their father. Janeen's way was to act as if she didn't care. But Ruth knew that she was as deeply affected as her sister.

With Christmas less than six weeks away, Ruth was desperate to make the holiday a time of healing. She'd set aside some money for a tree and some presents. But would that be enough? Where would the joy come from?

"Can I please have an Eggo, Mom?" Without waiting for an answer, Janeen opened the freezer, found the frozen waffles, and popped one in the toaster.

Count your blessings, Ruth admonished herself as she set a carton of eggs on the counter next to the stove. She had food on the table and a home for her family. She had a good job as custodian at the local elementary school. Her three children were healthy, and Ed was out of their lives. After a psychiatric examination had determined his fitness to stand trial on charges of kidnapping and attempted murder, he'd been sentenced to thirty years behind bars, without parole.

Things were all right now, maybe as good as they'd ever been. But for a woman whose life had been one long string of disasters, worry was second nature.

She was draining the bacon on a paper towel when she heard the sound of a squeaky bicycle wheel outside. That would be her fifteen-year-old son, Skip, coming home from his morning paper route. His footsteps crossed the porch, and he opened the door.

"That bacon smells great. I'm starved." He was a handsome boy, with light brown hair and blue eyes. His face was ruddy with cold. Since his stepfather's arrest, Skip had become the man of the family. He took his responsibilities seriously. Maybe too seriously, Ruth thought.

"Eggs over easy?" she asked.

"You bet. And maybe Janeen can toast me one of those Eggos."

"Toast it yourself," Janeen said. "Just because you're a boy, that doesn't mean I have to wait on you."

Skip just grinned. "I'll go wash up."

"Make it quick. And tell Tammy that breakfast is almost ready." Ruth cracked two eggs into the sizzling bacon grease. The electric stove was old, as was the house. But it was just a rental until she could sell her land and buy something nicer.

After Ed had dynamited their old farmhouse— with Skip and his friend Trevor barely escaping death inside—she'd counted on the insurance claim to pay for a new place. Then the letter had come from the insurance company. Since her husband had blown up the house himself, the loss had been ruled as arson, which wasn't covered by the policy. Her only recourse was to sell the forty acres of used-up land the house had stood on—land that had been in her family for three generations. So far, there'd been no offers.

"Mom, can I go to Trevor's today?" Skip asked as the family sat down to breakfast.

"Sure. I've got some errands to run after breakfast. Can I drop you off? It's chilly out."

"Thanks. That would be great."

Ruth was grateful her son had such a good friend. They'd been neighbors until the explosion last year. Now, with Ruth's move to town, and with Skip in high school while Trevor was in ninth grade, it was harder for them to spend time together. But they managed, usually on weekends.

With breakfast out of the way, Ruth took a few minutes to make herself presentable before going out. She'd never fussed much with her appearance. But now that she was single and had her own money, it was a pleasure to indulge in some good makeup and get her reddish-brown hair cut in a fashionable pixie.

She'd been a pretty, popular girl in high school before getting pregnant by her biker boyfriend.

Like Ed, Judd had gone to prison. She sure could pick them, she thought wryly. She'd never even told Judd about the baby. Instead, she'd found Tom Haskins—a good man who'd wed her while she was pregnant with Skip. They'd lived in Cottonwood Springs, where Tom had found a job managing a service station. She'd counted herself lucky—until her husband was killed in a robbery, leaving her with a young son to raise alone.

A few years later, still in Cottonwood Springs, she'd been working as a waitress when she'd met Ed McCoy. They'd married and moved back to the small farm she'd inherited outside Branding Iron. Good old Ed with his pretty words, volatile temper, and rock-hard fists. At least he'd given her two beautiful daughters.

No more men, Ruth vowed as she broke more eggs into the pan. Maybe not ever. Three tragic relationships were enough. Now that she was free, she would focus on what mattered most, building a better life for herself and her family.

Skip gazed out the car window at the bleak November countryside as his mother drove him to the Chapman ranch. He looked forward to visiting there. Trevor's father and stepmother treated him like family. And he always had a good time with his best friend—the friend who'd refused to leave him and flee to safety when Ed was threatening to blow up the old house.

Tammy and Janeen, too young to be left at home, sat in their boosters in the back seat. Dressed in their new winter coats, they'd been singing Christmas songs most of the way. But now they were quiet.

"Do you and Trevor have something special planned for the day?" Ruth asked as she turned off the highway onto the unpaved ranch road.

"Maybe. Trevor said something about visiting a neighbor's ranch. He's a man who makes custom saddles. Trevor says he's made saddles for movie stars, athletes, and lots of other famous people. I'd like to see how he does it."

"What's the man's name?" The car slowed as if Ruth had taken her foot off the gas pedal. Skip noticed how her voice changed. It sounded tense and uneasy.

"Sorry," he said. "Trevor told me, but I can't remember. He owns that big Angus ranch a couple of miles from our old place. And he drove the sleigh in last year's Christmas parade. Trevor says he keeps pretty much to himself, but he's nice once you get to know him."

"Well, don't trouble him too much." Ruth pressed the gas pedal again, and the old brown station wagon jolted ahead along the bumpy lane. "People who keep to themselves tend to have a reason for it."

"Like what?"

"Never mind that. He just might not be everything Trevor thinks he is. That's all."

Skip was about to ask her more when she swung the car through the ranch gate and pulled up to the Chapman house. Trevor's stepmother, Jess, had come out on the porch.

"Hello, Ruth," Jess said, as the side window came down. "Have you and the girls got time to come in? Maggie's here. We were going to make cookies this morning."

"Oh, please, Mom!" the girls chimed in from the back seat. They adored Trevor's eight-year-old cousin, Maggie.

"I'd love to, but I've got shopping to do and errands to run," Ruth said. "If I turn my girls loose in your house, they won't want to leave. I'll have a dickens of a time getting them back into the car."

"Well, why don't you leave them here while you do your errands?" Jess asked. "I know they love Maggie. Let them have fun while you take some time for yourself. Drive to the mall. Buy yourself a nice lunch. Do some early Christmas shopping. You can pick them up this afternoon when you come to get Skip."

"That would be asking too much, Jess. My daughters can be a handful. I can take them with me."

"Please, Mom!" The girls had unbuckled their booster seats and were tugging at their mother's coat. "Please, we'll be as good as gold!"

Jess laughed. "I think you've been outvoted, Ruth. They can help Maggie and me make cookies and watch videos afterward. You come on in, too. I'll make us some coffee."

Ruth relented and let the girls out of the car. Jess was a good friend—pretty much her only friend. It wasn't easy to bond with other women when you were being controlled and abused at home or when your husband was known to be in prison. Jess was the youth counselor for the school district. She'd supported Ruth and her children through the difficult period of Ed's trial and the divorce. She'd even helped Ruth find her job. Ruth would always be grateful—especially for Jess's genuine friendship.

With the girls skipping ahead of her, Ruth followed her friend into the remodeled ranch house. It was the kind of place Ruth had always dreamed of having—a cheery fireplace, a few live plants, shelves of books and a rack of music CDs, rugs, and cushions in warm colors. Trevor's border collie, Glory, dozing in front of the fire, raised her head, then settled back to sleep.

One door off the hallway was closed. "Cooper asked me to give you his best," Jess said. "He's bucking a deadline on one of his magazine articles. But don't worry, kid noises never bother him. Have a seat on the sofa. I'll have some coffee ready in a jiffy."

"Oh, please don't bother," Ruth said. "I need to be going soon. I just wanted to spend a minute with you and make sure the girls were settled."

"Your girls will be fine. They've already found Maggie in the kitchen. But as long as you're leaving soon, maybe you can drop the boys off at the Rankin place. They were planning to walk, but the wind is chilly out there. I can pick them up in a couple of hours."

"Of course." Ruth felt as if a clock had stopped inside her, the gears jammed and refusing to move. She forced a smile. "What will the boys be doing there?"

"When he last came by, Judd mentioned needing to clean out his storeroom. When Trevor offered to help, Judd took him up on it. Trevor's excited because, as he says, there's some cool stuff in that storeroom. And he's hoping Judd will show him some of his work."

"So he's not expecting Skip to come along?" Ruth forced her tight throat to form words.

"Not unless Trevor told him. But he won't mind. He's a nice man—although he's not very sociable. We only got to know him after he rented our pasture for his cows."

"All the same, Skip wasn't invited. Maybe I should just take him home and bring him another time."

"Nonsense. It'll be fine, Ruth. Skip can help with the work."

The debate ended as Maggie came bounding into the living room. A redheaded, eight-year-old dynamo, Maggie was the daughter of Big Sam Delaney, former sheriff and now mayor of Branding Iron. Her stepmother, Grace, a teacher, was Cooper Chapman's sister. Among her many talents, Maggie was an enthusiastic cook.

"Hi, Mrs. McCoy." She greeted Ruth with a friendly grin, then turned to Jess. "Aunt Jess, we're almost out of chocolate chips. Do you have any more?"

"Look in the bottom bin of the fridge," Jess said. "I put them there so they'll stay fresh and so nobody will find them and eat them."

"Like Trevor?" Maggie grinned.

"Yes, and like his father. Are Janeen and Tammy okay?"

Maggie nodded. "They're helping. We're having fun. I'll find the chips."

As she danced away, Skip and Trevor came out of the hall, wearing their warm coats, caps, and gloves. "We're ready to go, Mom," Trevor said.

"Okay, but Ruth will be dropping you off while I stay here and supervise the girls."

"I guess that's my cue." Ruth stood and found her keys in her purse. "Let's go, boys. Thanks for taking my daughters, Jess."

"No trouble at all. Remember what I said. Treat yourself. Have some fun. You don't get enough of that."

With the boys in the back seat of the station wagon, Ruth drove out through the gate and made a left turn onto the road that would take her to Judd Rankin's old family ranch.

Ever since learning that her first love was out of prison and back in Branding Iron, she'd avoided any contact with him—not an easy thing in a small town. But Judd had become reclusive, which made it possible. Ruth had kept a strict distance between them for her son's sake as well as for herself. But today, without warning, all her precautions were about to be tested.

Skip had always believed that he was the son of Tom Hastings—the kindly father he remembered from his early childhood. He'd seen the family photos—including one of a proud Tom holding him as a baby. That the two looked nothing alike had never seemed to trouble him.

When Ruth had married Ed, he'd given Skip his name, but Ed had never cared for his stepson. It was the memory of Tom's fatherly love that had kept Skip grounded growing up. What would it do to the vulnerable boy to find out his lineage had been a lie—and that his real father had been a biker who'd killed a man in a street brawl and served five years for manslaughter?

After Judd's arrest, Ruth could have told him about the baby in a visit or a letter. But for the sake of her child, she'd chosen to keep the truth from him. Given the chance, she would make the same choice again.

Now she could only let her son go to Judd and hope that neither of them would discover their connection.

She pulled up to the ranch gate and stopped the car. In the near distance, the rambling brick house, screened by bare cottonwoods, was just visible. "Here we are, boys," she announced. "You can walk the rest of the way."

"It's okay to come up to the house. Then you can meet Mr. Rankin," Trevor said.

"Thanks, Trevor, but I'm in a hurry today. I've got a lot to do." Ruth was trembling beneath her coat. "Maybe another time. Have fun, you two. But remember, you're there to help."

"Thanks, Mrs. McCoy." Trevor climbed out of the car. Skip followed him.

Ruth watched for a moment as the boys headed up the driveway, Trevor, slim and dark, Skip, taller, his body beginning to fill out. Tearing her gaze away, she forced herself to shift gears, turn the wagon around, and leave. She'd feared this day would come. Now that it was here, there was nothing she could do except hope for the best.

From where he stood on the porch, Judd Rankin watched the boys walk up the driveway toward the house. He'd been expecting Trevor. The second boy was a surprise. But Trevor bringing a friend shouldn't be a problem. Cleaning out the storeroom was a big job. He could always use an extra pair of hands.

He'd glimpsed a brown station wagon letting the boys off at the gate, then driving away. Somebody must've been in a hurry—or maybe they didn't want to deal with an ex-convict. That was all right, too. Judd had learned not to take things personally. Other people's attitudes were not his problem.

Trevor waved as he caught sight of Judd on the porch. A good kid. Judd liked him and liked his parents. He'd reserve judgment about the other boy.

Judd greeted the pair as they mounted the porch steps. "Thanks for coming, Trevor. And

I'm glad to meet you, young man." He extended a hand to the new boy. "Judd Rankin's the name."

The boy accepted the shake. His hand was chapped and roughened. "Pleased to meet you, Mr. Rankin. I'm Skip McCoy. My real name is Thomas, after my father, but I've always been Skip."

Judd's throat tightened. When he'd come home to Branding Iron, after five years in prison and a year in Australia, he'd learned that Ruth was married to a man named Ed McCoy. Could this young man be her son?

But no, the boy had said that his father was named Thomas. Probably no connection to Ruth at all.

In prison, Judd had hoped that Ruth would wait for him. Even after his letters were returned unopened, he hadn't stopped wanting her. But she'd wasted no time moving on. When she and her husband had moved back to Branding Iron a few years later, he'd resolved to stay out of her life. Even with Ed McCoy in prison now, that hadn't changed.

"Come on in, boys," he said. "I'll take you back to my workshop and get you started."

Skip followed Judd Rankin through the house. He liked what he saw. Polished wood on the walls and floor—real, not cheap imitation; a big, stone fireplace, copper lamps and fixtures, cushiony, well-worn leather furniture. Books

and magazines were stacked on the coffee table.
The framed western scene on one wall was a
real painting, not a print. And the big-screen TV
was enclosed in a wooden cabinet. If he ever
had the money to build his own place, Skip
thought, this was how it would look inside.

But one thing struck him as strange. There
were no photographs of people anywhere—no
parents, no friends or family, not even a picture
of Judd Rankin himself—a lean, rugged, Clint
Eastwood type who looked as if he'd stepped
out of a cowboy movie.

"Hurry up, Skip," Trevor called over his shoulder. "You're falling behind."

"Sorry, I was just looking around." Skip caught
up. "I really like your house, Mr. Rankin."

"Thanks. It's taken me years of work to get
the place the way I want it. You'll see some of
that work today."

"Are you going to have a Christmas tree?"
Trevor asked.

"I don't celebrate Christmas. When you're
alone, it's just another cold December day."

"You could come to our house," Trevor said.
"My folks would be happy to have you."

"Thanks, Trevor, but not this year. I've got too
much work stacked up. After the holidays, I may
take a trip somewhere. The fishing's supposed
to be good in Costa Rica. But we'll see about
that." He led them through a short breezeway
and unlocked a metal door. "Here we are. Come
on in."

The interior of the barnlike wooden building

was almost as large as the basketball court at the high school. Counters, tables, machines, and tools were organized for making saddles. A selection of beautifully tanned half hides hung from a sliding overhead rack. Their leathery aroma teased Skip's senses as he walked past them. Several unfinished saddles sat on wooden stands that looked like tall sawhorses.

A corner of the building was walled off with a closed door on one side. That would probably be the storeroom Mr. Rankin had mentioned.

"This is where I need your help, boys," he said. "Early on, when I started selling my saddles, I wanted to get them noticed. Some of the people who were interested—rodeo cowboys, barrel racers, small ranchers, and working cowhands—didn't have the cash, so I took items in trade, along with the buyer's promise to tell folks about my work. I've had these things so long that I can't remember where half of them came from.

"I need everything moved out into the open. Then I can go through the items and decide which I should keep, which I should haul off for junk, and which ones to donate for a big charity auction that's coming up in Fort Worth. I'll be here, working with you, in case you have questions or need help with something heavy. Got it?"

"Got it!" Trevor grinned. "This sounds like fun."

Judd Rankin laughed. "You might not think so by the time you've carried everything out. If you need a break, there are sodas in that little fridge over there. You can help yourselves. Ready?"

The boys nodded, eager to start. The door swung open, and they stepped inside.

"Wow!" Skip gasped as he came face-to-face with a mounted buffalo head.

"You'll need help with that. Here, I'll give you a hand. You can call me Judd, by the way. I'm not much for formalities. Here, I'll take one side and you boys take the other. Careful. I think this one is going to the auction."

They lugged the heavy head out onto the floor and laid it faceup on its mounting board. The animal must've been magnificent in life, Skip thought. Now it just looked sad.

They found several rawhide whips and lariats, a handmade bull riding rope, and a framed collection of gold-plated belt buckles. There were some paintings, a bronze statuette of a bucking horse, and a mounted pair of immense cattle horns. They carried out each item as they found it and laid them all on the cement floor. Suddenly, from the back of the storeroom, Trevor gave a shout.

"Oh, no! You can't give this away!"

He came out dragging a tangle of straps, buckles, and jingling bells. Skip recognized it at once. It was the double harness that the horses had worn to pull Santa's sleigh in last year's Christmas parade. In the weeks before, the boys and an elderly neighbor, Abner Jenkins, had finished building the sleigh. Judd had lent the harness for the parade and driven the horses, with Abner playing Santa.

"We're going to need that harness again," Skip said. "We'll need it every time we use the sleigh. Maybe the city can buy it from you, Judd."

"Good suggestion, but I wouldn't accept any money." Judd took the harness from Trevor and laid it out along one side of the floor. "Take a look. We made do with this harness last year, but it was so worn-out that it barely held together for the parade. When I unbuckled it and lifted it off the horses, it almost fell apart. See all the places where it's worn through?"

Skip gazed down at the harness. Judd was right. There were spots where the brass buckles had worn through the leather and were hanging loose, and others where the straps had rubbed and come apart. The bells, mounted on narrow leather strips, were tarnished and coming loose, their fasteners barely holding.

"When I took this harness in trade, I never planned to use it," Judd said. "It was just a way to get one more saddle out there for people to notice. I didn't realize what bad shape the harness was in until I hitched up the horses for the parade last year. I had to stick some places together with duct tape and hope it wouldn't show."

"Can't we mend it?" Trevor asked.

"The leather's too far gone," Judd said. "Even if we could piece it together, the harness wouldn't hold up on the horses, especially if they got spooked or stubborn and needed some firm handling. I think Abner's got an old harness he used for hauling hay. That might do."

"I've seen that harness in Abner's barn," Trevor said. "Abner is the best Santa ever, and the sleigh is perfect. But that ratty old harness would spoil it all. And look at the bells—they still ring but they're not shiny. And the strips could break when we put them on the horses. How can we have a sleigh without sleighbells?"

Judd's frown deepened. Skip could tell he didn't want to make this his problem. But Skip had an idea. Maybe it would help.

"The metal parts of the harness—the buckles and rings—are still good," Skip said. "And the collars would be okay with some polish. Could we just replace the worn leather straps?"

Judd frowned. "We could. But it would take a lot of time. And I have saddles to finish before Christmas."

"We'd help," Trevor said. "Wouldn't we, Skip? I'll bet Maggie would help, too. Hey, we finished the sleigh last year. If we could do that, we can fix a harness."

Skip could tell that Judd was hesitant. He'd be taking on a lot, especially with his own work to finish. And he hadn't planned on a couple of kids hanging around, getting in the way. If he said no, Skip wouldn't blame him.

"Let's put the harness aside while we finish this job," Judd said. "Then we'll talk about it. Don't be too disappointed if I say no. I've got customers waiting for their saddles. They need to come first."

"We understand," Skip said although the look on Trevor's face made him wonder whether he'd spoken for both of them or just himself.

They carried more things out of the storeroom—a silver-plated trophy cup, a moth-eaten buffalo robe, a handwoven Navajo rug, a pair of beaded moccasins, a guitar autographed by Willie Nelson, a pair of sheepskin chaps, a set of mounted moose antlers, an antique shotgun . . .

As Trevor put it, this stash of treasures would make the ultimate yard sale.

At last, the end was in sight. Aside from a few closed boxes, just one large object remained in the back corner of the storeroom. It was loosely covered with a dusty canvas tarpaulin.

"Do you want us to bring that out here?" Skip asked.

"No, leave it," Judd said. "That's not going any-where. It's—"

"Oh, wow!" Trevor had pulled the tarp aside. "This is unreal! A Harley-Davidson Road King!" He ran a hand over the leather seat of the classic motorcycle. "Is it yours, Judd? Do you ride it?"

"Yes, and no." Skip, standing close to Judd out-side the storeroom, noticed the way the man's body tensed as he spoke. "Cover it up and come out here, Trevor. It's a souvenir from another time, that's all."

Entranced, Trevor stared at the bike. "I have a book about motorcycles at home. I love them. What model is it?"

"Never mind, Trevor. I said cover the bike and come out of the storeroom."

"I'll help him." Skip dashed into the room and nudged his friend, who seemed mesmerized by the vintage bike. "Come on, Trevor. Do as he says." He grabbed the edge of the canvas and started pulling it over the bike. Trevor helped him. They finished the job and came out of the storeroom together.

"Those boxes can stay where they are," Judd said. "Let's take a break, and then I'll show you the saddles."

"Have you got any Mexican Cokes in that fridge?" Trevor asked.

"You bet." Judd smiled. "And I think I saw a couple of bottles with your names on them. Help yourselves. I need to check something on my computer. Oh—if you need it, there's a bathroom just inside the door to the house."

He disappeared into what Skip assumed was his office. In the miniature fridge, the boys found glass bottles of Coca-Cola from Mexico.

They popped off the caps. Skip took a deep swallow. "Man, this is good," he said, taking another swig.

"I know. It's sweetened with sugar cane, not corn syrup. I've only tasted these Cokes here. Wish I knew where Judd gets them." Trevor lifted the bottle to his lips again. "And I wish I could have a ride on that sweet motorcycle."

"That's not going to happen," Skip said. "He didn't even like you looking at it. Something about it being a souvenir of another time."

"A man with a mysterious past." Trevor laughed. "Just like in the movies."

"My mother would say that his past is none of our business," Skip said. "I just hope he's willing to help us with the harness. We can't fix it without him."

Chapter Two

After lunch and some early Christmas shopping at the Cottonwood Springs Mall, Ruth picked up her three children at the Chapman Ranch. The girls, who'd left with a covered bowl of homemade cookies, were so tired that they dozed off in their booster seats. But Skip couldn't stop talking about his new friend, Judd Rankin.

"He's got this beautiful home, Mom. And this big workshop, like a warehouse, where he makes saddles—Trevor told me that they sell for thousands of dollars. He showed us the different forms and machines he uses, and the different parts of the saddle. And we got to see the leathers that people can choose from—not just cowhide, but bison and elk and antelope, even ostrich."

"I hope you did some work for him." Ruth

spoke in a flat tone, as if she were reading aloud from a seventh-grade history book.

"We did. We carried a ton of stuff out of his storeroom—not just ordinary junk, but cool things he'd taken in trade—like this huge stuffed buffalo head. He offered to pay us, but we said we wouldn't take money. Instead, he's going to let us rebuild the harness from last year's Santa sleigh. The old one's falling apart. He says it wouldn't be safe to use it on the horses."

Ruth took a moment to let the words sink in. "So . . . you and Trevor will be going back?"

"Uh-huh. He said he'd cut the leather for the new straps, and we could start work the week of Thanksgiving break. If you don't have time to take me, don't worry. I'll figure out a way. I can always ride my bike if the weather isn't too bad."

"Are you sure that's a good idea, son? I mean, Mr. Rankin has his own work to do."

"We know that. But we'll be doing most of the work ourselves. He's going to show us how, and then we'll be on our own. Don't worry, Mom. Judd made it clear that he doesn't have time to babysit us."

"So now you're calling him by his first name?"

"He asked us to."

Ruth felt her stomach clench. Her son might not know the truth about Judd, but the situation was already getting out of control. If she took a stand and forbade him to go back to the ranch, he would want to know why. And she knew better than to lie to him. Skip didn't deserve to be treated like a child.

She held her tongue for the moment, fearing that anything she said about Judd might reveal too much.

"I can tell you're worried, Mom," he said. "But Judd Rankin is a good man. Trevor's folks know him. So does Abner. And his saddles are famous. He's made them for athletes and movie stars and for horse competitions. This year's champion cutting horse wore one of his custom saddles."

"Then I have a different question for you," Ruth said, hoping to change the subject. "Who put you in charge of making sure the harness was ready for the parade?"

He frowned, then shrugged. "I guess we put ourselves in charge. Nobody on the parade committee has said anything about it. They must've assumed the harness would be with the sleigh at Abner's place. We didn't think of it either until Trevor found the harness in Judd's storeroom."

"What about Maggie? Surely, she'd have remembered where it was. Wasn't she the one who organized the first parade last year?"

"She was. And she did a great job, starting a petition for the parade and getting people to help. But the Branding Iron Events Committee's taken it over this year. They didn't even include her. Maggie hasn't said much about it, but I think her feelings were hurt."

"But her dad's the mayor. Couldn't he just put her on the committee?"

"Big Sam wouldn't do that. And I don't think Maggie would want him to. But when we get the harness farther along, and if Judd doesn't mind, we might ask her to come and help us. That way, Maggie won't feel left out."

Ruth sighed. The conversation had circled back to the subject she'd done her best to avoid. "All right, Skip. If you've made up your mind to do this, it's fine. Just don't get carried away. Fix the harness and be done with it. Mr. Rankin isn't there to be your friend. He has work to do and a business to run. The less you interfere with his time, the better. Understand?"

"I do. And you don't need to worry, Mom. I've grown up, and I'm not looking for a father figure."

Ruth's pulse slammed. She swerved the car slightly, righted it, and pretended to laugh. "Father figure? Where did you learn that expression? Was it in that psychology class you're taking?"

"No, I think it came from some stupid sitcom on TV."

"Well, never mind." Ruth changed the subject again. "I need to stop talking and pay more attention to my driving. I'd planned to look in on Abner today. He's alone in that big old house and not getting any younger. Now look what I've done. I've missed the turnoff to his place."

"We're going to Abner's?" Janeen had popped awake in the back seat. "Can we come in with you? We can give him some of our cookies."

"We'll see. I don't want to bother him if he's napping. But first I'll have to turn this car around." Ruth slowed down, pulled off the road, and checked for oncoming traffic before she swung the station wagon around and headed back the other way.

Abner Jenkins, an aging widower, had been a godsend to her family after Ed's arrest. He'd given Ruth and her children a roof over their heads while she found a new place to live. In the interim he'd become like a grandfather to Skip and her girls. He'd befriended Trevor and Maggie as well. And he'd won the hearts of Branding Iron as Santa in last year's Christmas parade.

As Ruth pulled up to the old two-story farmhouse, Abner came out onto the porch. A big man, portly enough to wear the Santa suit without padding, he leaned on a cane as he walked. Butch, his shaggy brown mutt, bounded across the yard. The girls, who'd climbed out of the car, squealed with laughter as the dog licked their faces.

"Hey, Abner, we brought you some cookies!" Keeping a grip on the plastic bowl, Janeen broke away from the dog and raced toward the porch. "See?" She opened the lid. "Maggie helped us make these, and she showed us how, so we can make them at home. You can have all you want."

Abner helped himself to a cookie. "Yum, chocolate chip. My favorite. I'll just have a few of these. You can take the rest home."

"I'll put some on a plate for you." She hurried past him into the house with her sister trailing behind. Ruth and Skip climbed out of the station wagon and followed them onto the porch, a chilly wind whipping at their coats.

"Come on in." Abner held the door for them.

"If you need warming up, I can make you some hot chocolate."

"Never mind, Abner. We're fine." Ruth caught her breath in the entry as the door closed behind them. "I just picked up my children at the Chapmans', and the girls wanted to share their cookies with you." She glanced down at the cane. "How's the knee? Are you favoring it more today?"

"It's paining me some, but it's just the weather. Might be a storm blowing in. Come on into the parlor. I've got a fire going. That'll warm you up." He ushered Ruth and Skip into the next room. Being in Abner's house was like taking a step back into the 1950s—the furnishings and décor were long outdated but cozy. Family photos of Abner's late wife and their children, all married and gone, decorated the walls. Ivory lace curtains hung at the windows. A hand-crocheted afghan lay over the back of the faded sofa. A corner shelf held old children's books, photo albums, old school yearbooks, and other mementos.

An iron stove insert had been added to the redbrick fireplace, which made for more efficient heating. The room was warm and cheerful.

Ruth and Skip sat on the sofa, with Abner facing them in his worn La-Z-Boy recliner. The girls settled by the bookshelf, where they could choose their favorite picture books.

"How are you doing, Abner?" Ruth asked. "I've meant to come by sooner."

"Now, Ruth, you know I'm always glad to see

you and your youngsters," Abner said. "But there's no need for you to check on me. I'm doing just fine. You're not even my first visitor of the day. Alice Wilkins came by to see me this morning."

"Alice? The mayor's wife—I mean ex-mayor's wife?" Ruth pictured the officious woman with her mink coat and Cadillac—which she'd hung on to even after her husband confessed to personal use of public funds and was removed from office.

"One and the same. She's the chairman of the new Branding Iron Events Committee. She stopped by to make certain I'd be available to play Santa for the parade and the ball."

"I hope you said yes."

"I did—although she was so pushy about it that I was tempted to put her off."

"Alice Wilkins." Ruth shook her head. "When I used to clean houses for a living, she was one of my clients—and not my favorite. I know exactly what she's like. And now I know why Maggie isn't on the committee. Alice has never forgiven Sam Delaney for replacing her husband as mayor, or Maggie for being his daughter."

"It's the committee's loss," Skip said. "Maggie's had some great ideas. Without her, we might not even be having a parade. And the Cowboy Christmas Ball would still be just a boring dinner."

"Will you be okay to play Santa?" Ruth asked. "I noticed the way you were leaning on that cane. You're hurting, Abner."

"I'll be fine—though I might need help getting in and out of the sleigh, just like last year. I just hope Judd Rankin will be handling the horses again. He did a fine job of controlling the team in that crowd last year. His skill kept everybody safe, including me. But he might not want to do it again. Judd's a very private person—although I can't blame him for being the way he is. Spending five years in prison will do that to a man."

Ruth stole a glance at her son. Skip's expression had frozen on his face, but he said nothing.

She stood, forcing herself to smile. "I've taken enough of your time today, Abner. I've got things to do, and we don't want to wear out our welcome. I'll come by again in the next few days. Let me know if I can bring you anything. Come on, girls. We need to get going."

"Hold your horses." Abner put up a hand. "If you can stay another couple of minutes, I've got something to ask you. I keep remembering our big Christmas dinner last year and thinking how much I miss having friends around my table. If you don't have other plans for Thanksgiving, how about coming here for dinner? I'd buy the turkey and most of the trimmings if you'd help me cook."

"Oh, say yes, Mommy, please!" Janeen was on her feet, with Tammy clapping her hands. "That would be so much fun!"

"So how about it?" Abner asked. "We could invite some neighbors like last year and have a grand old time."

"We'd love to come." Ruth's answer was easy.

"But I can't speak for the other folks. Trevor's and Maggie's families might have plans of their own."

"Well, if they do, we could celebrate by ourselves. Or I could invite an old friend or two. Hank Miller at the hardware store is alone."

"Then by all means, invite him. The guest list is up to you, Abner. But let's count on it and start making plans. My goodness, Thanksgiving is just a week away. Where does the time go?"

Skip had fallen still after the remark about Judd. After taking leave of Abner, he followed Ruth and the girls out to the car and climbed into the passenger side. Ruth started the engine and headed back down the lane to the main road. As she drove, her son's silence was like a burning fuse. In the back seat, the girls were playing with an old portable radio, changing stations, looking for music they liked. The sound would keep them from overhearing any conversation up front, but for now there was nothing to hear.

At last, Skip cleared his throat and spoke, "Did you know that Judd had been in prison?"

"It's no secret. Most people around here do know—at least, the ones who've been around long enough to remember. If I didn't tell you, it was because I didn't think it was any of my business—or yours."

"What did he do?"

Ruth sighed, the memory like a knife in her flesh. "According to the story, he was out one night with some biker friends. There was a fight with a rival gang. A man he hit fell and struck his head against a curb."

"The man died?"

"Yes. Judd served time for manslaughter." Ruth struggled to block the memory—gripping his leather jacket, begging him not to go out with his wild friends that night. Judd had laughed, climbed onto his motorcycle, and roared off down the street.

"We saw his bike," Skip said. "It was in the storage room, under a canvas. Judd told Trevor to leave it alone. He seemed almost angry."

Ruth's throat tightened. It was hard to believe he still had that vintage Harley. Maybe his parents had stored it for him before they passed away. She forced herself to speak. "So, now that you know about him, are you still going to his place to work on the harness?"

"Sure. Why not?"

"And are you going to tell him what you just found out?" Ruth's hands tightened on the steering wheel as she waited for Skip's answer.

After a moment's thought, he shrugged. "Not unless he asks me. After all, as you said, it's none of my business. And he paid for his mistake."

"That's wise, I suppose." Ruth forced her hands to loosen their grip on the wheel. She felt as if she were walking a tightrope without a safety net, and the slightest misstep could plunge her into disaster.

She'd never wanted this to happen. When Judd had gone to prison and she'd married Tom, she'd closed a door on the past and locked it

tight. Now that door was threatening to burst
open and spill all the old heartbreak out into
the world. And the one who stood to suffer most
was her son.

Judd finished fitting the quilted leather seat,
backed with sheepskin, onto the rawhide-
covered wooden saddle tree. It was an exacting
task, tiring because of the concentration it re-
quired, but satisfying, too, like seeing a work of
art come together piece by piece.

Time tended to fly while he was working. This
saddle was a presentation model, to be awarded
to the all-around winner of a national rodeo
competition. Judd could only hope that it would
be used for work, as his saddles were meant to
be, and not just mounted and set in a display
case.

He'd learned the basics of saddle-making in
prison. After his release, he'd arranged to go to
Australia for a yearlong apprenticeship with a
master saddlemaker. Returning to Branding
Iron, where he'd inherited the family ranch,
he'd sold enough pastureland to set up his own
workshop. The black Angus cattle he raised had
been his financial mainstay at first. Now he was
making more from the saddles. But the beef cattle made for a nice safety net.

Moving away from the bench, he walked
across the floor to stretch his legs and work the
kinks out of his hands. The broken sleigh harness lay strung out where the boys had left it. He

could see where the straps had rubbed thin and where the leather had worn through at the buckles. Making it usable, let alone parade-worthy, was going to take a lot of work.

What had he gotten himself into? Given more time, he might have paid for a new harness and donated it to the parade committee. But finding a ready-made double harness could involve weeks of searching. And since the parade was to be held on December 19—the last Saturday before Christmas—that gave them less than a month to get the harness ready.

With pre-Christmas orders coming due, the last thing he needed was one more project, to say nothing of two teenage boys hanging around the shop, making noise and asking questions. If they wanted that harness in time for the parade, they'd better be prepared to do most of the work themselves.

But he had agreed to cut the leather strips for them. That would mean sacrificing an entire side of cow leather. At least it was for a good cause, he reminded himself. But even that would take all the time he could spare.

The boys appeared to be good kids, polite and respectful. He'd met Trevor last year, along with his family. The new boy, Skip, was a little older and perhaps more levelheaded. He'd seemed interested in everything around the shop. Judd could only hope he wouldn't ask too many questions.

And he hoped Trevor would leave the subject of the bike alone. Judd had almost forgotten about it until the boys had uncovered it in the storeroom. Just seeing it had brought back memories Judd had hoped to bury forever.

Once again, he was flying along the back roads, under a star-studded night sky, the Harley purring between his legs, and Ruth on the seat behind him, her arms circling his waist, her head resting against his back, and her jeans-clad legs fitting behind the curve of his own. They usually wore helmets but had left them off tonight. Her long, mahogany hair fluttered behind her on the wind. She was so beautiful. And she was his. All his . . .

Judd's hand clenched into a fist. Maybe he should just sell the damned bike. He could donate the money to some worthy cause and be done with it—forget that he'd ever owned it.

Forget her.

Ruth's life had been hard, he knew. Back in the day, he'd dreamed of giving her every good thing she deserved. But one reckless moment had killed that dream forever. Five years later, he'd walked out of the prison gates only to learn from old friends that she'd married another man and had a young child. Even now, with her husband in prison, he knew better than to contact her. He was an ex-convict, a branded man, and she had her own life. There could be no going back and picking up where they'd left off.

He'd seen her in town a few times, but always from a distance. She was still beautiful, but she appeared so careworn that it almost broke his heart. Once he'd glimpsed an ugly bruise on her cheek, but the anger that surged in him had no place to go.

Forget her. He had his ranch. He had his work. And he had no need to prove his worth to anybody. Now it was time to stop brooding and get back to the saddle, which sat half-finished on the stand. The pieces had been cut and intricately hand-tooled, but countless hours of trimming, fitting, and sewing remained before it would be finished and ready for shipping.

And meanwhile, there were the new leather strips to be cut for the harness. He might as well do it now, Judd told himself. That would give him one less thing to worry about.

He was examining the sides that hung from the sliding overhead rack when his phone rang. Not many folks had his number—just a few neighbors and business connections. It was most likely a customer waiting on an order.

He strode to the phone and picked up the receiver.

A familiar voice replied to his hello. "Howdy, Judd. This is Abner, your neighbor."

"Hey, Abner. Is everything all right? I hope my cows haven't gotten loose on your property again."

"No, everything's fine. I know what a busy man you are, but I'm calling to offer you an invitation."

"An invitation, you say?" Judd wasn't interested in socializing, but he was curious.

"That's right. Like I say, I know you're busy, but a man's got to eat. I'm inviting you to an old-fashioned Thanksgiving dinner, Thursday afternoon at my place."

* * *

"Have a happy Thanksgiving, Mrs. McCoy." The towheaded fourth grader gave her a grin as he headed for the front door. His plaid wool coat looked as if it had been remade from a larger garment, and his hair appeared to have been cut with sewing scissors.

"Same to you, Robert." Ruth paused in emptying a wastebasket into the trash barrel. The best part of her job was being around the children. She'd memorized the names and faces of every child in the school, and she loved seeing them light up when she recognized them. Having her own daughters here—Janeen in first grade and Tammy in preschool—made her life easier as well. After school, with permission, they could wait in the faculty room until she was ready to go home.

With the holiday coming tomorrow, school had been dismissed at noon. Students and staff were going home early. But Ruth still needed to leave the building ready for Monday. She'd emptied the wastebaskets and scrubbed the restrooms and was headed for the utility closet to get the floor polisher when Grace Delaney, who taught second grade, passed her in the hall, wearing her coat and carrying her purse.

"Goodness, Ruth, you're going to be the last one out of here. It hardly seems fair."

"Maybe not, but it beats having to come back on the weekend," Ruth said. "Abner mentioned he was going to invite you for Thanksgiving dinner. Has he called yet?"

"Yes, but we can't make it," Grace said. "Sam's cousin in Lubbock is hosting a big family reunion. We'll be taking Maggie and driving there tonight. But I believe Cooper's family is going to Abner's."

"Oh, that'll please Skip. He'll enjoy having Trevor there. I won't keep you any longer, Grace. You have a safe trip, now."

As she ran the polisher over the floor, Ruth's thoughts skipped ahead to the list in her purse. Abner had given her his credit card to pick up what they needed for dinner. He'd offered to go himself, but with his arthritic knee, Ruth knew he'd have a hard time walking the aisles. She'd talked him into letting her go in his place.

The new Shop Mart, south of town, should have most of what she needed, including a fresh turkey. But pies and rolls from Stella's Bakery on Main Street were a must. Since she'd had no time to order ahead, she would go there first and hope they weren't sold out. If they were, she'd have no recourse except to buy the mass-produced frozen ones at the store.

Ruth finished her work, locked the school doors, loaded her girls into their boosters, and drove downtown. Main Street had been cordoned off to vehicles while city workers strung colored lights back and forth over the street, anchoring them to the lampposts. More lights were going up on the tall blue spruce in the park. On Friday, all the lights would come on, signaling the start of Branding Iron's Christmas season.

Ruth parked on a side street, took her girls by the hands, and walked around the corner to the bakery. Petite, blond Wynette Winston, who managed the business, was married to Branding Iron's young sheriff. Last year she'd been a Christmas bride. This year she was due to become a Christmas mother.

"Hello, Ruth!" Her belly was straining the buttons of her pink smock, but she was as bubbly and cheerful as ever. "And I see you've brought your young ladies. How would you girls each like a sugar cookie?"

"Yes, please." Janeen held out her hand, accepted two cookies, and gave one to her sister. "Thank you, Mrs. Winston," she said.

"Such nice manners." Wynette smiled. "What can I do for you, Ruth?"

"I know it's late, but I'm hoping you have some dinner rolls and pies left."

"We're sold out. But I have a message for you. Jess Chapman came in early this morning and picked some up. She said, in case you came in, to tell you she'll be bringing them to Abner's tomorrow."

"Oh, thank goodness!" Ruth exhaled with relief. "I suppose you'll be having dinner with Buck's family. They must be excited about the baby—it's a boy, right?"

"Right. Buck's sisters already have little ones, so he'll have plenty of cousins growing up." She pulled down her smock where it had begun to ride up over the bulge. "The doctor says everything looks good. I'm hoping the little guy will stay put until Christmas. But every day gets harder. I feel like a big, lumbering cow."

"You? Never. You're radiant, Wynette."

"For that, you deserve a treat." Wynette passed her a sugar cookie like the ones she'd given the girls. "You ladies have a great holiday."

Ruth loaded her daughters into the station wagon and drove to Shop Mart. The big-box store was packed with shoppers, every aisle a traffic jam of carts. Fulfilling her list and getting through the long line to the cash register took almost two hours.

At last, she had everything she needed. But by then, the girls were tired and hungry. She'd planned to drive out to Abner's place and unload the groceries there, to have them ready and waiting in the morning. But she was worn-out, and with two whiny little girls in the back seat, it hardly seemed worth the trouble. She could just leave the bagged groceries locked in the back of the station wagon. With the cold weather outside, everything should be fine, even the turkey.

In the morning, she would get up early and leave for Abner's place. Skip could watch the girls at home while she unloaded the groceries, got the turkey stuffed and in the oven, and started on the rest of the fixings. Once everything was safely underway, she would take a break, drive home, freshen up, and fetch her children. If Jess arrived early to help, that would make the plan even easier. But either way, she could manage.

She pulled the station wagon up the driveway and left it securely locked next to the house. Skip was home, watching a basketball game on TV. The house was warm, the table cleared for supper. Ruth heated some leftover chili and made grilled cheese sandwiches. There wasn't much conversation at the table. Ruth and the girls were tired, and Skip's attention was focused on the ball game.

After supper, she gave the girls their baths, helped them into their pajamas, and tucked them into their beds. "Is tomorrow Thanksgiving?" Tammy murmured drowsily. "Will Daddy be here?"

Ruth's memory flew back to last year's Thanksgiving in their old house. She'd fixed a nice dinner and even helped Janeen make pilgrim and Indian hats out of colored paper and Scotch tape. After the meal, Ed had started drinking, and she'd asked Skip to take the girls out to play with the barn cat's new kittens. By the time Ed passed out, he'd loosened her tooth and left a swollen bruise below her right eye. Ruth had called the sheriff to take Ed away, then told the girls she'd tripped over the rug. Skip, of course, had known better, but there was nothing he could do. Two days later, yet again, she'd dropped all charges and brought Ed home for the sake of their family.

This year, she vowed, everything was going to be different.

"No, sweetheart," she answered her little one. "Daddy won't be coming home. But we're going to have a lovely dinner at Abner's, with turkey and potatoes and pie. Yummy!"

"Yummy!" Tammy smiled as she closed her eyes.

"Mom?" Janeen whispered from the other bed.

"What is it, dear?" Ruth bent over her.

"Can we get a dog for Christmas? Daddy would never let us have one. But we could get one now, couldn't we?"

Ruth shook her head. "I know you want a dog. But we're not allowed to have pets in this rental house. When we find a home of our own, then we'll talk about it. Okay?"

Janeen sighed. "Okay. But don't forget."

"I'm sure you'll remind me. Tomorrow morning, early, I'm going to Abner's to start dinner. I'll come back and get you later. But Skip will be here. So mind what he says."

"Can I make some decorations? We've got orange paper left from Halloween."

"Sure. Sleep tight, now." Ruth bent and kissed her daughter's forehead, then stole out of the room.

Skip was still watching the game. "I'm going to get ready for bed," she told him. "You know the plan for tomorrow. I'll call you from Abner's when I'm ready to come home. Make sure the girls are ready to go."

"Got it." His gaze remained focused on the TV. "Can I go home with Trevor after dinner?"

"We'll see. That'll be mostly up to his parents."

Ruth showered, washed and dried her hair, laid out her clothes for tomorrow, and set the alarm. By then she was ready to end her long day. She was so tired that her head had barely settled onto the pillow before she sank into slumber.

She slept soundly, barely aware of the racket made by the neighbor's dog sometime in the dark hours. Not until her alarm went off at six o'clock did she stir and come fully awake.

Moving quietly, she dressed in jeans and a clean sweatshirt, washed her face, dabbed on a little foundation, lipstick, and blush, and finger-combed her hair into submission. After a quick cup of instant coffee, she put on her coat, checked on her sleeping children, grabbed her purse and keys, and stepped out the front door onto the porch.

The morning wind was bracing. Sullen clouds roiled across the sky, promising a gloomy day, maybe even a storm later on. Tugging her thin trench coat around her, she made her way down the steps, crossed the winter-brown lawn to her station wagon—and stopped short. A sickening sensation welled in her stomach.

Shards of broken glass from the rear window littered the ground behind the open tailgate. Inside, the rear compartment of the wagon was empty. The bagged groceries she'd bought last night were gone.

Chapter Three

Ruth stared at her pillaged vehicle. She tried to tell herself that this was a bad dream. But then reality crashed in. This was no dream. She had Thanksgiving dinner to prepare and not a morsel of food. Everything she'd purchased last night was gone.

Whoever had broken into her station wagon must've had a desperate need. At least some other family wouldn't go hungry today. But what was she going to do now?

There was only one answer to that question. She would have to buy everything again and get it to Abner's in time to cook the meal.

Fortunately, the list she'd made was still in her purse. And Shop Mart would be opening at seven o'clock. There was still time to save the day. But one problem remained.

Abner had given her his Visa card to pay for the food. She still had the card in her wallet. But there was no way under heaven she would allow her friend to be charged a second time—especially since the loss of the groceries had been her own fault. She would pay for everything herself—easier said than done.

Two years ago, Ed had declared bankruptcy to clear his debts. Since Ruth's name had been included in the bankruptcy, she couldn't qualify for a credit card of her own. She would have to write a check—and with payday four long days off, her account was down to eleven dollars and forty-three cents.

Since the divorce, Ruth had been scrupulous in the handling of her finances. But this morning she could only write the check and hope it wouldn't clear the bank until Monday. If the check bounced, she would just have to pay the fine and accept the blot on her record.

Shivering in the chilly wind, she closed the tailgate and drove to Shop Mart. By the time she arrived, the big-box store was open. There were several cars and a black pickup in the parking lot. At least the aisles wouldn't be crowded this morning.

Inside the store, she found the list in her purse and grabbed a cart. One of the wheels thumped as she pushed it, but she didn't have time to be choosy. Thumping along, she hurried back to the meat counter to get a turkey.

* * *

Judd had yet to decide about Abner's invitation to dinner. The idea of socializing made him edgy. But Abner was a good neighbor, and with his family gone, he was probably lonely. Turning him down without a solid reason could create hurt feelings and strain their relationship.

In any case, Judd didn't want to show up empty-handed. A couple cartons of premium ice cream should be welcome. And if he changed his mind about going, he could save them for later.

He made a habit of shopping early. It involved fewer people, shorter wait times, and less chance of running into someone he knew from the old days. Everyone who'd been around back then would know what had happened and where he'd been, and they'd probably want to talk about it—or they'd just nudge each other and stare. No thank you. Get in, get out, and get going—that was his mode of operation.

He was standing in front of the freezer case, perusing the Ben & Jerry's display, when a rhythmic, thumping sound caught his attention.

At first, he ignored it. But then, as the sound paused, he happened to glance toward the end of the aisle, toward the meat cases. The woman, wearing a well-worn tan trench coat, her short, auburn hair curling over the collar, stood with her back toward him. But Judd recognized her erect carriage and the tilt of her head. He would have known Ruth anywhere.

She turned partway, showing him her profile

as she hefted a plastic-wrapped turkey into her cart. She looked thin and tired, her expression showing strain. She used to say that he could read her like a book. That hadn't changed.

But seeing him would only add to her stress—and to his. As she swung the cart in a different direction, he grabbed two half-gallon cartons of ice cream—vanilla and something else—out of the freezer and strode toward the front of the store.

At this hour, only one checkout was open. The line ahead of him was short, with most people buying just one or two last-minute items. This shouldn't take long. A few more minutes, and he'd be on his way.

But he couldn't stop thinking about Ruth. She couldn't be having an easy time of it, with her abusive husband in prison and three children to support. No doubt she was sacrificing to give them a good Thanksgiving celebration.

What he did next was done without thought, but it felt right. As he presented his Amex card to pay for the ice cream, he spoke to the cashier, a girl barely out of her teens.

"There's a woman in the store—tan coat, short hair—she'll be buying a turkey and some other things. I need to go, but please put her charges on my card. Can you do that?"

"Maybe." The girl looked doubtful. "If she was right behind you, it would be easy. But since there are other people in line, I'd have to run the card again, and you said you needed to leave."

"Then let's do it this way," Judd said. "Just

ring up an extra hundred dollars as cash on this purchase. That should cover what she's buying. But don't tell her who paid. If she asks, it was just a customer, and you don't remember. All right?"

"All right." The girl giggled. "This is fun!"

Judd carried the purchased ice cream out to his truck. Parked a few spaces away was an old brown station wagon with the rear window busted out. The shards clinging to the frame suggested the damage might have just happened.

A few weeks ago, a car like this one had passed him on the way to town. The driver, briefly glimpsed, had been a woman who looked like Ruth. Was this her car? It seemed likely. But he couldn't wait around to find out. He could only hope that having her groceries paid for would make her holiday easier.

As he pulled out of the parking lot, Judd glanced in his rearview mirror. Ruth was just coming out of the store with her loaded cart. She was headed straight for the brown station wagon.

Ruth lifted each bag from the cart and placed it in the rear of her wagon. Broken glass littered the rug she'd laid over the worn-out carpeting. She would clean it up later. Right now, she needed to get to Abner's and start on the turkey.

She would keep quiet about the theft of her groceries. And she certainly wouldn't mention the Good Samaritan who'd paid to replace them. The grocery tally had come to $88.71—a generous gift. Ruth knew she should be grateful. But she was equally puzzled and disturbed. She'd seen no one she knew in the store. Did she look like a charity case? Or worse, was she being stalked? Would someone contact her, demanding a favor in return?

But she was overthinking things. This was a day of giving thanks. She should be grateful for what was likely a simple act of kindness.

It was almost eight when she pulled up to Abner's house. She'd hoped to get the groceries unloaded before he saw the damage to her wagon. But she was out of luck. He was waiting for her on the front porch, his big shaggy dog at his side. By the time she had the tailgate down, he'd propped his cane against a chair and hobbled out to help her.

"Sorry to be late," she said. "I had to stop at Shop Mart on my way here."

"What the hell happened to your back window?" he demanded.

"I'm not sure. It was like this when I came out of the store." It was a half-truth. But she didn't want to upset him.

"Did you call the sheriff?"

"There wasn't time. I needed to get here. Don't worry about it, Abner. I'll just get the window replaced."

"You'd better, or you'll freeze. Feels to me like a storm's blowing in."

"I'll be fine. And I can get these bags in by myself. You need your cane."

"Stop fussing over me." He'd picked up two bags and was headed back to the house. Ruth grabbed the turkey and caught up to steady him as he reached the front steps. She supported him until he'd gained the porch.

"I'll bring the rest," she said. "Then I need to get this turkey stuffed and in the oven."

The morning flew past. With the eighteen-pound turkey stuffed, wrapped in foil, and cooking in the oven, Ruth started on the other dishes—potatoes to be peeled and mashed, green bean casserole, baked sweet potatoes, salads, and homemade cranberry sauce.

Around eleven o'clock, after Abner had gone to his room for a nap, Jess Chapman arrived with the pies and dinner rolls. "Sorry I didn't show up until now," she apologized. "If I'd realized you were doing this all on your own, I'd have come sooner. You look a little frayed, Ruth. Is everything all right?"

Ruth managed a tired chuckle. "I thought I was holding up pretty well. Trust a psychologist to see right through me."

"I saw your station wagon outside." Jess took a potato from the bag and began peeling it. "What happened to the rear window?"

"I found it like that. Somebody must've smashed it." Ruth didn't want to mention the stolen groceries or her mystery benefactor, not even to her friend. "I only have liability insurance on the car. I'm hoping Silas at the garage can find me a replacement from a junkyard. Still, it won't be cheap to fix, and with Christmas coming, the timing couldn't be worse."

"If you need my help, just ask—although something tells me you won't," Jess said. "Your strength has been amazing this past year—what you've been through, divorcing Ed and losing your home, finding a job and a new place to live, and protecting your children the way you have. You'll get through this, too."

"Sometimes I wonder." Ruth began grating the carrots she'd scrubbed to make one of the salads. "Speaking of children, did Trevor tell you that he and Skip are going to rebuild the parade harness at Judd Rankin's place?"

"He did. It sounds like a lot of work, but it will keep the boys busy, and they might even learn a thing or two."

"And you're all right with their spending time there, given his past and all . . . ?" She let her words trail off, fearful of revealing too much.

"With Judd? Yes, Cooper and I are fine with it. We've known Judd for a year. He's worked hard to make a good life for himself. And he's very open about having served time. My only worry is that the boys will get in the way and distract him from his own work."

"So I shouldn't be concerned? Skip's at such an impressionable age, and he's looking for role models. I imagine Trevor is the same."

"I know how protective you are of your children, Ruth. But from what I know of Judd, he'll be nothing but a good example."

Ruth muttered as the grater nicked her finger. She stopped working long enough to get a Band-Aid from the cabinet and wrap the tiny but painful cut. Jess was wise and a good judge of people. But she didn't know about Ruth's history with Judd or his relationship to Skip. Ruth didn't plan to tell her, or anyone else. That was a secret she meant to keep forever.

Working together, the two women finished most of the dinner preparations. The table was set, the salads and other dishes assembled. Only the last-minute tasks waited for the turkey to be done and the guests to arrive.

"Why don't you go home now, Ruth?" Jess said. "You'll have time to rest a little before you bring your children back here for dinner. I can keep an eye on things while you're gone. I hear Abner stirring. He'll be around in case I need help."

"Thanks." Ruth untied her apron and hung it behind the kitchen door. "My feet could use some time off. And thanks for showing up to help, Jess. You've made everything easier—and more fun."

Jess grinned. "Run along now. Get some rest. You deserve it. I'll see you in a couple of hours."

After a quick phone call home, Ruth put on her coat and went outside. Abner had been right about the storm blowing in. The clouds she'd seen earlier were darkening the sky like spilled ink. A frigid wind whipped her coat against her body as she crossed the yard and climbed into her station wagon.

With the engine running, she punched the heater up all the way. By the time she'd reached the highway, warmth was blasting out of the vents, but most of it was flowing out of the broken rear window. Ruth was still shivering. With a storm coming, she would need to cover the opening as soon as she got home. Maybe Skip could help her find something that would work.

The house was warm, and the girls were watching the Disney Channel while Skip read a science fiction novel from the library. Ruth called her son outside to look at the damage to the station wagon.

"We can't drive around with the window out," she said. "The girls will freeze. It's got to be closed off before we go back to Abner's. Any ideas?"

Skip took a moment to think. "Remember when we moved into this house, we painted the living room? We bought some plastic drop cloths to protect the rug. There might be one or two we saved. Maybe that would work. I'll check the storage space."

The storage space was little more than a gravel-floored hollow under part of the house. The rickety stairs went down from the laundry room. It was windowless, lit by a single flickering bulb, and populated by spiders. Ruth disliked going down there. Even now, as her son descended the stairs, she felt a nervous prickle. Time seemed to crawl before she heard his voice.

"Found it!" Seconds later, he emerged with a plastic-wrapped packet. "Now let's hope it works."

Outside, the wind had picked up. Leaning into it, they staggered to the vehicle and opened the tailgate. The plan was to wrap the transparent drop cloth around the frame of the broken window, then slam the tailgate shut to hold it. It took both of them, fighting the wind and wrestling with the blowing plastic, to do the job. But finally, everything was in place. On the count of three, they closed the tailgate. The plastic held.

Skip raised his hand. Ruth slapped it in an enthusiastic high five. "Thank you!" she said. "I could never have managed it myself. Now let's get inside before we blow away!"

Ruth was proud of her son, and the way he'd grown up to become a responsible young man. His actions had worried her for a time—making mischief, cutting school, and sneaking out at night. But those behaviors were behind him now. He had good friends, and he appeared to be on the right path.

His father would be proud of him if he knew . . .

But where had that thought come from? Ruth scrambled to blot it from her mind. Even if he were to want children, Judd didn't deserve a son like Skip. And Skip deserved better than a man who would surely break his young heart— just as Judd had broken hers.

Dinner had been scheduled for three o'clock. Ruth made sure her family was ready to leave the house by 1:45 so she could arrive at Abner's in time for the last-minute preparations: mashing the potatoes, making gravy, dishing out the stuffing, carving the turkey, and making sure other dishes were hot. By now, the storm had moved in. Sleet splattered the windshield, but the plastic over the rear window was holding up. The station wagon was warm inside.

Janeen had made paper turkeys to decorate the table. She carried them in a bag. "I made them with my hand," she said. "You trace your fingers—the thumb is the head and the other fingers are the tail. Then you draw on them. I wanted to write names, but I didn't know who was going to be there."

"I've got a pen in my purse," Ruth said. "There should be time to write names after we get to Abner's. I'll be busy, but you can ask one of the grown-ups to help you."

"I know some of the people who'll be there." Janeen began counting on her fingers. "Abner and the four of us—that makes five. And there's Trevor and his mom and dad. That's three more. How many is five and three?"

"Think about it and tell me."

Janeen counted her fingers again. "Eight. Is Maggie coming?"

"Maggie's family is going out of town. So no, she and her parents won't be there. But Abner said he might invite Hank, the man who runs the hardware store," Ruth said. "I don't know if he's coming, but that would make one more."

"So, that's nine. Anybody else?"

"Not unless Abner surprises us. We'll see."

A few minutes later, Ruth drove through the gate and pulled up to Abner's house. Out front, through the blowing sleet, she recognized Jess's Toyota and Cooper Chapman's black SUV. An older pickup probably belonged to Hank Miller, who managed the hardware store. Sheltering the girls with her coat, Ruth ushered her brood through the storm and onto the sheltered porch. Warmth and the fragrance of delicious holiday food greeted her as she opened the door. Tammy raced ahead of her into the living room. "Yay!" she shouted. "We're here! Let's eat!"

Abner chuckled. "Hold your horses, young lady. Wait till the food's ready."

Hank Miller was seated on the couch, his prosthetic leg extended at an angle. A balding man in his forties, he'd lost the leg a few years ago in a terrible farm accident. The bouts of depression and drinking that followed had cost him his wife and young son. He'd since pulled his life together, stopped drinking, and now had a good job at the hardware store. But his family was gone.

"It's great to see you, Hank," Ruth said, giving him a friendly smile. "I was hoping you'd accept Abner's invitation."

"How could I turn down a chance for good food and friends?" Hank asked. "This is so much better than a turkey TV dinner at home."

"Mom!" Janeen was calling from the dining room where the table had been extended with extra leaves and set with a holiday cloth and elegant china that had been passed down in the family of Abner's late wife.

"Mom! Come here!" Janeen demanded again.

"What is it?" Ruth hurried to find her daughter scowling at the table. She was holding a pen and the paper bag that contained her turkey cutouts.

"Look. We counted nine people in the car. There are ten places at the table. Did you make a mistake?"

"I wasn't the one who set the table, dear. But I'm sure it's all right. Maybe somebody else is coming. Or maybe the extra place is there to welcome any guest who stops by. Some people like to do that."

"But what about my turkeys? I need to write names."

Ruth sighed. It had been a long day, and it was far from over. "Why don't you go and ask your brother, dear? I need to help in the kitchen now."

"Skip and Trevor are watching sports on TV. They won't want to help."

"Then maybe Abner will. Or why don't you just write the first initial of the names? You can do that by yourself. I've got to go, honey."

Before her daughter could protest, Ruth hurried off to the kitchen. Jess would be needing her help to make sure all the different dishes were ready at the same time.

It was 2:45 when Judd swung his pickup through the gate and drove up to the house. He'd gone back and forth about accepting Abner's invitation. He had work to do, and he'd never been much for social niceties. But in the end, wanting to be a good neighbor and lured by the thought of an old-fashioned Thanksgiving dinner, he'd relented.

Several vehicles were parked out front. Through the blur of sleet that battered the windshield, he recognized Cooper Chapman's SUV and his wife's red Toyota. The older pickup probably belonged to Hank Miller. Abner had mentioned he might be coming to dinner. Then Judd's gaze fell on the last vehicle in the row.

His mouth went dry.

There could be no mistaking the brown station wagon with the broken—and now patched—rear window. It was Ruth's—the same vehicle he'd seen that morning at Shop Mart.

Judd had never considered himself a coward. But the thought of facing Ruth over dinner, making inane conversation as if the past had never happened, turned his insides to jelly. They'd spent years avoiding each other and the pain they'd chosen to forget. Judd muttered a curse. Why did this have to be the day when he finally had to face her?

There was still time to leave, he rationalized. He could turn his truck around and explain to Abner later that he'd had a sudden sick spell.

But no, it was already too late. Abner had come out onto the porch, smiling and waving at him. Steeling his nerves, Judd parked his truck, picked up the insulated bag that held the ice cream, and opened the driver's door. The flying sleet struck him like a barrage of birdshot, the wind almost tearing the door out of his hand as he closed it.

"Come on in, Judd," Abner greeted him as he made it to the shelter of the porch. "You're just in time. We'll be eating in about fifteen minutes."

"Thanks for inviting me, Abner." Judd brushed the moisture off his jacket. "I didn't realize there was going to be a crowd."

"What's Thanksgiving dinner without friends at the table? You can toss your coat on the rack." Abner opened the door. Judd was greeted by a rush of warmth and the rich aromas of a holiday dinner. His eyes swept the living room. No sign of Ruth, but as he hung up his jacket, he saw her tan trench coat hanging next to it.

Abner took the insulated bag Judd had brought and peeked inside. "Yum! Ice cream! I'll put it into the freezer for you. It'll taste great with the pie." He disappeared through the swinging door into the kitchen.

Cooper Chapman rose from the couch to greet him. Trevor and Skip were watching TV. So Skip must be Ruth's son after all. But the boy had mentioned that his father's first name was Thomas. Judd had understood that Ruth was married to Ed McCoy. Had she married more than once? And was she still married to Ed? Maybe the next hour would answer those questions.

Judd was just beginning to realize how little he knew about Ruth's life. He'd seen her with the two little girls who were sitting on the rug, petting Abner's dog. They resembled their mother. But Skip had a different look about him—lighter coloring, sharper bones. Judd would never venture to ask Ruth about her past. But maybe Abner could tell him something later.

"Sit down and get warm, Judd." Cooper motioned him to a seat on the couch. "That storm's a wicked one. Let's hope it blows over before we need to head out."

"I'm afraid I won't be staying long," Judd said. "I hate to eat and run, but I've got work piled up at home and customers wanting their saddles before Christmas."

"Trevor tells me that he and Skip will be repairing that harness for the Christmas sleigh. Won't having them in your workshop slow you down? You know what they say. 'One boy is a boy. Two boys is half a boy. And three boys is no boy at all.'"

"I can't let them slow me down. All I can do is show them what to do and turn them loose. And at least there won't be three of them."

Cooper chuckled. "Not unless you get Maggie as well. She wants to help, too. But don't count her out. That girl can do anything she puts her mind to."

Judd felt a touch on his knee. He glanced down to see the older of Ruth's two little girls. She was holding a pen and an odd-looking paper turkey shaped like a hand.

"Hello, mister," she said, thrusting the pen into his hand. "My name is Janeen. I need you to write your name right here on this turkey. Okay?"

"Maybe." Judd couldn't hold back a smile.

"But first tell me why you need my name on a turkey."

"It goes by your plate at the table, so you'll know where to sit." She was a charming child with her mother's hazel eyes.

"Well, in that case, of course." Judd laid the turkey on the coffee table and printed his first name across its belly. "There you are."

"*J, U, D, D.*" She studied the letters, reading them out loud. "Thanks. It's almost time to eat." She took the turkey and skipped off into the dining room.

"Ruth's done a great job with those kids, considering the hell Ed put the family through," Cooper said. "Jess and I hope she can move on and find herself a good man this time."

"So she's divorced?"

"For almost a year now. With her husband in prison, the judge didn't make her wait. Say, you're single, Judd. Maybe you ought to think about—"

"Oh, no. Not me. I'd never have the patience to take on a family, especially one that isn't mine. That takes a special kind of sainthood."

Just then, Janeen skipped back into the room, ringing a small handbell. "Dinner's ready!" she announced. "Everybody to the table. Skip, Mom says to turn off the TV."

Everybody was hungry. They trooped into the dining room. Judd found his name near the foot of the table, with Skip on his left. There was still no sign of Ruth, but he could hear women's voices in the kitchen. A moment later, Jess came out through the swinging door with a platter of carved meat. She set it in the center of the table before taking her seat on Judd's right.

Everyone was seated except Ruth. Judd found himself churning inside. His appetite had fled. Did she know he was here? Was she avoiding him? Lord help him, he should never have agreed to come.

However he played this encounter, it was going to be awkward as hell.

His heart seemed to stop as the kitchen door swung open.

Chapter Four

Ruth had come in from the kitchen carrying a bowl heaped with mashed potatoes. At the sight of Judd sitting at the table next to her son, her fingers seemed to freeze. The bowl started to slip from her hands. She recovered and grabbed it just in time to keep it from crashing to the floor.

She'd known that sooner or later she would have to face him. But why now, when she was frazzled and unprepared?

"Hello, Judd," she said as Jess reached out to rescue the bowl and take it from her. There were more things she might have said, but everyone at the table was watching and listening.

"Welcome to our celebration," she added.

"Thank you. I'm grateful to be here." He

sounded as uneasy as she was. She'd been aware of him over the years, even glimpsed him now and then. But she'd made every effort to avoid him. She was married to Ed McCoy, and her son had been legally adopted by his stepfather. Any familiar contact with Judd might lead to questions—the wrong questions.

The years had changed him. The shaggy-haired biker who'd broken her heart was long gone. The man she was seeing now was in his midthirties, with handsome but timeworn features. His light brown hair was prematurely streaked with silver, his blue eyes framed by leathery creases. He had the look of a man who'd found peace and purpose, she thought. But no joy.

"Have a seat, Ruth," Abner said. "Then we can say grace and dig into this wonderful feast."

The only empty place was between her girls, directly across from Judd. Ruth pulled out her chair and sat down. There appeared to be no rhyme nor reason to Janeen's seating arrangement.

After joining hands around the table, Abner offered a heartfelt prayer of thanks—for their friendship, for good health, and for the ways life had blessed each of them in the past year. Ruth stole a glance across the table at Judd. His eyes were lowered but not closed. He looked as if all he wanted was to get up and leave. She had to assume that, when he'd agreed to Abner's invitation, he hadn't known she would be here.

All they could do now was make polite con-

versation, as if the past had never happened—
even if the living evidence of that past was sitting right next to him.

He'd written to her from prison. She'd returned his letters unopened. By then she was
married to Tom, and any future they might've
had together was gone.

The prayer ended, and the feast began with
dishes moving around the table and murmurs
of pleasant conversation. Ruth filled her daughters' plates with small amounts of food she knew
they would like and buttered Tammy's roll. The
meager helpings on her own plate were for
show. Her appetite had fled.

Across the table, Skip was talking enthusiasti-
cally to Judd. Only now, with the two of them together, did she see the striking resemblance.
Skip was like a youthful reflection of his father.

Surely, given time, Judd would notice. Then
all he'd have to do was find a way to check Skip's
birth certificate. He would see that Tom Haskins was listed as the father. But the birth date
would be enough to unmask the lie.

Would things have been different if Skip had
known that his real father was in prison? Tom
had wanted only to protect the boy and to raise
him as his own. A robber's bullet on a winter
night had ended that plan. But at least Skip had
grown up believing his father to have been a
kind and honorable man—something he'd
needed during those dark years with Ed. Wasn't
that enough to justify the deceit?

"Mom?" Skip caught her attention. "Judd says
he's got the straps cut for the harness. If Trevor

and I can go home with him after dinner, we can get started on the work. Will that be all right?"

Ruth forced a smile to hide her anxiety. "Maybe," she said. "But it's storming out. You'll need a way home."

"I can drive him home, Ruth," Judd said. "I saw your car outside. You won't want to drive back out here and get him in this weather. Not until you get that window replaced."

"Please, Mom. We've got to have that harness ready for the parade," Skip said.

Ruth sighed. "All right, then. But what about tomorrow?"

"We'll need to spend most of the weekend working," Skip said. "Can you take me back in the morning if the storm's over?"

"I suppose so. I can stop by Silas's garage on the way home and get an estimate on the window."

"What happened to it?" Judd asked.

Ruth shrugged. "Somebody smashed it while it was parked. Maybe they were just in a bad mood. I came out and found it that way this morning. Skip helped me cover it."

"Are you driving yet, Skip?"

"Not yet. I won't be sixteen till next April. I'm counting the days."

Ruth's pulse slammed. Her son had just given away her secret. If Judd suspected anything, all he'd have to do was count the months backward. But he appeared not to have noticed the slip.

"Goodness!" Desperate for a distraction, she

rose from her chair. "I'm looking at a lot of empty plates. Who's ready for pie and ice cream? I'm taking orders."

Jess stood. "You take orders. I'll start serving." Bracing the door open, she bustled into the kitchen.

The diversion worked, for now at least. Dishing out plates of delicious apple, pumpkin, and pecan pie and scoops of ice cream marked the grand finale to the meal. Judd and the two boys finished their dessert and left to work on the harness. Everyone else pitched in to clear the table and put away the extra leaves. Ruth and Jess were left in the kitchen to box the leftovers and load the dishwasher.

"Well, I'd call that a success, thanks to you," Ruth said. "Thanks for pitching in. I could never have managed it alone."

"Of course I pitched in," Jess said. "It was a group effort. Even Janeen with her cute little turkeys helped out."

"She'll be happy to hear you said that."

"But I sensed something below the surface between you and Judd," Jess continued. "I didn't realize you already knew each other."

"It was back in the day. I was in high school. He was a few years older—wild guy in a biker gang. He gave me a couple of rides on his Harley. But that's water under the bridge now. Today was the first time we'd spoken in years."

"Is that why you were worried about letting Skip spend time with him?"

"Not so much that. It's just . . ." Ruth paused

to think. "In spite of his dark past—or maybe even because of it—Judd is like the Pied Piper— the air of mystery, the trappings of success, the cowboy charm. And Skip is so hungry for a man's approval. I don't want him to get drawn in and end up being hurt. He's already been hurt enough. You were there last year when Ed almost killed him."

"Judd's been a good neighbor. And I can't imagine him hurting anybody—physically or mentally. He would have seen enough of that in prison." Jess rinsed a plate and slipped it into the last space on the rack. "If you'd rather not have to bring Skip back out here in the morning, he could stay with us tonight. There's an extra bunk in Trevor's room."

"That's very kind of you," Ruth said, meaning it. "But you know the boys wouldn't get much sleep. And I like having Skip at home. He's growing up fast, and soon I won't have much control over him. But for now . . ." She shrugged. "I'll take what I can get."

"I understand." Jess added detergent to the dishwasher, closed the door, and pushed the start button. "That storm isn't letting up, and I'm sure your girls are tired. I can finish up here if you want to leave now."

"You're sure? I really do need to get them home."

"No problem. Don't forget your share of the leftovers. They're in those plastic boxes in the fridge, the ones with the red lids."

Ruth stacked the boxes in a paper bag and

went to round up her daughters. She found Abner watching TV with Cooper. He gave her a smile. "Many thanks for your hard work, Ruth. You made an old man happy today."

"And you made us all happy, Abner. Thanks for hosting a wonderful celebration—oh, and here's your credit card."

"One last thing," he said, taking the card. "I invited Judd because I sensed you were uneasy about letting your boy spend time with him. Now that you've gotten to know him, I hope you're feeling all right about it. He's a good man."

"Yes, thank you for telling me." Abner didn't know the truth, of course. Nobody did.

She found the girls, got them into their coats and out to the station wagon. As she buckled them into their booster seats, a stray thought passed through her mind.

Earlier, Judd had mentioned the damage to her vehicle. It had been no more than a passing comment. But now the question struck her. How had he known the station wagon was hers?

There had to be a simple explanation. She'd been working in the kitchen when he'd arrived. Had he assumed that only a single mother with three children would drive such an old beater? Had he made a lucky guess? Or was she looking at a puzzle with a missing piece?

With sleet battering the wagon, she'd drove home at a crawl, with the passenger-side wheels anchored on the graveled shoulder of the road. She was driving like an eighty-year-old, she knew.

But with four balding tires and her little ones in the back, she couldn't risk a skid.

By the time she pulled into the driveway, both the girls were asleep. At least the plastic wrapping over the broken window had held up. The interior of the vehicle was tolerably warm. Janeen woke up when she opened the door. Tammy was so deeply asleep that she had to be carried inside, undressed, and tucked into bed.

Janeen danced into the house and turned on the TV. "The Christmas cartoons are on, Mom. Frosty, Rudolph, Charlie Brown, and all the ones we like. Let's make some popcorn and watch, okay?"

Ruth was dead on her feet, but she gave her daughter a hug and put a popcorn bag in the microwave. With the buttery aroma filling the air, they snuggled on the couch and watched the old animated features, singing along with the music. The Christmas season had begun.

Judd had given up hope of completing his own work. The two boys were eager to get busy on the harness, but they couldn't start without his help. He began with a lecture.

"Your job," he'd said, "is to get this harness ready in time for the parade. We want it to be beautiful, yes. But more important, it has to be usable. That means, first things first. Look at all the straps. Which ones should be fixed first— either because they're worn through, or because the harness won't work without them? I'll

be giving both of you pieces of colored chalk.
You're each to mark six straps that need to be
fixed. We'll worry about the rest later.

"One more thing before we start." Judd had
gestured toward the harness, which was spread
on the floor. "The harness has two sides, one for
each horse. They're like mirrors of each other,
and they need to balance. That means if you
replace something on one side, you replace it
on the other side, the same way and at the
same time. So, everything you do will be double. Got it?"

"Got it!" Trevor exclaimed. "Let's get started!"

"All right. Here's your chalk. Red for you,
Trevor. You take the right-hand side. Blue and
the left side for you, Skip. Work together. The
repairs will be easier if you can match the mark-
ings on both sides. Remember, stop when you've
made six marks. Now, go."

Judd stepped back and watched them work—
Trevor making snap decisions; Skip taking his
time to study the straps and how they fit together.
He was slower than Trevor, but his choices were
always good.

Despite having suffered more hardship than
any woman deserved, Ruth had managed to
raise a fine boy. And her little girls were charm-
ers. If things had turned out differently, they
might have been his children. But maybe that
was just as well. Some men weren't cut out to be
fathers. Men like him.

Judd was still recovering from the impact of
facing Ruth today. She'd been a beautiful young

girl. Now she was a beautiful woman. Her finely etched features seemed barely touched by the years, but strength and sorrow shone in the depths of her expressive eyes. Her work-worn hands told a story of courage and survival.

According to Abner, she'd been single for almost a year. Maybe there was a chance . . . But Judd killed that idea before it could take root. The wild young man on the Harley and the beauty who'd ridden behind him, with her hair flying in the wind, were long gone. Two care-worn people had taken their places. No chance, Judd told himself. Too much time had passed, too much regret, and too much pain.

"I've got six!" Trevor said.

"Hang on, I'm almost finished," Skip muttered. "There, it's done."

"Good choices," Judd said. "Now, working together, pick one strap on each side—the same one—to replace. Then I'll walk you through the process. You've got a big job ahead of you."

"What about the bells?" Trevor asked.

"Keep them safe for now. The harness has to come first. If we run out of time, the bells will have to wait. Understand?" He glanced at the boys. They nodded. "Good. Now, let's get started."

At nine o'clock, when the Christmas shows ended, Ruth turned off the TV and tucked Janeen into bed. By nine thirty, she'd begun to worry. The storm was still raging outside, and Skip hadn't come home. Maybe he'd decided to spend the night with Trevor. But wouldn't someone have called her?

Were the boys still working at Judd's? Could they be stranded somewhere in the storm?

Worried, as only a parent can be, she watched the second hand creep around the face of the wall clock. Maybe there'd been an accident on the road. Perhaps if she turned on the TV again, she'd get some news.

She recalled that long-ago night when the police had come to tell her Tom had been killed—the feeling that somehow it was a mistake, and that any minute he would walk through the door and everything would be fine. What if the same thing were to happen again?

Stop it! she told herself. She was working herself into a frenzy over nothing. Forcing herself to sit down, she picked up a novel from the coffee table and found her place.

It was after ten when she heard the roar of a big vehicle turning into the driveway. Dizzy with relief, she hurried out to the porch. A black pickup with oversized tires had stopped behind her station wagon. Skip was climbing out of the passenger side. As he ran around the truck to the porch, the driving sleet plastered his hair to his head. Slicking it back with one hand, he opened the door and went inside, leaving Ruth on the porch.

The driver's side window came down. "Sorry to get him here so late." Judd's raised voice could be heard above the storm. "The boys were working, and we lost track of time."

"I was worried about the roads, that was all," Ruth called back. There was something oddly familiar about that truck, and suddenly she knew why. It had been parked a few spaces away from her that morning, in the Shop Mart parking lot. And she'd noticed it leaving when she came out of the store. The Good Samaritan who'd paid for her groceries had to be Judd.

If that was true, she wasn't about to let him get away without settling things between them.

"Come on in," she heard herself saying. "I'll get you some coffee and leftover pie to fortify you for the trip home. And I have something to say to you."

"Sounds good to me." The truck door opened. Long, boot-clad legs emerged and slid to the ground. "Even with four-wheel drive, that highway was tough going."

Maybe asking him in had been a bad idea. But it was too late for Ruth to regret her invitation. He strode onto her porch, moisture dripping down his canvas coat.

"Wait." He slipped off the coat and shook it lightly. "I'll just leave this out here, so it won't drip on your floor." He hung the coat over the back of an Adirondack chair that Ruth had been too busy to put in storage. She ushered Judd inside and closed the door behind them.

Skip had gone back to his room, leaving them alone in the kitchen. Ruth measured coffee and water and switched on the coffeemaker. As she turned away, the back of her hand accidently brushed his sleeve, and a shimmer of warmth passed over her skin. She struggled to ignore it.

"The coffee will be ready in a minute." She was babbling, filling the awkward silence with empty words. "How about some pie? Your ice cream got left at Abner's, but I can give you a choice of apple or pecan."

"Never mind the pie," he said. "I don't plan to trouble you long. But you mentioned that you had something to say to me. Please feel free to say it now."

"All right." She took a deep breath. "Correct me if I'm wrong, but I believe I owe you eighty-eight dollars and seventy-one cents for groceries. I'm going to write you a post-dated check to hold until Monday. After that, I expect you to cash it."

For an instant he looked startled; then he shook his head. "What if I were to tell you I don't know what you're talking about?"

"Then I'd tell you that you were lying. I saw your truck parked a few spaces away from me this morning. And when I came out of the store, it was just pulling out of the parking lot. It was a nice gesture, Judd, but I can pay my own way. I don't take charity."

"Oh?" One eyebrow tilted upward. "Is that why you want me to hold the check until Monday? Were you going to write a rubber check to the store and hope it didn't bounce before you got paid? What am I missing here, Ruth?"

The coffee was ready. Remembering he liked it black, Ruth handed him the steaming cup. "I don't owe you an explanation," she said.

"That sounds to me as if there's something to explain." His stern expression softened. "There's a story here. And I'm not leaving until I hear it."

She sighed. "If I tell you, will you take the check?"

He took a sip of coffee. "I'll take it. But I'm not promising to cash it. Come on, let's sit down."

They pulled out chairs and sat at the kitchen table, facing each other across the checked cloth. "You're not having any coffee?" he asked.

"I'm not the one who has to drive home in the storm."

"In that case, I'll drink, and you talk. I'm waiting to hear that story."

She told him then, the full account of using Abner's credit card, leaving the groceries locked in the rear of the wagon overnight, and coming outside the next morning to find the window smashed and the bags gone.

"There was nothing to do but go and buy more. Of course, I couldn't charge Abner's card again. And I didn't have a card of my own—Ed dragged me through bankruptcy with him a couple of years ago. And my checking account was almost empty."

Strange, how natural it was to talk with him after all these years. She'd expected some awkwardness. There was none.

"So, you were prepared to write a bad check and face the consequences." Judd was smiling now.

"My paycheck is scheduled for direct deposit on Monday. I was hoping . . ." She managed to laugh. "I was really worried. At least you saved me from that. But that doesn't mean you're getting away with this prank. What possessed you to pay for my groceries anyway? Did I look like that much of a hard case?"

"I was buying ice cream when I noticed you—that thumping cart was hard to ignore. You didn't look like a hard case. But you looked like you might be having a bad day. I was going through the checkout lane when I thought, why not? It was an impulse, that's all."

Ruth rose from her chair and walked to the counter where she'd set her purse. She opened the clasp, whipped out her checkbook, and found a pen. "Well, impulse or not, I'm writing you this check. And if you don't cash it, I'll be insulted. As I said, I don't take charity. I've got a job, and I can afford to pay you back." She scrawled the check and tore it free. "There." She thrust it toward him. "I've been through some tough times, but I've never taken a handout. Don't you dare spoil my perfect record."

"I'll think on it." He folded the check and slipped it into his shirt pocket. "You always were a proud little thing."

"I had to be. With a father on disability and a mother working as a maid for some rich lady, pride was all I had."

"But you were respected. And you were still the prettiest girl in Branding Iron High School."

"Don't," she said. "Don't go back. We can't."

"No. Sorry, you're right." He stood. "It's late. Time for me to hit the road. Thanks again for the coffee. Will you be bringing your boy to-morrow?"

"I suppose. I'll let him off out front. He can go home with Trevor, and I'll pick him up there."

"That's fine, though you're welcome to come in and see what the boys are doing. I like your son. He's well-mannered and has a level head on his shoulders. His father must've been a good man."

"Yes." Ruth's throat tightened. "Yes, he was."

He headed for the door. "Don't come out. You'll just get cold. Thanks again."

He opened the door far enough to slip out and closed it before the cold wind could blow into the room. A moment later she heard the truck's powerful engine start up and fade into the storm.

Knees giving way, she sank back onto the chair. She'd never wanted to see Judd again, let alone have him in her home. But he had been right here—sitting across from her at this very table, drinking coffee, and talking to her almost like an old friend.

This couldn't be allowed to go on—not for Skip, not for any of them. The secret she kept could crush them all.

His father must've been a good man. Judd's words came back to haunt her. She thought of Tom Haskins, who'd been a father to Skip in every way but one. Yes, Tom had been the best. Not handsome, not romantic, but a good man in every respect.

Her parents had thrown her out of the house when they'd learned she was pregnant. She'd fled to her older, married sister, JoAnn, who lived in Cottonwood Springs. Determined to make her own way, she'd found a job waiting tables in a diner. Her pregnancy was just beginning to show when she met Tom—just out of the army and ready to build a future. He'd fallen for Ruth and proposed with the full knowledge that she was carrying another man's baby. Then, when Skip was born, Tom had loved him like his own. They'd talked about trying for another child before it all ended, late one night when he was closing the station. He'd died instantly from a gunshot to the head.

Had she loved Tom? She had in her way. Not with the dizzying teenage passion she'd felt for Judd. But if gratitude and respect amounted to love, then yes, she'd loved him. Short and stocky with curly black hair and a prominent nose, he didn't have the looks to make her heart flutter. But Tom's goodness had gone all the way to the marrow of his bones.

She hadn't fully appreciated that goodness until after she'd married Ed.

The house was quiet. Even Skip's radio, which he liked to play in his room before going to sleep, was silent. Rising, she tiptoed down the hall and cracked the door far enough to look into the room. In the faint light, her son lay sprawled in his bed, fast asleep.

Her heart contracted with love. He must've worn himself out working on that harness tonight. She would let him sleep in the morning. There was no need to get him to Judd's at an early hour—especially since it meant getting the girls up to go with her.

A phone call had confirmed that Silas's garage would be open until noon the next day. On the way back, she would stop by and get an estimate on the window. Then, if the weather had cleared, she would take the girls to the park on Main Street to see the lights and hear the Christmas songs playing over the speakers. They would love that.

But her thoughts would be with the son she'd entrusted to the man who could break his heart. At dinner, seeing the two of them together, Ruth had realized that Skip's fate was beyond her control. Sooner or later, the truth would come out. And she was too late to stop the heartbreak that would follow.

For fifteen years she had lived with a lie. Would the price of that lie be the loss of her son?

She could only wait and pray for forgiveness.

Chapter Five

Judd drove the pickup into the shed and made his way to the house. The storm was letting up, but given the freezing temperature, the roads could be coated with ice in the morning. He couldn't risk Ruth driving out here under those dangerous conditions

Ruth's phone number was on the check she'd given him—which he had no intention of cashing. If the highway was bad in the morning, he would give her a call and tell her to wait.

He was too tired to go back to work but too restless to sleep. Sinking onto the sofa, he found the remote on the coffee table and switched on the TV. There was nothing on at this hour but a choice between a ranting televangelist with a gold Rolex and an antiquated Japanese horror movie, with a giant lizard man stomping around in a rubber suit. He chose the movie, hoping it would numb his mind to the point that he could go to sleep without thinking about Ruth.

She'd begged him not to go out with his friends that night. What if he'd listened to her? Or what if events had gone differently?

The confrontation between two biker gangs had taken place in an alley on the outskirts of Cottonwood Springs. One of the rivals had cornered Judd's friend, Digger, and was using a club to pound him to a pulp. Digger's eyes were swollen shut, his face a mass of blood and bruises. Judd had fought his way to his friend's side. A sharp uppercut with his fist had landed a blow to the husky biker's jaw. The man had staggered, reeled backward, and gone down, striking his head on the concrete curb. Seconds later, sirens had announced the arrival of the police. By then the man was dead.

Ruth had never contacted Judd again. When his letters were returned unopened, he had come to accept that she'd moved on. He'd never blamed her. Five years was a long time for a young girl—too long to wait for a man who'd thrown away their future in one reckless act. Still, he'd never stopped thinking about her and hoping for a miracle—a miracle that had never happened and never would.

Judd's musings were cut short by the sound of the doorbell. He switched off the TV and pushed to his feet. It was after eleven. A visit at this hour generally meant one thing—trouble.

The bell chimed again. Judd strode to the door. The thought flitted through his mind that maybe he should grab a pistol. But he was over-reacting. This wasn't the Wild West.

He switched on the porch light, then opened the door.

The man who stood in the circle of light was a half head shorter than Judd. Unshaven, with battered features, he was dressed in a thick army surplus coat with a hood. A backpack lay next to his booted feet.

He appeared to be a vagrant who'd wandered onto the property seeking shelter from the storm. Judd wasn't in the habit of taking in strangers, but he could hardly leave the man outside to freeze.

"How can I help you?" he asked.

The stranger grinned, showing nicotine-stained teeth. "Don't you know me, Judd? It's your old pal, Digger."

Thunderstruck, Judd stared at the man he hadn't seen in sixteen years. He remembered his last glimpse of the paramedics loading the injured Digger into an ambulance. After that there'd been nothing—no appearance at the trial, no visits to the jail, no letters in the long years that followed. It was as if his friend had vanished from the face of the earth.

Now here he was. And Judd's instincts were screaming caution. Why here? Why now?

He found his voice. "Digger! I'll be damned! You look like forty miles of bad road. How did you find me—and how did you get here?"

"I asked at the convenience store in town. They were just closing, but they gave me directions. I'd have been here sooner, but my bike ran out of gas about a mile back. I had to walk the rest of the way. Hell, it's colder than a gravedigger's butt out here. Aren't you going to invite me in?"

"Of course." Judd stepped aside to let the man enter. "Come in and warm up. Are you hungry? I'm low on groceries, but I could make you a roast turkey sandwich and some coffee."

"That sounds good, thanks." Digger wiped his feet on the mat, stepped inside, and dropped his heavy pack next to the door. Judd took his wet coat and hung it on the rack. Underneath it, Digger was wearing a faded plaid flannel shirt. His scalp gleamed white through long, thin strands of hair.

"Come on in the kitchen and have a seat at the table," Judd said. "We can talk while I fix you a plate. I'll be interested in hearing your story. The bathroom's down the hall if you need to wash up."

"No need. I haven't had a bite to eat since breakfast. I could eat a horse."

"I'm afraid a turkey sandwich will have to do." Judd turned on the overhead light in the kitchen, started the coffeemaker, and rummaged in the fridge for the Thanksgiving leftovers that Abner had insisted he take home—a few slices of turkey meat, several dinner rolls, and a piece of pumpkin pie. At least he had food to offer. For the past couple of weeks, he'd been too busy with work to do much shopping.

"Don't worry about the coffee," Digger said. "But if you've got a beer, I could go for that."

"Sorry, I gave up alcohol years ago. I can't

even keep it around, or I'd get weak and fall right off the wagon. But I've got sodas if you want one."

"Nah. Coffee will be fine. Black."

Using two of the dinner rolls, Judd slathered the cut surfaces with mayo and mustard, added a slice of cheese and most of the turkey. As he turned to give it to Digger, he noticed how the overhead light cast a ghostly pallor over the man's skin. Judd knew that look. After five years with a minimum of sunlight, he'd been just as pale in the weeks after his release.

He filled a mug with coffee and passed it across the table. "So, Digger, how long have you been out?"

"About three weeks." Digger's surprise morphed into a slow grin. "I guess it takes one to know one."

"How long, and what were you in for? Since you're sitting at my table, I have a right to ask."

"Four years. Dealing. Crystal meth, mostly. And a little heroin. It wasn't like I hurt anybody. Just giving folks what they wanted."

Judd didn't have to ask whether Digger had done drugs, too. They all did. "And what now?" he asked. "Are you clean?"

"Hell, yes. My parole officer's in Cottonwood Springs. Mean sonofabitch. I gotta pee in a cup every time I check in."

Judd studied his old friend from across the table as Digger took a big bite of the sandwich, washed it down with coffee, and wiped his mouth on his sleeve. Saving Digger on that long-ago night had ended one man's life and cost Judd five years of his freedom, not to mention any chance of a future with the girl he'd loved.

Seeing this wreck of a man and what he'd become made Judd feel sick inside. All that loss—and Digger probably didn't even care.

Judd took a deep breath, dismissing the thought for now. "So, what brings you out this way, Digger?" he asked.

Digger shrugged. "I heard you'd cleaned up your act and made good on your old family ranch. I want to do the same—turn my life around and make a fresh start. But for now, I've got no place to go. I was hoping you could give me a bed and some work, just till I can get on my feet."

Judd sighed. He should have known this was coming. If he had any sense, he would just say no. But how could he turn a needy man out in weather cold enough to freeze fingers and toes?

"I can't offer anything in the way of work," he said. "My herd is sold down to breeding stock for the winter. A couple of cowboys who live with their families show up every day to take care of the cows and horses. And my saddle-making business is strictly a one-man operation."

Digger was gazing at him like a sick puppy. Judd willed himself to ignore a jab of guilt as he continued.

"My house isn't set up for company. But since you've no place to go, you can stay in the bunkhouse for a few nights. There's an electric space heater and a kitchenette with a hot plate and a microwave. There might be some coffee and a few cans on the shelf, and I'll load up a bag of staples from this kitchen. I wish I could be more accommodating, but this is my busy season. I'm up to my ears in work, and I didn't plan on having anybody drop in. You'll be on your own."

"I understand." Digger finished the last of his sandwich. "I've got just one more favor to ask. If you've got a can with gas in it, could you drive me out to my bike? I don't want to leave it in the weather all night."

It was a reasonable request. Judd rose to his feet. "Sure. There's a full can in the shed. We'll take the truck. And I'll turn on the heater in the bunkhouse before we leave, so it'll be warm when you get back."

Digger grinned. "Thanks, Judd. You're a real pal. You saved my life once, and I promise not to make you sorry."

Judd was already sorry.

As he filled a paper bag with eggs, bread, butter, jam, and a few frozen dinners, Digger's words sank home. They were calculated to put him at ease, he knew. But they had the opposite effect. His old friend was a drug dealer, a free-loader, and an opportunist who had his own reasons for being here.

He didn't want the man in his house, and he didn't want him around the boys who'd be coming to work tomorrow. But he couldn't turn a dog out in weather like this.

The bunkhouse was frigid, but the heater was working. Judd turned it on and left the groceries on the counter and the backpack on a chair. Then, with the gas can in the bed of the truck, they set off back down the lane. The storm was moving out, but the road was icy. Even with four-wheel drive, Judd had to keep the truck to a crawl.

"Say, what became of that pretty girl who used to hang out with you?" Digger asked. "Ruth. Wasn't that her name? You two were hot and heavy, as I remember. I wouldn't mind looking her up, just for old times' sake."

Judd felt a rush of cold anger. Ruth didn't need this kind of trouble. "She was smart enough not to wait for me," he said. "By the time I got out of prison, she was married. End of story."

"Well, she didn't waste any time. I was in the hospital for two weeks after that beating I took. When I got out, she was gone. But I saw her one more time about a year later, at a restaurant in Cottonwood Springs. She was with this square-built, dark-haired guy, and they had a baby. I figured he must be her husband, so I didn't try to talk to her."

Judd's jaw tightened. He swallowed hard. "Watch the roadside for your bike," he said, closing the subject. "Tell me if you recognize the place where you left it."

A few minutes later they found the bike under some trees. Judd used the spotlight mounted on the truck to give Digger some light while he filled the tank.

The bike, what Judd could see of it, looked more like a high-end Yamaha than a Harley, not the sort of machine he'd expect a hard-core traditionalist like Digger to be riding. But he'd have to process that later. For now, all that mattered was getting home and out of the cold.

He waited until the bike had started. Then he drove home with the headlights on and Digger riding the bike behind him.

"You can put your bike in the shed, next to the truck," he told his visitor. "The bunkhouse should be warm by now. You'll need to turn the water heater on. I'll be up early in my shop. The less I'm disturbed, the happier I'll be. As I said, you're on your own, free to come and go as you like."

"Thanks, friend," Digger said. "You've saved my life a second time. I could've frozen to death out here. Now, I know you'll be busy with work, and I don't mean to put you out any. But if there's anything I can do to earn my keep, just let me know. I don't want to wear out my welcome."

To Judd's way of thinking, his old friend had already worn out his welcome. The challenge would be making sure his stay didn't last too long. "Good night, Digger," he said. "Make yourself comfortable in the bunkhouse."

"Thanks again, buddy. I'll owe you big-time."

"Forget it." Judd turned and walked toward the house. Glancing back from the porch, he saw the lights come on in the bunkhouse. Everything appeared to be under control. But he'd be a fool to lower his guard.

In bed, he lay staring into the darkness as thoughts clashed in his mind. What if he hadn't struck the blow that had killed a man and sent him to prison? Would Digger have lived to become a petty criminal? And what about the man who'd died? What would have become of the life he'd lost?

But these were questions without answers. Only the present could be controlled. Digger could be lying—just as that fancy motorcycle of his could be stolen. If his former friend was on the run, Judd could be found guilty of harboring a fugitive. He could end up back in prison. He could lose everything.

In the morning, after the workday had started, he would make a discreet call to Sheriff Buck Winston, alert him that Digger was here, and ask him to do some checking. If Digger was on the level, then no harm would be done. If he was on the wrong side of the law . . .

Judd exhaled and rolled onto his side. Tomorrow would be a busy day, with work to be done on the saddles. Having Digger here would only add to the pressure. And the boys would be coming to work on the harness.

Ruth would be dropping off Skip. If Digger were to see and recognize her, that could be awkward for all concerned. Digger wouldn't be above taking advantage of their shared past.

The next morning, Judd was measuring coffee after a sleepless night when the phone rang. He was surprised to hear Jess Chapman's voice.

"Hello, Judd. I hope I didn't wake you, but I thought I'd better let you know. Trevor woke up with a nasty cold this morning. He really wanted to work on the harness, but I'm keeping him at home for now. He needs to rest, and I don't want him giving that cold to anybody else."

"Sorry, Jess, that's too bad. Thanks for letting me know. Oh—did you happen to call Ruth? She was supposed to drop Skip by this morning."

"I tried. But there was no answer. She's probably on the road."

"Thanks. I'll watch for her."

Judd hung up the phone. If Ruth was on the road, she should be here soon. He could watch for her, but a better idea would be to go and look for her. Skip probably wouldn't want to work without Trevor. If he could stop Ruth on her way here and turn them back, that would lessen the chance of her meeting Digger.

Pulling on his coat and gloves, he grabbed his keys and headed out the door.

As he crossed the yard, he saw that his two hired men had arrived and were parked out back taking care of the stock. So far, there was no sign of Digger. He was probably asleep. But his bike was under the open shed. It was, as Judd had guessed, a high-end Yamaha, probably expensive. He'd try to get its serial number before he called the sheriff. But right now, he needed to head off Ruth.

He was about to get into the truck when she drove in through the gate and pulled up to the house. Skip climbed out of the passenger door.

By then, Judd had reached them. Ruth lowered the side window. She looked fresh and pretty, her cheeks pink with cold. The girls were bundled into their booster seats, a blanket laid over them for extra warmth.

"I hope we're not too early," she said. "Skip was anxious to start on that harness."

"I was just about to come and find you," Judd said. "Jess called me a few minutes ago. Trevor's got a bad cold. He won't be coming this morning. So Skip might want to make other plans."

"No, I want to stay," Skip said. "I can work alone. I know what to do. If I leave, the harness won't be ready in time for the parade."

Judd sighed. "All right. But I won't have time to help you. I'll be busy with the saddles."

"That's fine," Skip said. "You showed us a lot yesterday. I'll just have to do Trevor's side of the harness as well as mine."

"Then it's okay with me, as long as it's all right with your mother." Judd looked down at Ruth and caught the worried expression on her face. Maybe she didn't want to leave her son alone with an ex-convict. "It's your call, Ruth," he said. "If he stays, I'll drive him home."

He could sense her hesitation, but she nodded. "All right. I can tell he really wants to stay. If there's any trouble, let me know."

"Mom, there won't be any trouble," Skip protested. "I'm here to work."

"Don't worry, Ruth. He'll be fine." Judd couldn't help wondering if Digger was awake and whether he was watching. The sooner he got Ruth off the ranch, the better. "I'll take it from here, so you can be on your way," he said. "Be careful on the roads."

"I'll be fine." She raised the window. Judd stepped back, giving her space to turn the vehicle around. He exhaled with relief as she drove out of the gate and disappeared down the lane. At least Digger hadn't come out to talk over old times. Judd understood why she might want to put the past behind her, especially for her children's sake. He owed it to her to protect her privacy—and to protect her son.

Skip had noticed the Yamaha in the shelter of the open shed. "Hey, that's a cool bike," he said. "I didn't notice it yesterday. Is it yours?"

If he was to protect this curious young man, nothing would do but the truth, Judd decided. "It belongs to an old friend of mine who dropped by for a visit," he said. "But pay attention, Skip. I didn't invite the man, and he's not a person you want to be hanging out with. Until I send him on his way, I want you to promise me that you'll stay in the shop and work. There's food for you in the fridge. If he happens to wander in, you can be polite, but don't get into a conversation with him. Understand?"

Skip looked startled, but he nodded. "I guess, if you say so."

"I do. And leave that bike alone. I promised your mother I'd keep you out of trouble. And trust me, that man could be trouble. Got it?"

"Got it."

Judd changed the subject. "Have you had breakfast? I could whip you up some pancakes."

"Thanks, but Mom fed me before we left home. I'm ready to start work."

"Good. Let's get—" He broke off as an all-too-familiar figure strolled around the corner of the house. Digger appeared to have showered, but his beard was as scruffy as ever, and he was wearing the same clothes he'd arrived in yesterday. Maybe they were all he had.

"Good morning, Digger," Judd said without giving him a chance to speak. "This is Skip, my assistant. He just got here from town, and he was about to go to work." He dug in his pocket for the keys and tossed them to Skip. "Go let yourself in. You know what to do. I'll be along."

Skip caught the keys. With a curious glance at Digger, he went into the house, from which he could cut through the breezeway and let himself into the shop.

"Nice-looking lad," Digger observed. "For a minute there, I thought he might be yours. He looks enough like you to be your kid."

"Can't say as I've noticed," Judd said with a shrug. "He's just one of the town boys. His mother dropped him off here a few minutes ago. He's doing a special project for me."

"I saw that old station wagon out the window. Pretty lady driving it, but then you know me, I've always had an eye for good-looking women."

Judd took a breath. At least Digger hadn't recognized Ruth, probably because of her short hair. Maybe it wouldn't matter if he had. Maybe Digger was nothing worse than a harmless derelict. But Judd's instincts told him to protect Ruth and her family from this man. They'd had enough trouble in their lives.

As soon as he got a moment to himself, he would make that call to the sheriff. His next step would depend on what he learned.

A flock of crows rose from a nearby field, spiraling against the sunless sky. The morning air was frigid. He thought of Ruth, driving her car on the icy roads. She'd made it here, Judd reminded himself. She should be all right driving back to town. Still, he couldn't help worrying.

But meanwhile, there was Digger, standing in front of him, the rank smell of weed wafting from his clothes.

"Did you get some breakfast?" Judd asked him.

"Instant coffee and stale toast. I guess that's better than starving." Digger's voice had taken on a whining tone. "And the shower was so cold I could barely stand it. But beggars can't be choosers, can we?"

"So, what's your plan, Digger?" Judd asked.

"For today, you mean? Or down the road?"

"Either." Judd took a deep breath. "You know you can't stay here. I don't have work for you, and I'm not equipped, mentally or financially, to take on a long-term guest. I'll give you a few days to get on your feet. But you need to start making plans."

"Plans?" Digger scratched the stubble on his chin. "Well, since I'm flat broke, I thought I'd just hang around here for now. I can't get very far without money, can I?" He brightened. "How about you advance me a few dollars—say, enough to fill my gas tank at the convenience store, maybe buy me a few snacks and a couple of beers?"

"All right. But you'll be expected to earn it first. There's a shovel in the shed, where your bike's stored. You can use it to break up the ice and clear it off the front steps and the walkway. I'll pay you now, so you won't need to bother me at work. But I want your word that you'll get the job done before you leave."

"It's a deal." Digger held out his hand. Judd took two twenties out of his wallet and slapped them across his palm. The amount was more than generous for the work to be done, but if it would get Digger out of his hair for a few hours, it would be worth the money.

Inside the house, he waited for the sound of the shovel scraping ice. When he felt sure Digger was busy, he picked up the kitchen phone and dialed the sheriff's office.

Helen Wilkerson, the department's longtime secretary, took the call. Having served under four sheriffs, she knew everyone in town and most of their past histories. Her discretion was known to be solid gold.

"What can I do for you, Judd?" she asked. "Is something wrong at your ranch?"

"Nothing urgent," Judd said. "I was just hoping that the sheriff could check the status of a man who showed up at my ranch last night. I knew him years ago, and I know he has a record. I just need to make sure he's not on the run."

"I understand," she said. "It makes sense that you'd worry about harboring a fugitive. But

Sheriff Winston isn't available. His wife went into labor early this morning. He's with her at the hospital in Cottonwood Springs. I promised I wouldn't bother him unless it was a life-or-death emergency, which this isn't."

"No, of course not," Judd said. "Just give him my message when he's in. Unless it's possible for you to—"

"No, sorry, I can't access the records you need. Nobody but the sheriff is authorized to get into those online files. But give me the man's name, and I'll pass it on to the sheriff. I'm sure he'll get to the matter as soon as he can. Meanwhile, Judd, don't worry about any legal issues. The fact that you made this call should cover you against any charges."

"That's a relief," Judd said. "But it's not my only concern. I have people to protect. If this man is a danger, I need to know."

"I understand," Helen said. "I'll give the sheriff your message as soon as I hear from him."

That was all he was going to get for now, Judd told himself. "Thanks, Helen," he said. "Give my best to the new parents."

He hung up the phone. The scraping sound outside had stopped. He could hear the sputter of the engine as the Yamaha started, then burst into a roar that faded away down the lane.

Ruth should be safe from meeting Digger by now. She'd probably be at the garage, getting an estimate on her station wagon. She ought to dump the old rattletrap and get a better vehicle. He'd buy her one himself if he thought she'd accept it. But Ruth was fiercely independent.

She'd never take help from a man—especially from him.

Now that Digger was gone, it might be smart to check inside his backpack for anything like weapons or drugs. But Digger would probably know his bag had been searched. *Leave it and get to work,* Judd scolded himself, turning back toward the breezeway. He'd wasted enough time this morning.

"That's an old vehicle, Ruth. It might take me some time to find a replacement for your window. Meanwhile, I'll be glad to patch the hole so you can open the rear door. That won't take more than a few minutes. No charge."

Silas Parker, young, skinny, and married less than a year, was the best mechanic in four counties. Trained in the army, he'd come home to Branding Iron, wed his sweetheart, Connie, and started his own auto repair business in an abandoned furniture store. His cluttered shop smelled of motor oil and exhaust fumes. From somewhere out of sight, a radio blared country music.

"I'm really hoping it won't cost too much," Ruth said. "The car's not insured for damage. I'll have to pay for it myself."

"I'll let you know the cost when I've located your replacement," Silas said. "Now, if you and your girls will take a seat across from the counter, I'll patch that hole with epoxy and a sheet of plastic. You won't be able to open the window, but at least it'll keep out the cold."

"Thank you, Silas, but I really must insist on paying," Ruth said. "How much do I owe you?"

He gave her a grin. "Well, I do accept payment in cookies," he said.

With the rear window patched and the wagon filling with warmth, Ruth drove up Main Street where the Christmas lights, strung back and forth above the street, glowed like festive rainbows.

"Oh, Mom! It's so beautiful! Like a Christmas fairyland!" Janeen exclaimed. "Can we get out of the car?"

"Of course," Ruth said. "That's why we're here. Just let me find a parking place."

By now, the shops were open, showing off their holiday gift displays. Cars filled the parallel spaces along Main Street. But Ruth found a diagonal spot along one side of the city park, next to an unfamiliar Yamaha motorcycle.

"Let's go!" The girls were out of their booster seats by the time Ruth opened the doors. Clasping a little hand on either side, she led them around the corner to where a sixty-year-old spruce tree rose in a tower of twinkling lights and glittering tinsel. Their mouths made round *O*'s of amazement.

"It's so tall!" Janeen gasped. "I can barely see the star on top!"

Tammy tugged at Ruth's hand. "Mommy, when can we get a Christmas tree?" she asked.

"We'll see. Maybe next week. We'll need Skip along to help us load it and set it up."

"We'll need decorations, too," Janeen said. "Our old ones got blown up in the house."

"Yes, I suppose we will." Ruth sighed. Lights and ornaments were expensive, just one more thing to buy. But if she wanted this Christmas to be special for her children, having a beautiful tree would have to be part of the plan.

The children were still looking up at the tree when she felt a chill of awareness creeping down her spine—the sort of instinctive warning that told her she was being watched. Turning abruptly, she saw a scruffy-looking man in a brown canvas coat standing a dozen paces away. His face was unshaven. Strings of dark hair dangled below his woolen cap.

As their eyes met, he grinned. Her pulse slammed.

Heaven help her, she knew him!

Chapter Six

"Hello, Ruth." The gritty voice was even more familiar than the battered, be-whiskered face. She and Judd had spent enough time with Digger to embed him like a splinter in her memory. Back then, they'd been friends. But looking at him now, it wasn't friendship she felt. It was more like dread.

Instinctively, she pulled her daughters against her coat.

"Hello, Digger," she said. "It's been a long time. What are you doing back in Branding Iron?"

"Just passing through. Judd's letting me bunk at his place for a few nights while I make some plans. I thought that might be you this morning, driving up to the house to let that boy off. Is he your son?"

"Yes, by my first husband." Ruth struggled to

keep her voice from quivering. Digger had been in the hospital, recovering from head injuries, when she'd left Branding Iron. He wouldn't have known about her pregnancy, but he'd been aware that she and Judd were intimate. Now his big mouth could cause serious damage. The worst of it was, he was staying with Judd while Skip was working there. Alarms were going off in her head, but there was nothing she could do.

"You've cut your long hair, Ruth," he said. "I always thought it was so pretty."

"We all grow up," she said. "We all change. Right now, I need to get home. The girls and I were just leaving."

"Mom!" Janeen wailed in protest as Ruth gripped her hand and tugged her away from the tree. "You said we could stay!"

"Not now. We can come back tomorrow." Ruth quickened her step, pulling her girls along with her. Tammy had begun to cry. She howled, turning heads all the way to the car.

As she helped the girls into their booster seats, Ruth glanced back toward the park, fearing that Digger might be following her. But he was nowhere to be seen.

Her hands kept a death grip on the steering wheel all the way home—not because she feared any physical danger from Digger, but because he knew enough to upend her precious family. Skip's birth date and his resemblance to Judd were like two disconnected pieces of a puzzle. If Skip were to learn that she and Judd had been lovers before Judd's arrest, the pieces would fall into place, and he would know that he'd been lied to all his life—this when he already carried more burdens than a teenage boy should have to bear.

Judd would be affected, too, and he would no doubt be angry with her. But that was the least of her worries. Her first concern had to be protecting her son.

Judd had offered to bring Skip home at the end of the day. That would be the time to pull him aside for a private talk. But what would she say? How much should she tell him?

"Who was that man in the park, Mom?" Janeen asked. "I could tell you didn't like him."

"I was surprised. That was all, honey," Ruth said. "I knew him a long time when I was in high school. Hey, let's listen to some Christmas music!" She switched on the car radio and dialed up the volume. The mellow voice of Gene Autry singing "Santa Claus Is Coming to Town" filled the station wagon.

They sang along all the way home.

Judd laid aside the piece of hand-tooled leather skirting and paused to rest his eyes. Creating a custom saddle involved a lot of close work, and he wasn't getting any younger. By this time next year, he'd probably be due for eyeglasses.

His gaze found Skip, measuring a length of harness strap at the other end of the workshop. By now, it was late afternoon. The boy had worked steadily through the day, barely stopping at lunchtime to grab a sandwich and Coke from the fridge. He was getting more done alone than he and Trevor had accomplished as a team.

And, judging by what Judd had seen of it, Skip was doing good quality work—the cuts precise and even, the strap edges smooth, the placement of holes and buckles exactly matching the old pieces. It was too soon, certainly, to say that Ruth's son possessed a talent for this kind of work. But Judd couldn't have been more pleased with him.

The one task Skip had yet to do was the machine stitching. The heavy-duty sewing machine, its steel needles made to pierce layers of tough leather, was similar to the ones sold for shoe repair. Operating it was tricky and could even be dangerous.

Skip had cut a leather strap to fit a brass buckle. With the buckle in place, the cut end needed to be glued down with rubber cement to hold it, then stitched.

"If your mother uses a sewing machine, it works about the same way," he said as Skip sat down at the machine table. "Just take it slow and be careful." Judd guided the strap into place and lowered the presser foot. "Now hold it steady with one hand and turn the wheel with the other. That's it. Now put it in reverse and go back the other way. Good. Let's call it a day. You can do the other side tomorrow."

"Are you sure?" Skip asked. "I could stay longer if you'll let me. This isn't work—I'm having a good time."

Judd had heard Digger's bike come back around noon. His unwelcome guest had probably gone to sleep in the bunkhouse. But he could show up at any time, touching off another awkward encounter.

"If I don't get you home, your mother will worry," Judd said. "You've done enough for today."

Skip sighed. "Okay. I'll get my coat."

As he turned away, he noticed the hand-tooled skirting piece, with its design of cactus flowers, lying on the workbench. "Wow! Did you do that?" he asked. "It's cool!"

"I did the tooling," Judd said, "but the pattern came from a book. If we have time tomorrow, I'll show you how it's done."

"Thanks. That would be great." He went to get his coat, which he'd left on a chair. Judd took a moment to pick up his phone to check for voice messages. He was hoping to hear from the sheriff, but there was nothing.

"Let's go," he said.

They drove back to town in the truck, taking it slow because the icy road that had thawed during the day was beginning to freeze again.

"How did you learn to make saddles?" Skip asked.

"I learned the basics in prison. They had a workshop where we were trained to make saddles for a company that sold them on the outside. Sometimes bad things that happen to you can turn into good."

"I already knew you were in prison. My mom told me. She said you killed a man in a fight."

"I didn't mean to. He was beating my friend with a club. I stepped in and punched him. When he fell, his head hit the curb. Do you know what manslaughter is?"

"Yes, I know. What happened to your friend?"

"He was badly hurt. By the time he got out of the hospital, I was in jail. For a long time, I lost track of him."

"And then what? Did you ever find him again?"

"Not until last night, when he showed up at my house. You met him this morning. Digger's friendly, but he's done time for dealing drugs, Skip, and probably using them, too. That's why I don't want you even talking to him."

"You killed a man and went to prison so your friend could live and become a drug dealer?"

"Yup. I think that's called irony."

They'd turned off the highway and onto Main Street. Shoppers hurried to their cars as the daylight faded. The glow of Christmas lights was reflected in the icy street.

"What time do you want me back tomorrow?" Skip asked as they turned the corner onto the side street where he lived. "I can come out to the ranch as soon as I've done my Saturday morning paper route."

"That's not up to me. It's up to your mother. Let's see what she says." Judd pulled the truck up to the curb. As he switched off the engine, the front door of the house opened. A small figure stood framed by the light. It was Tammy. She was jumping up and down with excitement.

Judd had weighed the wisdom of letting Skip

off and driving away. But that wouldn't do. Ruth would have questions. He owed her the best answers he could give.

"Hurry up, Skip!" the little girl called as Skip and Judd came up the walk. "Mommy said we could get a Christmas tree when you came home."

"I didn't mean tonight, Tammy." Ruth appeared in the doorway, pulling her daughter back into the room. "I meant we could go later, anytime Skip was here to help."

"But why not tonight?" Janeen demanded. "Mr. Judd is here with his truck. He could haul the tree for us, so we wouldn't have to tie it on our station wagon."

Judd had entered the house in time to hear most of the discussion. "Hey, I'd be glad to help get your tree home," he said. "It would be no trouble at all."

The look Ruth sent him clearly said, *You're not helping.* "I'm sure Mr. Judd has better things to do. Besides, I don't get paid till Monday. We can get a tree next week."

"I bet Mr. Miller would let you pay next week," Janeen argued. "Please, Mom, it'll be so much fun!"

"But we don't have any decorations." Ruth appeared to be weakening.

"We can get them later," Janeen said. "Just think, with a tree inside, our whole house will smell like Christmas!"

"Something tells me you've been beaten, Ruth." Judd stepped into the fray. "Come on, let's do it."

Ruth sighed. "All right. But only if you'll join us for chili afterward. Just let me turn off the stove."

"It smells delicious. You've got yourself a deal," Judd said. "Come on, let's go get a tree."

Bundled into their coats, they piled into Judd's truck. Since there were no boosters, Ruth sat buckled into the rear seat with her arms around the girls to keep them secure. Skip sat in front with Judd.

Christmas music was playing on the radio, the girls singing along. As he drove back down Main Street, Judd reflected that he hadn't celebrated Christmas since before his time in prison. It had become just another day to spend at home alone, mostly working. Being with a happy family— Ruth's family—felt strange, like stepping into the past. But it wasn't unpleasant.

The Christmas tree lot, surrounded by a high chicken wire fence, was set up in a vacant field adjacent to the hardware store. Hank Miller, the manager, had made a festive occasion of the opening night. Strings of Christmas lights twinkled above the trees. Music was playing. Helpers passed out candy canes and free cups of cocoa. The fragrance of fresh evergreens perfumed the air.

The girls raced among the trees, looking for the perfect one. Skip followed to keep an eye on his sisters, leaving Judd and Ruth to stand on the sidelines and watch.

Judd stepped to the refreshment table, picked up two Styrofoam cups of cocoa, and handed one to Ruth. "You've done a fine job of raising that boy," he said. "He's responsible, caring, courteous, everything a young man should be."

"Skip has pretty much raised himself. He's had to." Ruth sipped her cocoa in silence for a long moment. "I saw Digger in town today. We exchanged a few words. He said he was staying with you."

"He showed up and I let him sleep in the bunkhouse. I didn't have the heart to turn him away in a storm. But it won't be for long. I'll see to that."

"I don't want Skip around him, Judd. Digger knows too much about the old days—and he always was a talker."

"That's not the worst of it," Judd said. "He's done time for dealing drugs, and I've smelled weed on him. I've told Skip he's not to go near the man."

"Can't you just throw him out?"

"I could. But there might be repercussions. He could even show up on your doorstep next. I've been trying to reach the sheriff to see if there are any warrants on him. I'm still waiting to hear back."

"Meanwhile, you can't expect me to let Skip anywhere near your friend," Ruth said. "I've never told anybody about you and me, and I intend to keep that secret."

An image flashed through Judd's memory— Ruth lying beside him in the long summer grass, the stars overhead, her breathing soft in the darkness . . .

But that was a long time ago, and their love

had ended in heartbreak. He forced the thought from his mind.

"Digger was wild back in the day," Ruth continued. "And it appears he hasn't changed. I can't trust him around my son."

"I understand," Judd said. "But Skip's doing some fine work on that harness for the parade. He'll be crushed if he's not allowed to finish it in time."

"Worse things could happen. The sleigh could always be pulled with a tractor. But nothing is worth having my son—or Trevor—hurt in any way."

She stood in silence, watching her daughters flit like fireflies among the rows of Christmas trees. Skip stood by the refreshment table, sipping cocoa and talking with a pretty girl while he kept an eye on them.

At last Ruth spoke again.

"Could the harness be moved to Abner's barn, so the boys could work on it there? That's where they built the sleigh last year."

"I wish it was that easy," Judd said. "But they need the machines to cut and sew the straps, and those can't be moved. Digger has orders to stay out of the shop, and I'll be there the whole time. Knowing how strong your feelings are, I'll make sure Digger doesn't get anywhere near the boys."

Ruth sighed. "All right, we'll try it tomorrow. But as long as Digger's there, I won't be driving to your place. I don't want him to get any ideas. If Trevor's well enough to work, I can leave Skip at his house. If not, I'll leave Skip at Abner's and pick him up there. He can walk the rest of the way. But if anything goes wrong, anything at all, my son won't be coming back. Understand?"

"I understand." But Judd wasn't sure he understood his own feelings. He'd never wanted the boys working in his shop. But he'd just begged Ruth to let Skip come back. Maybe he was getting soft.

"Mom! We found our tree!" Janeen was waving. Tammy was bouncing up and down. Leaving Judd, Ruth hurried to join them.

The tree was perfect—not too tall for the house, but beautifully shaped, full and fresh, its needles fragrant with the scent of pine. But Ruth's heart sank as she saw the price tag. The amount was almost double what she'd planned to pay.

"Are you sure this is the one you want?" she asked the girls. "There are plenty of other nice trees here."

"No!" Tammy tugged at her coat. "Please, Mommy! We want this tree. It's the prettiest one of all."

Ruth sighed. She had never known a time when she didn't have to count every cent. Tonight was no different. But standing here with her girls gazing up at her and "White Christmas" playing over the speakers, she remembered her vow to make this the best Christmas ever for her children. For Skip that would mean the bicycle she'd put on layaway at the Target in Cottonwood Springs. For Janeen and Tammy, it would mean the dolls they'd chosen from the Sears Roebuck catalog—and the perfect tree.

She would make up the difference somehow.

Opening her purse, she found a pen and her checkbook. Leaving the girls with the tree, she joined the short line to the cash register. Hank Miller, who was collecting payment, gave her a smile. Ruth could only hope that meant he'd be willing to take her check and hold it till Monday.

She reached the front of the line and laid her checkbook on the counter.

"You won't need that check, Ruth," Hank said. "Your tree's been paid for, along with a stand to hold it. Look."

Ruth followed the direction of his nod. Judd and Skip were carrying the tree out to the truck, with the girls dancing along behind.

She knew she should be grateful. But she could feel her stung pride lashing like the tail of an angry cat. Taking the pen, she scrawled Judd's name on the check, filled in the amount, and signed it. With a nod to Hank, she strode out of the lot to the truck.

The tree had been laid in the bed of the truck. Skip had helped his sisters into the rear seat and climbed into the front. Only Judd remained standing outside. She thrust the check at him. "Take it. Cash it. I know you're expecting me to thank you, but you're wrong. I've been paying my own bills and making my own decisions for most of my life, and I've managed fine. You're treating me like a child."

"Understood." Judd took her check, folded it double, and tucked it into his shirt pocket. "I won't apologize for wanting to help. But next time I'm tempted I'll remember that it makes you feel patronized."

"And you'll cash the checks—both of them?"

"I'll give it some thought. Let's go. A bowl of your chili sounds mighty good to me right now."

While Ruth reheated the chili, sliced some homemade bread, and helped Janeen set the table, Judd and Skip got the tree set up on the stand and the reservoir filled with water. Watching them work side by side, laughing and joking, Ruth was struck by how comfortable they seemed together. Judd was already becoming the wise, gentle father figure Skip had missed growing up.

It would be all too easy to let things take their natural course. But the risk for heartbreak was too great. Judd would never forgive her for depriving him of his son. Skip would never trust her again after the lie she'd told. She could even lose him. But short of moving away, how could she stop what was happening?

Supper was pleasant enough, with Janeen and Tammy's chatter filling any lulls in the conversation. The girls had taken to Judd. After being raised by a father who cursed, drank, and hit their mother, seeing a different kind of man at their table had to be good for them. But letting them get too attached could break their trusting young hearts.

As their mother, it would be up to Ruth to protect them.

With the meal finished and the dishes cleared away, Skip and the girls went down the hall to their bedrooms. Judd lifted his coat off the rack. "Would you mind walking me outside, Ruth?"

His request startled her, but she managed a smile. "Not at all. Let me put on my jacket."

They stepped out onto the porch. Judd closed the door behind them. The night was surprisingly warm and breezy, the kind of weather that heralds a wet storm. Clouds scudded across the moon.

He stood facing her, his features cast in shadow. "Thanks for letting me tag along tonight," he said. "I lead such a solitary life, I'd almost forgotten how it feels to be with a family. I enjoyed it. You have amazing children."

"Thank you. My children are my reason for living. My only reason."

She thought he would turn and go then, but he stood looking down at her, his gaze warm and questioning. Old memories gave rise to new desires. She imagined being in his arms again, his kisses burning her with need. Long-buried urges stirred in the depths of her body—yearnings that she mustn't let herself feel again—not for him.

Then he spoke.

"I'm only going to say this once, Ruth. We've both been through some hard times—you more than me. I stayed away from you because you were married and because you deserved better than an ex-convict. But now that we've been pulled back into each other's lives, I can't help wondering if we've been given a second chance."

"What are you saying?" Ruth's throat was so tight she could barely whisper. This couldn't be happening.

"We had a good time tonight," he said. "I'd like to spend more time with you and see where this leads. We could take things as slow and easy as you want—just be friends for now. Maybe that will be all that happens. Maybe we'll decide we were happier apart. Even that would be all right, as long as I know we didn't miss out on something good."

When she didn't reply, he waited a moment, then spoke again. "I told you I was only going to say this once. If you need time, that's all right. I'll understand. But for now, what do you think of the idea?"

Ruth stared down at her boots, her thoughts crashing like waves in a storm. Part of her had never stopped loving him. She wanted him. She wanted the hot intensity they'd once shared. And there were other, practical reasons to say yes. Her children liked him. And he had the means to provide for them and keep them all safe.

But she was through depending on a man. And she was through taking time from her children to pursue a relationship. She'd made that mistake with Ed, and her children had paid the price. Then there was the secret she'd kept for sixteen years and vowed to keep forever.

There was only one answer she could give him—an answer that would close the door once and for all.

"All I can say is no, Judd," she said. "You were wrong about tonight being a second chance. We only had one chance, and it ended the night you walked away from me to ride with your wild friends. You took everything from me—all my hopes, all my plans for a lifetime together. I can't forgive what your selfishness did to me.

"I know Skip wants to finish the harness," she continued. "I'll allow that. I'll even deliver him to Abner's place, or to Trevor's, and pick him up. But once the harness is ready for the parade, that will be the end of it. Do you understand?"

His expression had hardened. "I understand. You can't blame a man for trying, but I won't ask you again. Good night, Ruth."

He turned and walked out to his truck. Without looking back, he climbed into the cab and drove away. Ruth watched the taillights disappear around the corner. Only then did she force herself to move her feet and go back inside.

Had she done the right thing? There was no point in wondering. It was too late to change her mind and call him back.

The house was warm, the air fragrant with pine. The tree, beautiful even without ornaments, stood in front of the window, waiting to be decorated and surrounded with gifts. Christmas was a month away. There would be presents to wrap, cookies to bake, carols to sing, and parties at school. But for Ruth, much of the joy had faded from the season.

Sinking onto the couch, she buried her face in her hands.

Judd slammed on the brakes as a deer leaped across the highway. The truck screeched to a stop just in time to avoid a collision.

Pay attention! he chastised himself as the animal flashed off into the trees. At least the roads weren't icy tonight. Otherwise, he'd be dragging a dead deer off the hood of his truck—as if he hadn't already made a spectacular fool of himself.

What had he been thinking tonight? Being with Ruth, buying a tree, sharing supper in her house, chatting with her children—it had all felt so natural. Looking at her across the table in that shabby little house, he'd burned to give her and her children the security they'd never had. And Ruth, so warm and brave and beautiful. How he'd wanted her.

Had it been overconfidence or sheer desperation that had led him to say those words to her on the porch? He'd given her an ultimatum—practically backed her into a corner. No wonder she'd turned him down.

Her refusal had been right on point. His decision to ride with his bike gang, even after she'd begged him not to, had changed not only his life but hers. The first husband—Skip's father—who'd tragically died; the grinding poverty and hard work; the brutal second husband who'd abused her. If he'd listened to her that night, everything would have been different.

Driving through the ranch gate and passing the sheds, he noticed that the Yamaha was missing. Maybe Digger had moved on. But no such luck. His pack lay on the rumpled bed in the bunkhouse. Judd curbed the temptation to undo the flap and look inside. Digger would know if anything had been disturbed. He should at least wait until after he'd spoken with the sheriff.

In the house, he checked his voice mail. Nothing. Maybe his message hadn't been passed on. He would try the sheriff's office again in the morning.

Meanwhile, it was barely ten o'clock. Sleep was out of the question, and he was too restless to read or watch TV. Work was the only diversion that made sense. It might not take his mind off Ruth, but if he could put in two or three hours, at least he'd be making progress. He took a few minutes to brew some coffee. Then he carried the cup back through the breezeway and set to work on the presentation saddle.

There was a pay phone in a booth outside the convenience store. After changing a couple of bills into quarters, Digger closed himself inside the booth and placed a call to the Hutchins State Jail in Dallas.

Getting a prisoner on the phone wasn't easy. But there were a few guards who would grease the wheels in exchange for small favors like cigarettes, smuggled drugs, or information. One of them should be on duty now.

After entering the extension he'd memorized, Digger listened to the ring and waited for the night guard to pick up. He swore under his breath as the phone rang again, then again. At last, the familiar nasal voice answered.

"This is Damian Schmidt," Digger said, using his given name. "I'd like to speak with Ed McCoy."

Chapter Seven

"It's about time you checked in, Digger."
Even over the phone, Ed McCoy sounded like a bully. In the nine months they'd been cellmates, Digger had survived by being smart enough to flatter the man and become his prison lackey—a relationship that had continued after Digger's release.

"You'd better have some news about my wife." Ed's voice lowered to a growl. Digger knew better than to remind the big man that Ruth was no longer his wife.

"I managed to track her down," Digger said. "She's still here in Branding Iron, living in a rented house with her children—"

"You mean *my* children. I don't give a damn about that boy, but those little girls are my flesh and blood. And the bitch better not forget it. Just because I'm in here doesn't mean I'd ever give up my rights. Has she found herself another man?"

"Hard to say. She's been friendly with her old boyfriend, Judd Rankin, the saddlemaker. They were a hot item back when Ruth was in her teens."

"Then why didn't she ever tell me about him?"

"Don't ask me. Her boy's been working for Rankin. That's all I know."

Ed snorted. "Well, you keep an eye on them. Let me know everything they do."

"Sure, Ed." Digger knew better than to remind the big man that Ruth was free to do whatever she chose, and he was helpless to stop her. Where his ex-wife was concerned, Ed had a jealous streak a mile wide.

Digger deposited two more quarters at the prompt, then cleared his throat and changed the subject. "Now about that promise you made me."

"What promise? Maybe you'd better remind me."

Digger cursed silently. He should have known that Ed wouldn't make things easy. "You promised me that if I got you word about your wife and kids, you'd tell me where you stashed that coke you hid before you got arrested."

Ed laughed. "I guess I did. But you haven't done enough to earn it yet. You need to find out more about Ruth and that Rankin bastard. If there's a way to ruin him, I want to find out what it is. He's got a record, too, you know."

"Yes. The whole town knows that." Digger had never told Ed about his part in the fight that led to Judd Rankin's arrest. Now wouldn't be the best time to tell the big man that Judd had saved him and gone to prison for it.

"Damn it, Ed, you owe me something," Digger said. "If you can't make it worth my time, I'll throw up my hands and leave town, and there'll be nothing you can do about it."

"All right," Ed said. "I'll give you a hint. There were two packages, not one. They're hidden in two different places. The first is somewhere inside that old brown station wagon of Ruth's. Bring me another report in the next few days, and I'll tell you where to find it."

"What about the other package?"

"All in good time, little man. Keep doing your job and I'll let you know."

Before Digger could reply, the line went dead.

Never mind, he told himself. At least he had something to go on. But finding the stash in Ruth's beat-up station wagon was going to take some planning. Ed must've figured that if the police got wise about the drugs, at least they wouldn't think to look in his wife's vehicle.

Leaving the phone booth, Digger climbed onto the Yamaha, which he'd "borrowed" from outside a smoke shop in Fort Worth. Before going back to the ranch, he swung past the house he'd learned was Ruth's. The station wagon was parked in the driveway. The old clunker probably wasn't even locked. But rummaging through it here would attract too much attention. He would have to watch for a less risky time in a less exposed place.

He'd had a crush on Ruth back in the day.

But she'd been Judd's girl; a homely little no-body like him didn't stand a chance with a beauty like her. He still fancied her, but some things never changed. When he'd greeted her at the town park, she'd looked at him as if he was something she'd cleaned off the sole of her shoe.

She'd bewitched Ed McCoy, too. The fool was obsessed with her. But that was his problem. All Digger cared about now was finding Ed's co-caine stash and selling the white powder for enough money to set himself up somewhere be-yond the reach of the law.

Twenty minutes later, he drove through the ranch gate and cut the Yamaha's noisy engine. The black pickup truck was in the shed, the workshop's high windows brightly lit. Judd must be working late.

Digger would have welcomed the chance to sit down with his former friend and talk over old times, maybe learn more about Ruth. But Judd was a loner, and he'd made it clear that he didn't want to be disturbed—didn't even want his old buddy in the house. Any notion of friendship was out the window.

For now, there was nothing to do but stretch out in the bunkhouse with a joint, a cold beer, and the girlie magazine he'd bought under the counter at the convenience store.

His pack was on the bed, the single long hair he'd laid over the flap still in place. At least Judd hadn't been checking his personal things. He hadn't found the Ziploc bag of weed or the

9mm Glock Digger kept wrapped in a dirty undershirt. Parolees weren't supposed to have guns or drugs, but this was a free country—and as soon as he got his hands on Ed's stashes, he'd be where no damn parole officer could ever find him again.

Judd was making his morning coffee when the phone rang. The caller was Helen Wilkerson. "Hello, Judd," she said. "Do you still need to talk to the sheriff?"

"I do. Thanks."

"If you don't mind holding for a few minutes, I'll put you in the queue. He's got a lot of catching up to do this morning."

"That's fine. I'll hold—and Helen?"

"Yes?"

"I was just wondering about his wife and baby. Is everything all right?"

She laughed. "Everything's fine, thank goodness. Wynette gave birth to a feisty little six-pound boy. He was three weeks early and needed to go into an incubator overnight, so there was some worry. But he's doing great now. Eating like a champ. Hang on, I'll put you on hold."

Judd willed himself not to watch the clock as the minutes crawled past. At last, the young sheriff's voice came on the line.

"What can I do for you, Judd?"

"First of all, Buck, congratulations on your new son," Judd said.

"Thanks. Being a dad will take some getting used to. But I'm sure it'll sink in once we take the little guy home."

"I can't imagine how that feels," Judd said. "I don't suppose I'll ever know. But to get to the reason I called you. I need a quick check on a visitor of mine, an old friend."

As briefly as he could, Judd summed up Digger's story. "He claims to be on parole, but I don't trust him. For now, all I need from you is a check for any warrants. And I need to get the VIN on the bike—I should be able to check that online. I don't want to be a Judas, but you know my history. If he's a fugitive, I can't afford to have him around."

"And if he's clean?"

"Then he's my problem. I'll think about giving him some help."

"Got it. I'll run a check on the name and get back to you. It might take me a few hours. I've got a lot on my plate today."

"I understand. No rush. And thanks again."

Judd ended the call, filled a mug with coffee, and carried it out onto the porch. The sun was up, the day already warming. But the clouds billowing in the west promised a weather change.

There was no sign of activity from the bunkhouse. But from where he stood, he could see the rear end of the Yamaha where it had been parked next to the truck. This could be his best chance to get the VIN.

In the house, he found a small flashlight, a notepad, and a pen. Then, with a quick look at the bunkhouse, he walked out to the shed.

On most motorcycles, the VIN would be etched into the metal steering neck. Judd switched on the flashlight and quickly found what he was looking for. He cursed. Most of the VIN numbers had been scratched away. There'd be no way to know whether Digger had done the job or someone who'd had the bike before. Either way, the Yamaha was untraceable.

Shoving the flashlight into his pocket, he walked back outside. In the distance, he could see Skip coming along the lane from the direction of Abner's farm, where Ruth would have brought him. Sending Judd her precious son, even after learning that Digger was here, was an act of pure trust. He would honor that trust, Judd vowed. Nothing was more important than keeping the boy safe.

Ruth stood on the porch of Abner's house, watching her son disappear behind the trees. He was growing up fast, gaining height as his limbs lengthened. His voice was beginning to deepen, as well, and she'd caught him inspecting his upper lip in the bathroom mirror, probably looking for the first sign of a whisker.

He was being transformed into a man before her eyes. And every day he was growing to look more like his father.

Like Judd.

"When are you going to tell them, Ruth?" Abner had come out onto the porch. As his question penetrated, her mouth went dry.

"How long have you known?" she managed to ask.

"I'd suspected something of the kind for years. I was around when you were in high school—had a daughter close to your age. There was talk at the dinner table about you and your biker boyfriend. I even saw the two of you together a couple of times, riding around on that motorcycle looking like you were ready to take on the world.

"When Judd got arrested and your parents threw you out of the house, it wasn't hard to guess the reason why. Then a few years later you came back here married to Ed, with that boy who looked nothing like him. Still, I wasn't sure—not until Thanksgiving when I saw Skip sitting next to Judd at dinner. It was as plain as day. I can't believe they haven't noticed the resemblance." He shrugged. "Maybe it's because they can't see themselves side by side, the way I did."

"I don't know what to do, Abner." Ruth's voice broke. A tear trickled down her cheek. "I know it's only a matter of time before they discover the truth—especially now that Digger's come back."

"Digger?" Abner shook his head. "That boy was always a bad apple. But Judd stood up for him—and paid with five years of his life for saving him. I can't imagine what he's doing back here, unless it's to somehow take advantage of Judd."

"Digger knows everything," Ruth said. "He knows about Judd and me, and by now, he will have guessed the rest. All he has to do now is open his mouth."

"Would that be so bad?" Abner asked. "Judd's a good man. He could be just the father Skip needs after those rough years with Ed."

"What if Judd doesn't want to be a father? And what if Skip hates me for lying to him his whole life? Tom, my first husband, was a fine man. I used to remind Skip of that when things were bad with Ed—that his father had been a good person. Now he learns that his mother can't be trusted, and his real father was in prison when he was born. What is that going to do to him?"

"You're shivering," Abner said. "It's chilly out here. Come on back inside and get warm."

He opened the door and followed her into the house, where Janeen and Tammy were playing with the dog, petting it and scratching its ears, giggling as its big pink tongue licked their faces.

Ruth stood back, watching them for a moment. A dog was what the girls really wanted for Christmas. But until they had a home of their own, a pet was out of the question.

She took a packet of wet wipes out of her purse and gave one to each of the girls to clean their hands and faces. "I suppose we'd better be going," she said. "I need to drop some cookies off to Silas for patching my window, and then I promised to take the girls to the park to see the lights. After that we'll be looking at ornaments for our tree—even though I can't buy any till I get paid next week."

"You need Christmas tree decorations?" Abner asked. "I've got boxes full. My late wife loved decorating for Christmas. But in the years since she passed away, I haven't even had the heart to open a box. Take them all. You'd be doing me a favor."

"That would be wonderful, Abner!" Ruth turned to her daughters. "How about it? Should we take Abner's decorations home? We can decorate our tree tonight."

The girls cheered and clapped their hands.

There were several boxes, none of them heavy. It didn't take long to load them in the station wagon and buckle the girls into their booster seats.

"Thank you again, Abner." Ruth hugged him on the porch. "Knowing how precious these ornaments were to your wife, I will handle them with respect and love."

"Just enjoy them." Abner returned her hug. "And don't worry about your boy. He's got a good head on his shoulders. He'll find his way."

If only I could be sure of that, Ruth thought.

The girls laughed and sang along with the radio all the way back to town. Ruth loved seeing them so happy. She would do everything she could to make the day—and this holiday season—special for them.

As she pulled up in front of the garage, Silas came outside to greet her. Balancing the plate of chocolate chip cookies she'd made, she climbed out of the station wagon. "Here you are." She thrust the cookies toward him. "Payment for patching my rear window."

"Yum." He tasted one. "Paid in full, I'd say. I'll share them with my helpers. Oh—and I've got some good news for you. I've tracked down a replacement for your window. The vehicle's in Cottonwood Springs with a smashed front end. It shouldn't take too long to remove the glass and ship it down here. I'm still negotiating the price, but it shouldn't cost you too much."

"Ballpark?"

He gave her a number that was less than she'd expected. "I'll call you when it's in. Figure on about a half day to install it."

"Thanks, Silas. We're off to do some Christmas celebrating." She climbed back into the station wagon. The girls waved as she drove away. Silas waved back.

Main Street was crowded with early Christmas shoppers and people who'd just come to see the lights and hear the music. Ruth found herself glancing around for any sign of Digger. She didn't see him, but she'd resolved ahead of time that she wouldn't allow him, or anyone else, to spoil the day for her children.

They walked around the park, admiring the lights on the smaller trees and exclaiming in awe over the glittering spectacle of the tall spruce crowned by a golden star. A stand on the corner was selling giant pretzels. Ruth bought one and divided it for the girls.

The shops along Main Street were open, their windows decorated with tempting gifts—dolls and toy trains, miniature kitchens, baseball gloves and bats, bikes and tricycles, glamorous party gowns, fancy shoes, and jewelry.

One window displayed chocolates in elegant gold boxes. Another window had a winter scene with stuffed toy animals riding in a sleigh.

The girls filled their eyes with Christmas wonders until Ruth's feet began to complain and Tammy began to drag. "We've seen enough," Janeen said. "I want to go home and decorate our tree."

"The tree will have to wait until your brother comes home," Ruth said. "But if you promise to be very careful, we can open the boxes that Abner gave us and see what's inside. Would you like that?"

"Yes! Let's go!"

Chattering and dancing, the girls tugged their mother back toward the car.

Trevor was still recovering at home. But Skip didn't seem to mind working alone. It was as if he'd found a hidden rhythm in the cycle of measuring, cutting, smoothing, fitting, and sewing that carried him from one piece of the harness to the next. Pausing in his own work to watch him, Judd was surprised at how much progress the boy had made in just a few days' time.

Midway through the morning, Judd heard the Yamaha start up and leave. Another worry. He didn't trust the little man, and Ruth seemed to trust him even less. Judd remembered his conversation with the sheriff. At least Buck would be checking Digger's record. But Judd wouldn't rest easy until he had more answers about his old friend. Was Digger the harmless derelict he appeared to be, or had he shown up with some darker scheme in mind?

Around noon, the pizza delivery Judd had ordered from Buckaroo's showed up at the door of the workshop. Judd paid, adding a generous tip, and pulled up a chair to split the pizza with Skip. "Help yourself," he said.

"Thanks." Skip chose a middle-sized piece, took a bite, and closed his eyes for a moment, savoring the taste. "Wow. This is better than the energy bar I stuffed in my pocket for lunch. Mom will have a good supper for me when I get home, but that's a long time off."

"I get the impression your mother has her hands full."

"She does—and it's all for her family." Skip helped himself to another slice of pizza. "For as long as I can remember, she's worked herself ragged—at least since my father was killed. She was waitressing till she met Ed. After that, when she couldn't hold down a steady job because the girls were babies, she cleaned people's houses. Things are better now that Ed's gone. He used to get drunk and beat her. The sheriff would lock him up—she'd go and bring him home again because, as she said, her kids needed a father. It was awful for me, not being big enough to protect her from him."

Judd's jaw clenched at the thought of what Ruth had endured at the hands of her monster ex-husband. This was on him. If he hadn't gone off with his friends when she wanted him to stay, she might have become his wife—and he would have treated her like a queen. This winning boy might have been his.

"She's got a good job at the elementary school now," Skip continued. "We even get health insurance. But money's still tight. I try to help out, but a paper route doesn't pay much."

The thought surfaced in Judd's mind that he could hire Skip as a part-time assistant for a fair wage. He could use the help, and the boy had shown a real aptitude for the work. But Ruth would have none of it. She'd made it clear that once the harness was finished, he was to cut off all contact with her family.

"The farm where our old house stood before Ed blew it up is hers," Skip said. "If she could sell the land, we'd have enough money for the down payment on a house. But so far, nobody wants to buy the place. And with winter coming, Mom figures nothing's going to happen till next spring, at least."

"Interesting." Judd filed that bit of information away and changed the subject. "Go ahead and take that last slice of pizza, Skip. Have you talked to Trevor? How's he doing?"

"Better. Just a bad cold. But his mom wants to keep him home until school starts on Monday. After that, I can come here with him on the bus. We can work for a few hours every afternoon."

"That's fine. What about tomorrow? It's Sunday."

"Mom likes us all to go to church and have a nice dinner at home that day—maybe invite Abner or take him some food afterward."

"Then that's what you should do. I'll be working tomorrow, but I won't expect you to show up."

Skip had finished the pizza. "One more thing. Could I ask a favor, Judd?"

"You can ask." Judd gathered up the pizza box, napkins, and soda cans and carried them to the trash. "Go ahead."

Skip stood. "Yesterday you offered to show me how you did the flower design on the leather. I know you're busy, but would you show me now? We might not have time later, and I'd really like to learn about it."

Judd couldn't have been more pleased, but he tried not to show it. "I guess I could spare a few minutes. Let's wash our hands. Then come on over to the workbench."

Skip followed him to the bench where he'd been working on the skirts for the presentation saddle. One of the pieces was done. He'd started on the other one.

"These are the tools." He pointed out the pencil-sized metal stamps—the background textures, the edgers, the bevelers and shader pieces, and the different mauls for striking a stamp into the leather.

"This piece is ready to be worked," he said. "Pick it up. Feel how damp the leather is. It needs to be soft to take the design."

"And this is the design?" Skip touched the stenciled pattern with a cautious fingertip.

"Right. I've already outlined the flowers with a blade. Now we texture the background, so they'll stand out. Here, I'll show you." He chose a stamp with a textured end, placed it along the side of a flower, and struck the top end lightly with the maul. "See? We'll fill in the background with this texture." He held out the stamp and the maul. "Want to try it?"

Skip's eyes widened. "I'd better not. I could ruin the whole thing."

"No, you won't. I trust you. Try it." Judd guided the placement of the stamp next to the previous one. "Now, just a sharp little tap with the maul. That's it. See? It looks fine. Now, try another one, by yourself this time."

Skip placed the stamp on the design again and tapped it with the maul. "Hey, that looks cool." He made several more impressions, then laid the tools on the bench. "I'd really like to learn how to do this, Judd. Could you teach me—not now, but maybe after Christmas?"

Judd would have enjoyed saying yes. But he remembered Ruth's bitter words. He wouldn't be seeing her son after the harness was finished.

"I wish I had time, Skip, but I have to say no, at least for now. Talk to your industrial arts teacher at school. Or check out the district night classes. Or you might find something useful online."

"I'll check," the boy said, struggling to hide his disappointment. "But nothing's going to happen until the harness gets done. Thanks for showing me." He walked away, his shoulders sagging a little. The next time Judd looked up to check on him, he was working on the harness again.

* * *

For Ruth and her daughters, opening Abner's boxes was a magical experience. Lovingly packed between layers of quilt batting, the Christmas ornaments were precious. Some of them were charmingly old-fashioned, like souvenirs from Christmases long past. And the newer decorations were beautiful.

The girls exclaimed in wonder as they took each piece out of the box and lined it up with others on the kitchen table. There were little animals dressed in Santa suits—mice and rabbits, cats, dogs, and lambs. There were small angels with wings like butterflies and one large angel dressed in white and gold like a queen, with wings made to look like real feathers.

There were strings of lights that twinkled and even bubbled. There were boxes of jewel-like glass ornaments and strings of glittering tinsel and a star that had its own light inside.

"Mommy, I want to put *everything* on the tree," Tammy said.

"There won't be room for everything," Janeen said. "The tree will look too crowded."

"But you can choose what goes on the tree, starting with your favorite things." Ruth made a neat pile of the empty boxes. One box remained, not large but sturdy, with a weight that she could feel when she lifted it. "What do you suppose is in here? Who would like to open this box?"

"You open it, Mom," Janeen said. "We opened the other boxes."

"All right. Here goes." Ruth raised the snug-fitting lid and gasped. In the box, lovingly cushioned, was a complete manger set—but not just any manger set. Ruth had seen a similar one last year when she cleaned the mayor's house. His wife, the formidable Alice Wilkins, had pointed out the set, which she had arranged on the mantel.

"Don't you even touch these," Alice had warned her. "They're made by a company in Spain called Lladró, and they're very expensive, practically priceless. You won't see anything this fine in Branding Iron, I guarantee you that."

Ruth remembered thinking that Alice's manger set was beautiful. But this set was larger and more detailed, the figures elegantly tall in their flowing robes. Her hand shook slightly as she picked up the Joseph statuette and saw the Lladró stamp on the bottom.

Surely Abner hadn't meant to give her this treasure. She would close the box and take it back to him tonight when she went to pick up Skip.

"What's in the box?" Tammy asked. "Can we see?"

"You can look." She held the box so the girls could look inside. "But don't take anything out. I'm going to take these back to Abner. I'm sure he didn't mean to give them to us. They're worth a lot of money."

"How much money?" Janeen demanded. "Enough to buy a house?"

Ruth sighed. "No, dear, not that much. And the money belongs to Abner. That's why we're going to give these beautiful things back to him."

By now the girls were tired. Ruth fed them each a cookie and a glass of milk and sent them to their room to lie down. With luck, they'd go to sleep and give their mother some peace and quiet.

Needing fresh air, she slipped on her jacket, stepped out onto the porch, and sank into the Adirondack lawn chair left from warmer days.

The late-November weather was unsettled, just as she was. Clouds churned in the west, the wind blowing in restless gusts, changing directions as it stirred the last of the fallen leaves in the gutters. Was she doing the right thing, allowing Skip and Judd to spend time together without either of them knowing they were father and son? How long did she think she could keep up the charade—especially with Digger around—before the situation blew up in her face?

She'd believed her life would be easier once Ed was in jail and the judge had granted her an instant divorce. But things weren't any easier now, just different.

Leaning back in the chair, she closed her eyes to rest them a moment. She might have begun to drift, but the growl of an approaching engine startled her to full alertness. As the growl became a roaring crescendo of sound, she saw a vaguely familiar Yamaha bike rounding the corner and heading down her street. Her heart sank as she recognized the driver.

She stayed where she was as Digger's bike

neared the house. What was he up to? Did he expect to be invited in? Had he come to threaten her? To tease her?

But he didn't even slow down as the bike came up to her front yard. Instead, he made a spectacular doughnut turn, and raised the front wheels, like a cowboy on a rearing horse, before he sped back the way he'd come.

Seconds later, he was gone, as if he'd never been there. But Ruth had glimpsed his face as he put on his brief show. His cocky grin was sending her a message—one she understood without the need for words.

I know where you live. I know your secret. And I know how to use it.

Chapter Eight

It was late afternoon. Skip had just left when Judd got the call from Buck Winston. "I don't know if this will come as good news or bad," the sheriff said. "Your friend has met the conditions of his release. His parole officer is in Cottonwood Springs. He says Digger has reported in right on schedule. He's passed every drug test. All he needs to do is find a place to live and a job, and he'll be a solid citizen."

"In other words, if I don't want Digger hanging around, I'm on my own," Judd said. "I'm glad he appears to be following the law, but damn it, something doesn't smell right. I don't trust him."

"Did you check the VIN on the motorcycle?"

"No good. It's been gouged out. But that doesn't prove Digger stole it."

"Then all I can do is wish you luck. But keep your eyes open and trust your gut. If you find out he's up to something, let me know."

"Thanks, Buck." Judd ended the call and returned to the latigo he was tooling. Maybe he was wrong about Digger. Maybe his old friend had paid his debt to society and just needed help to make a new start. Didn't he deserve a chance to prove himself?

Trust your gut. That was what the sheriff had told him. Judd respected the younger man's judgment. But he had to be fair as well. Years ago, he had saved Digger's life. Was he justified in turning his back on the man now?

But this was no time to ask that question— not when he had more pressing responsibilities. Ruth had trusted him with her son, and Trevor would be under his care as well. As long as the boys were here, he owed it to their families to keep them safe. That included keeping them away from a convicted drug dealer.

For now, the safest decision was no decision. He would keep an open mind, taking things one day at a time, protecting the boys, and giving Digger enough rope to either prove himself or hang himself.

Meanwhile, he would remember Buck's words and trust his gut.

When Skip arrived at Abner's house, his mother and sisters were already there, waiting for him. The girls were playing with Abner's dog in the parlor. Through the kitchen doorway, he could see Ruth at the kitchen table drinking coffee with Abner. When he noticed the way she sat, with her spine clear of the chair's back, he knew she had something on her mind.

"Is everything all right, Mom?" he asked.

She rose and hurried toward him.

"Everything's fine," she said, clearly lying. "I was just worried about you. It's getting late."

Skip glanced at the clock on the kitchen wall. "I said I'd be here at five thirty. I'm right on time."

"Oh—so you are. Come here, son. I want to show you something."

He followed her back into the kitchen, where an open box, well-padded and made of sturdy cardboard, sat on the table. When Skip looked inside, he saw a ceramic manger set—the ceramic figures elegantly tall and beautifully worked.

"These are Lladró," Ruth said, as if that was something he should know. "A set like this one is probably worth several thousand dollars. They were in with the Christmas boxes Abner gave us. His wife collected them over the years— one every Christmas until she had the full set.

"I tried to give them back. When Abner refused to take them, we had a long discussion. Tell Skip what we decided to do, Abner."

"I told this stubborn woman I had no use for knickknacks like these," Abner said. "So, we're going to sell them, probably on eBay, and put the money in the bank to start a college fund for you. How does that strike you?"

Skip could almost feel his heart drop. It was a generous gift—a fabulous gift. But a different plan had sprouted in his mind only today. He'd meant to keep it to himself for now, but that was fast becoming a problem.

"Well, Skip, what do you say?" his mother prompted him.

"Thank you." Skip stumbled over the words. "That's unbelievably kind of you, Abner. But here's the thing. I might not be going to college."

"What?" The word emerged as a strangled whisper from his mother's throat. "But of course you're going to college. You have to go to college. It's been my lifelong dream to see you get a good education."

"It may be your dream, Mom. But not mine. I've decided what I want to do, and I don't need college."

She folded her arms across her chest, her expression a wall of resistance. "Tell me what you're thinking," she said. "And this had better be good."

Skip took a deep breath. "I really love working with leather, Mom. It just feels natural and right to me—like nothing I've ever done before. I want to learn to make saddles, like Judd does."

Skip hadn't expected his mother's reaction to be a happy one. But when he saw her go rigid as stone, he knew he should have kept the news to himself.

"What gave you that fool idea?" Her voice was

taut with anger. "Have you been talking with Judd? Did he plant that notion in your head?"

"No, Mom. I came up with it by myself. It wasn't Judd at all. In fact, when I asked him to teach me, he said he didn't have time. I'd have to learn some other way."

"How would you learn? In prison, like he did?"

Skip's temper flared. "Judd's a good man. Why do you hate him so much? You won't even come to his house. What did he ever do to you?"

"That's enough, young man." There was cold steel in Ruth's voice. "I have something to settle. You stay here and keep an eye on your sisters. I won't be long."

Snatching up her purse, she stalked out the door to her station wagon. The tires spat gravel as she gunned the engine and headed for the road.

As she drove through the twilight, Ruth's hands gripped the steering wheel so hard that her knuckles ached. Was she angry or plain scared? Maybe both.

She could feel her precious son slipping away— drawn by the magnetism of the one man who could take him from her and ruin his life. She had to put a stop to it any way she could.

Taking deep breaths and willing herself to be calm, she drove through Judd's gate and pulled up to the house. The window lights were off, but his black pickup was in the shed, so he should be home. Maybe he was working.

She slipped her purse under the seat and pocketed the key before climbing out of the vehicle and mounting the steps to the front door. The bell, when she pressed it, was so loud that the sound startled her. It was probably meant to be heard when he was working.

She waited, hesitant to ring the bell again. Maybe he hadn't heard. Maybe he wouldn't come. But in the next moment, she heard a stirring from the rear of the house. The porch lights came on, and the door opened.

His tall frame filled the doorway before he stepped back to let her in and closed the door behind her. The living room was dark, but she could see him clearly in the light from the hallway. He was wearing jeans and a faded flannel shirt rolled up at the sleeves and open at the throat. The rich aroma of leather lingered on his skin and clothes. His shadowed expression was unreadable.

"Hello, Ruth," he said. "Is something wrong?"

The gentleness in his voice would have weakened her defenses if she hadn't been so angry. "Yes," she said. "And I need to set you straight before the situation gets any worse."

"This sounds serious," he said. "Come sit down and we'll talk."

"Since I won't be staying long, we can talk right here," she said, planting herself next to the door, giving herself a ready exit in case she needed to storm out.

"Fine. I'm listening." His voice had taken on an edge.

"I have two things to say. I'll start with the easier one. Your friend Digger has been harassing me. He came roaring up to my house this afternoon while I was on the porch. He showed off in the street, grinned at me, and roared off."

"Did he threaten you?"

"Only by implication—just letting me know he was there. But I won't put up with his driving up, disturbing the neighborhood, and scaring my children. Tell him that if he comes by again, I'll call the sheriff."

"I'll do that and more," Judd said. "I'm sorry he's bothering you. I'll see that it doesn't happen again. But you said there was something else you had to tell me?"

"Yes." Ruth lowered her gaze to his well-worn boots as she collected her thoughts. When she looked up at him, the words burst out of her.

"Leave my son alone, Judd!"

He stared down at her, his gaze shocked and questioning. At last, he spoke, "I think you'd better explain that. I don't know what he's told you, but I've never laid a hand on Skip."

"That's not what I'm talking about. It's what you're putting into his head that's troubling me. Tonight, he announced that he doesn't want to go to college. He wants to work with leather and make saddles—like you."

A low gasp emerged from his throat. "So help me, Ruth, I would never suggest anything like that. He asked me how I tooled the design on leather, so I took a few minutes to show him and let him try it. When he asked me to teach him more, I told him I didn't have time, and that if he wanted to learn, he could find some other way. That was all. I swear it. And whatever else you might think of me, I would never lie to you."

"Let's say I believe what you're telling me," Ruth said. "It doesn't change anything. Skip worships you. Every word you say to him, he takes to heart. If I could, I'd forbid him to come here, but then I'd have to give him a reason why."

"And what reason would you give him?" His gaze burned into her. "Would you tell him about the past—how much we loved each other, and how you turned your back when I got arrested? Is that what you don't want Skip to know? Is that why you're worried about Digger—because he remembers, and you're afraid he'll tell your boy the truth?"

"Stop it!" She was fighting the tears that welled in her eyes. "You don't know what it was like after you went to jail! You can't imagine what I went through—it was as if you'd died."

"And you don't know what it was like for me—waiting for a phone call or a letter, wondering why you couldn't at least have said good-bye. And lying awake at night, yearning to have you in my arms, aching to—"

With a muttered curse, he caught her close. His lips captured her mouth in an urgent kiss that swept like wildfire through her senses. Only as her resistance melted did Ruth realize how much she'd wanted him. The masculine scent

of leather enfolded her like a caress as she softened her mouth to meet his. The kiss felt the
way she remembered, clean and hot and hungry. She molded her body to his strength, as if
trying to pretend that the years had never come
between them.

But the years *had* come between them.

And making up for lost time wasn't the reason she was here.

Summoning every last vestige of will, she
pushed him away. They stood facing each other,
both of them breathing hard.

"We can't do this," she said. "I mustn't come
here anymore. And I don't want you trying to
influence my son."

Anger tightened the lines on his face. "What
kind of game are you playing, Ruth? I've never
tried to influence Skip. He doesn't need my influence. He's a fine boy, a credit to you and his
father. Why is this such a problem for you?"

Ruth's hard-won control snapped under the
strain. Trembling, she leaned toward him and
flung the words in his face. "You stupid, blind
fool! After all this time, haven't you guessed the
truth? You left me pregnant. Skip is *your* son!"

Judd reeled as if he'd been punched, then recovered enough to speak. "Why didn't you let
me know?"

"You were gone, my parents had thrown me
out, and I had to think of my baby. I went looking for a good man, and I found him. Tom
Haskins was no movie star, but he was kind and
honest and faithful—and he couldn't have

loved Skip more if they'd been flesh and blood. If he hadn't been killed, we'd probably still be married. If I'd told you I was pregnant, that would have complicated everything."

His mouth tightened as he took in what he'd just learned. At last, he spoke, "Does Skip know?"

"He has no idea. And for his own good, I want you to swear you'll never tell him."

"Shouldn't he know the truth?"

"Maybe when he's older. But right now, at his impressionable age, what he needs is stability. If he were to learn the truth, you never know what he'd do. Some morning, you could find him on your doorstep with all his gear. Or he could kick over the traces and start getting in trouble—just like you did."

"I get the picture, Ruth." He cut her off, his voice a snarl. "Fine, I won't tell him—I promise. But that doesn't mean I'm all right with your not letting me know."

"Maybe you didn't deserve to know—riding off with your buddies when I begged you to stay, getting in a fight. We could have been a family, Judd. Now that chance is gone."

"Is that why you didn't let me know you were pregnant—because you wanted to punish me?"

"No. I did what I believed was best for my baby."

"As the father, I had a right to know."

"You had no right at all. You gave up that right when you left me." She gulped back a sob. "I'll let Skip come here until the harness is ready. He's needed, and I know I couldn't keep him away. After that, it's over. And you're not to say a word about what you learned tonight."

"Fine." His jaw tightened. "If you've said all you came to say, I think it's time you were leaving."

"At least we agree on something." She turned away from him, opened the door, and stepped out onto the porch.

"Damn it, Ruth—"

Before he could say more, she closed the door. Her stumbling feet carried her down the steps into the yard. She had almost reached her station wagon when a voice from out of the twilight raised goose bumps on her skin.

"Well, if it isn't the lovely Miz Ruthie. Fancy meeting you here." Digger stood next to his motorcycle, blocking her way out of the yard. His face wore a mocking grin. "You look a mite upset," he said. "What's the matter? Did you and Judd have a lover's quarrel?"

Rage and fear made Ruth's head swim. She stood her ground, knowing that she couldn't let him intimidate her. "Get lost, Digger," she said. "If I see you anywhere near my home or my children again, I'm calling the sheriff, and you'll find yourself back behind bars."

"It's a free country," he said.

"Not for you, it isn't. Now get out of my way before I run you down."

She climbed into the station wagon, switched on the headlights, and gunned the engine. Taking his time, and still grinning, Digger walked his bike to one side, letting her pass. She shot down the lane and onto the gravel road that led back to Abner's place. Partway there, after making sure she was out of Digger's sight, she pulled onto the side of the road. Hands shaking, she switched off the engine and headlights, lowered the side window, and sagged forward with her forehead resting against the steering wheel.

The night breeze, blowing in through the window, was chilly enough to make her shiver. But her face felt hot and damp. She couldn't go back to Abner's looking like this. She needed a few minutes to calm down.

What a miserable mess she'd made of things tonight. She should never have gone to Judd's house. She should never have let him kiss her. Worst of all, she should never have told him about his son. Now it was as if everything that was troubling her had gone from bad to worse.

But it was too late for a do-over. All she could do was go home and try to create a memorable Christmas for Tammy, Janeen, and Skip. In the end, her precious children, and their happiness, were all that mattered.

As she started the engine and pulled back onto the road, the memory of Judd's kiss swept over her in a flush of heat. For that moment in his arms, she'd felt like her young, passionate self again, lost in the feel of his body against hers and the unforgettable taste of his mouth.

But then she'd come to her senses. She and Judd were different people now. Time and tragedy had wiped out the past. The wild, giddy love they'd shared was gone forever.

* * *

Sunday was gray and gloomy with a drizzle of freezing rain. When the sky failed to clear, Digger gave up waiting, donned his cheap nylon slicker, and set off for town on his motorcycle.

His mood was as dark as the weather. Last night, an angry Judd had taken him to task, laying down the rules in no uncertain terms—no alcohol, no weed, no speaking to the boys when they were here. And on pain of instant banishment, he was to leave Ruth strictly alone.

He would have six weeks to find a job and a place to live, preferably somewhere away from Branding Iron. After that, or if he violated any of Judd's conditions, his fate would be left to his parole officer.

Damn Judd Rankin! They'd been friends once. But Judd had been lucky after leaving prison. Now that he had a cattle ranch, a thriving business, and money in the bank, he was too good for his old pal. Digger would have enjoyed torching Judd's fancy place and watching it burn to the ground. But that wasn't going to happen. He'd be a fool to risk his freedom on revenge when what he needed was cash.

Lights were glowing up and down Main Street, but the shops were closed. Only the convenience store on the outskirts of town was open. Digger bought a beer and took the change in quarters for the phone. What he had to tell Ed should earn him more clues. But he was getting damned sick of this game. All he wanted was to find Ed's hidden cocaine stashes, sell the drugs to a dealer out at Rowdy's Roost, and hightail it over the border.

"This better be good, Digger," Ed growled as he took the call. "You woke me out of a sound sleep."

"It's good, all right." Digger related, with some embellishments, how he'd seen Ruth coming out of Judd's house. "Looked to me like she was pulling her blouse together," he lied, imagining the expression on Ed's face. "Now it's your turn to come through for me. I can't get close enough to that old station wagon to search it. If you ever want me to call you again, I need more to go on."

Ed sighed. "All right. You've got to raise the tailgate and pull off the panel. It's right there. I just wish I could count on you to kill that Rankin bastard for me."

"You know better than that, Ed. I'm not a murderer. Come on, tell me about that other big stash you mentioned. Where did you hide that?"

"Not yet. Maybe next time if you bring me something good."

Digger ended the call and drank the beer he'd bought. Damn Ed to hell. This game was all the power the brute had, and he was doing his best to pull Digger's strings, even from prison. Meanwhile, Digger was getting low on cash, and he could hardly ask Judd for more. Somehow, he had to find a way into that station wagon.

* * *

Judd had spent Sunday and most of Monday alone, working on the saddles. He had made decent progress but keeping his hands busy was one thing. Keeping his thoughts focused was another.

Skip was his son. His and Ruth's. And he had lived the past sixteen years of his life without knowing he was a father—years he would never get back again.

For the past two days, his emotions had ricocheted from joy and wonder to cold, black anger. Ruth could have let him know—sent him a letter, even a photo or two to buoy his spirits in that bleak hellhole of a prison. She could have waited. They could have been a family.

But faced with five years of struggling to raise a child on her own, she had put her baby's welfare first. It had been to her credit that she'd found a good man. She'd raised a fine son and two sweet girls despite the rough years with Ed McCoy.

But why couldn't she have given Skip's real father a chance to do right by his boy?

He glanced at his watch. Skip would be taking the school bus home with Trevor today. They should be arriving here soon. At least, with the two boys working together, he wouldn't be alone with his son. There'd be less chance of him saying too much.

Outwardly, nothing could be allowed to change. He would just have to get used to that, Judd told himself as he walked out onto the porch. There was no other good choice.

Now he could see the boys coming up the lane—Skip the taller of the pair, and Trevor a year behind him in growth. But now there was a third figure—a gangly little girl with fiery curls, striding along beside them. Judd recognized her at once. Everyone in Branding Iron knew Maggie Delaney, the mayor's eight-year-old daughter.

Judd sighed. He hadn't planned on babysitting—especially a meddlesome youngster like Maggie. With her poking into things and asking constant questions, not much work was going to get done. But he could hardly send her away.

As they neared the porch, Judd forced his gaze away from Skip. But stolen glances revealed details he'd never noticed before—the slope of his shoulders, the curve of a smile, the peaked hairline, and more. In so many ways, Skip was the mirror image of Judd as a teenager. Invisible strings seemed to tighten around Judd's heart. How could he not have guessed? How could he have denied the connection he'd felt to the boy?

Maggie had moved ahead. Right hand extended, she marched up the steps.

"Hello, Mr. Rankin," she said. "I'm Maggie. You might remember me. The boys said I could help with the harness."

Judd shook the small hand. "How do you do, Maggie? I hope the boys gave you a job, because there's a lot of work to be done."

"They did." She grinned, showing slightly crooked front teeth. "I'm going to be in charge of the bells. I'll clean them and make them all shiny. When the holes are punched in the new leather strips, I'll fasten the bells in place. Does that sound all right to you?"

"It sounds excellent." Maybe he'd been wrong, Judd thought. This precocious little girl might be just the distraction he needed today. "Welcome to the team, Maggie," he said. "Let's get to work."

On Wednesday of that week, Ruth took two phone calls in the school office. The first one was from the real estate agent she'd engaged to sell the farmland where her home had stood. "Good news, Ruth," the agent had said. "We've got a solid offer on that property of yours— from a qualified buyer, at full price. The paperwork might be a little slow with the holidays coming, but with luck, we should be able to close before Christmas."

"Oh . . . that's unbelievable." As her legs gave way, she'd sunk into a nearby chair. Thank goodness her divorce lawyer had been able to get her clear title to the land she'd inherited from her parents. With Ed's name still on the deed, the sale could have dragged on for months. Now, as soon as the sale closed, she could start looking for a house to buy.

The second call was from Silas at the garage. "Hey, Ruth, we've got the replacement for your broken window. If you don't mind dropping off your wagon after school today, we'll start on it as soon as we get time. Meanwhile, I'll have a loaner car for you to drive."

"Wonderful, Silas. I'll be there." Silas's loaner cars, cobbled from parts of wrecked vehicles, were a joke, but they ran fine. At least she'd have transportation.

Her step was light as she walked back down the hall to the tiny custodian's office. Two pieces of good news in the same day. What had she done to deserve that kind of luck? Ruth had never been superstitious, but she found the thought almost frightening.

After school she loaded her girls and drove to Silas's garage, where she traded the station wagon for an ancient Chevy Nova with unmatched doors and a missing back bumper.

"That's an ugly car, Mommy," Tammy complained. "I don't want people to see us in it."

"We're not going to keep it, silly," Janeen said. "We're just borrowing it until our car is fixed."

Ruth gave Silas the keys to the station wagon. "Thanks," she said. "How soon do you expect it to be done?"

"With luck, it'll be tomorrow," Silas said. "Give me a call after school."

Ruth transferred the booster seats and drove home in the Nova, with the girls giggling as they ducked down in the back to avoid being seen. Grace Delaney had offered to bring Skip home when she went to pick up Maggie. That made one less errand to worry about.

She wouldn't tell her children about the land

sale yet. She would wait until the papers were signed. But tonight, just to celebrate, she would order an extra-large superdeluxe pizza delivered from Buckaroo's. They could enjoy that without knowing the special reason.

Right now, it felt good just to sit with her stocking feet on the footstool, the lights twinkling on the beautifully decorated tree, and "Have Yourself a Merry Little Christmas" playing on the radio. Finally, for the first time this year, Ruth was beginning to feel the Christmas spirit.

"Mom, we forgot to check for mail," Janeen said. "Do you want me to run outside and look in the box?"

"Yes, thank you, dear." Ruth leaned back and closed her eyes.

"Here, Mom." Janeen was back with a single plain, white envelope. The postmark was local. Ruth's name and address were written on the outside, but there was no return address.

Running a finger under the flap, she opened the envelope. Inside she found two checks, the ones she'd written to Judd for the groceries and for the tree. He had voided them with a black marker. There was no message.

The checks fluttered to the floor as another thought struck her. There was no need to wonder who'd made the offer on her land. It must have been Judd.

Pride shrilled that she didn't want any favors from him, that she should turn down the offer and find another buyer, no matter how long it took. But no, she owed it to her children to accept. Judd wasn't doing this for her. He was doing it for his son.

She glanced at the clock. Skip should be home before long. If she ordered the pizza now, it would arrive hot and ready soon after he walked in.

She made the call, then settled back with the girls to watch a kiddie show on TV and wait. A few minutes later, the doorbell rang.

Strange, she thought. It was too soon for the pizza to arrive. Skip wouldn't ring the bell, and she wasn't expecting anyone else.

Leaving the girls on the couch, she hurried to answer the door.

Sheriff Buck Winston stood on the porch. The grim expression on his face told her this wasn't a social call.

He looked past her to where the girls sat on the couch. "Is there someplace where we can talk privately?" he asked.

She felt the blood drain from her face. "What is it? Has something happened to Skip?"

"He's fine, as far as I know. If you don't mind putting on a jacket, we can talk on the porch. This won't take long."

Her jacket was on the coatrack by the door. She slipped it on, went outside, and closed the door behind her. Her heart was pounding like a pile driver. "What is it, Buck? Is it something about Ed?"

Buck shook his head. "I've come from Silas's garage. One of his mechanics was working on your station wagon. When he took the panel off the tailgate to replace the broken glass, he found something. He showed Silas, and Silas called me."

Without waiting for another question from her, he pulled a plastic snack bag out of his pocket. It was half-filled with white powder. Ruth fought a wave of nausea as she realized what it was.

"There was a gallon-sized Ziploc bag filled with these, ready for sale," the sheriff said. "I'm not accusing you of anything, Ruth. But I'll need to talk to your son about this."

Chapter Nine

Ruth stared at the sheriff. "Surely you don't think these drugs are Skip's. He's always been a good boy. He would never—" She couldn't even say the words.

"I'm sorry, Ruth, but we have to look at all the possibilities. You're not a suspect. You wouldn't have taken your wagon to the garage if you'd known about the stash. But teenage boys have been known to use and sell drugs or to act as mules for traffickers. I hope I'm wrong, but Skip does have access to your vehicle. We can't rule him out."

"But where would he get drugs? He couldn't buy them."

"Skip's been working for Judd Rankin. Judd has a friend staying there who's done time for dealing drugs. He could have talked Skip into hiding the cocaine for him."

"No!" This was getting worse and worse. "Judd promised me he wouldn't let Digger near the boys." Her mind scrambled for some shred of hope. "Can't you dust the bag for fingerprints? That should tell you something."

"We plan to. Digger's prints are on file. We could fingerprint Skip, or I could take something of his, like a glass or a soda can, and get the prints off that. That way, if the prints clear him, I won't have to bring him in. I'd do that as a favor to you."

"Thank you." Ruth's heart was still pounding. "There's a water glass in his room. I know better than to handle it myself. Do you want something of mine, too?"

"That could be helpful." He handed her two plastic bags.

"I'll hurry," she said. "Skip will be home any minute. I don't want to upset him unless I have to."

She went inside, hurried to Skip's room, and slipped one bag over his glass. Then she took a small mirror from her purse and put it in the other. Thank goodness it was Buck handling the situation. A different lawman would have barged in, terrified the girls, and dragged Skip off to lockup.

This has to be a mistake. Dear God, it just has to be!

Ruth rushed back outside and handed him the bags. "Will you call me as soon as you've checked the prints?" she asked.

"Yes. It'll probably be tomorrow morning."

"And, Buck, one more thing."

"Yes?"

She squared her shoulders and raised her head. "If you find my son's prints on those drugs, I promise I'll bring him in myself. All right?"

The sheriff nodded. "All right, Ruth. Let's hope it won't be necessary."

As he turned and left the porch, a pair of headlights rounded the corner, coming toward her house. Was it Grace, bringing Skip home?

But no. It was only the pizza delivery. She ran to get her purse as the young man came up the sidewalk. "Keep the change," she said, handing him a $20 bill. "And thank you."

The girls, who'd paid no attention to the sheriff's visit, danced around her as she carried the pizza box to the kitchen table. "One piece each," she said, putting the cheesy slices on two paper plates. "You can have more when your brother gets here."

The pizza was still hot when Skip walked in, looking tired but happy. She wouldn't tell him about the sheriff's visit, Ruth resolved. Not until she knew the outcome of the fingerprint examination. Why give him a night of worry?

Her hungry children wolfed down the pizza. Ruth nibbled a single small piece, her appetite gone. Tonight was supposed to have been a celebration. Now it was just a meal. Even the lights on their beautiful tree seemed less bright.

After the children were asleep, she would phone Judd. If he'd allowed any contact between Digger and Skip, especially if it had led to lawbreaking, she would never forgive him.

* * *

Judd was getting ready for bed when Ruth's call came. As soon as he heard her voice, he knew that something had pushed her to the edge.

"What is it, Ruth?" he demanded. "Did Skip make it home all right?"

"That depends on what you mean by 'all right.'" Her voice quivered with strain, like a wire stretched to the breaking point. "You and your drug-dealing friend may have ruined my boy's life!"

Judd forced himself to speak calmly. "That doesn't make sense," he said. "Skip was fine when he left here. Tell me everything."

Bit by agonized bit, her story emerged—how the mechanic at the garage had found a bag of cocaine in the tailgate of her station wagon, and Skip was suspected of hiding it there.

"The sheriff is checking a sample of his finger-prints against the ones on the bag," Ruth said. "He promised to call me in the morning."

"This can't be serious. How much does Skip know?"

"He wasn't home when the sheriff came. I haven't told him anything yet. I don't want to worry him before we know the truth. But there's no way a boy could get his hands on thousands of dollars' worth of cocaine—not un-less somebody gave it to him to hide."

"Damn it, Ruth. I promised you I'd keep him away from Digger, and I have. Skip has been with me in the workshop the whole time. Digger hasn't been near him. There has to be some other explanation."

"Then why don't you ask your friend? Let me know what he has to say."

"I'll do that right now," Judd said, but he spoke into a silent phone. Ruth had hung up.

Judd strode outside. Nothing Ruth had told him made sense—especially Skip's alleged involvement. But if Digger was dealing drugs, the man was going to find himself back behind bars.

He cursed out loud as he saw that the bunkhouse was dark, and the Yamaha was missing from the shed. Digger was gone. Whatever he might have to say would have to keep until the bastard showed up.

Judd walked slowly back to the house. He thought about calling Ruth. But he had nothing to tell her. All he could do was wait.

Headlamp turned off, Digger rode the motorcycle past the corner where Silas Parker's garage stood. The building would be locked tight—maybe even with a security system. But the lot in the rear, where vehicles waited to be worked on, was surrounded by a sagging chain-link fence. Crawling under it should be easy.

Stopping next to the fence, he looked around to make sure he was alone. Then he turned on his flashlight and swept the beam over the enclosure, where perhaps a dozen vehicles were parked. His pulse clicked into overdrive as he saw it—the old brown station wagon with the glass missing from the rear window frame.

At last.

Digger had seen Ruth deliver the wagon after school, but he'd forced himself to stay away until the late hours when the town was asleep. Now his goal was in sight. All he had to do was get under the fence, find the stash inside the tailgate, and get out again.

Leaving his bulky leather jacket on the bike and, sticking a screwdriver in the hip pocket of his jeans, he dropped to the ground, raised the lower edge of the wire barrier, and squirmed underneath. Keeping low, he crept across the lot to the station wagon. The night was chilly, but he barely felt the cold as he crouched in the shadow of the vehicle. The back was closed, but with nothing in the space where the window would be installed, getting to the stash should be easy. He wouldn't even have to open the latch. With the screwdriver in one hand, he pushed to his feet and reached over the bottom of the window space to pry off the panel.

The panel wasn't there. All his groping fingers could feel was the hollow inside the door and the gears that rolled the window up and down.

He was beginning to sweat.

Finding the latch, he raised the tailgate. When he shined the flashlight beam upward, he could see a space where the stash might have been hidden. But it wasn't there. Nor was it on the floor, under the seats, or anywhere else.

It was gone. Either somebody else had already found it, or Ed had lied to him.

Mouthing obscenities, he crawled back under the wire and climbed onto his motorcycle. What was he going to do now? And what in hell's name was he going to say to Ed?

After a sleepless night, Judd was at work the next morning when the phone rang. His pulse lurched when he heard Ruth's breathless voice.

"Have you heard anything?" he asked.

"Yes. I just got off the phone with Buck. The prints had a match. But not to Skip."

Thank God.

"So, Skip is all right?"

"Yes. He's in school now. He doesn't even know about the drugs."

The breath Judd had been holding ended in a long exhalation. "So, whose prints were on the drugs? Were they Digger's?"

"No." She paused. He could hear her breathing. She sounded emotionally drained. "They were Ed's. He must've hidden them sometime before he was arrested. I had no idea he was involved with drugs. We were so poor—if he was making money, it wasn't going to support his family. I don't know if he'll be charged or not. Right now . . ." Her voice broke. "Right now, I don't much care. I just want this to be over."

The thought of Ed making drug money while Ruth worked her fingers to the bone cleaning people's houses made Judd want to drive his fist through a wall, but he controlled the urge.

"Where are you, Ruth?" he asked.

"At school. There's a phone in the conference room."

"Can you get away for a little while? I'd like to take you to Buckaroo's for coffee and pie. We could both use the break."

She hesitated, perhaps remembering last night's emotionally charged phone call. But then she sighed. "I should be able to get away as long as I leave word at the office."

"Good, I'll meet you out front in about fifteen minutes," he said.

Ruth arranged to leave for a short time, then put on her coat and went outside to wait. Not wanting to start rumors in her workplace, she chose a spot away from any windows or doors in the building.

She stood gazing up at the trees that fronted the parking lot, their branches a dark tracery against the pewter sky. A V-shaped flock of geese flew overhead, their cries as faint as echoes. With Christmas barely three weeks away, the days were getting shorter and colder.

What would the holiday bring? A month ago, she'd planned a calm season of peace and plenty, a time of making new traditions with her children. But she no longer knew what to expect. Every day seemed to bring a new crisis—and at the heart of it all stood the man she'd sworn to forget.

A few minutes later, Judd drove up in his truck. With the motor still running, he came around to open the passenger door and help her onto the high seat. Her hand was cold, but the warmth of his big, leathery palm, enclosing hers, seemed to radiate through her body. She settled back into the seat, savoring the blast from the heater.

"Are you still good for Buckaroo's?" he asked.

"It's all I have time for," she said.

They turned the corner and headed down Main Street with the Christmas lights glowing above them. As they passed the park, with its glistening tree, Ruth found herself wishing they could stop there and enjoy the lights, sounds, and aromas of Christmas. She'd promised to be back at school in forty-five minutes. There wouldn't be much time. Still . . .

"Are you thinking what I'm thinking?" His voice interrupted her thoughts.

She gave him a grin. "You read my mind. Let's stop."

It was early yet. Main Street was far from crowded. He pulled into a handy space and helped her down from the truck. Side by side, they walked along the pavement that wound through the park. In the old days, he would have taken her hand. But that was then. This was now.

"Are you cold?" he asked. "That jacket looks thin."

"I'm fine," she said, but her teeth were chattering.

"Let me fix that." He was wearing a down vest over a heavy wool Pendleton shirt. Slipping off the vest, he held it so that she could slide it on over her jacket. It enfolded her in cozy warmth. She snuggled into the lingering heat from his body.

Most of the refreshment vendors were still setting up, but the heavenly fragrance of hot chocolate was drifting on the wintry air.

"I promised you coffee," Judd said. "Would you settle for chocolate—maybe with a marshmallow or two?"

"That sounds even better than coffee this morning," she said. "But no marshmallows. They're too sweet."

He chuckled. "I remembered that you didn't like them. I was just wondering if you'd changed your mind. Have a seat by the tree. I'll be right back."

Benches were arranged in an open semicircle with a view of the Christmas tree. At this hour most of them were empty. Ruth chose one and sat down. She was aware that Judd wanted to talk, and she wasn't looking forward to what he had to say. But for now, she allowed herself to enjoy the moment, gazing up at the tree with its traditional decorations, filling her senses with the aromas of spruce, cinnamon, bayberry candles, and freshly baked cookies.

The speakers had come on, playing a beautiful new song called "Candlelight Carol." Ruth had heard it only a few times, but she loved it. Skip had mentioned that the school choir, of which he was a member, would be singing that song in their Christmas concert, here in the park, on the last day of classes. She could hardly wait to hear their performance.

She was feeling almost sentimental by the time Judd returned. His hands balanced two Styrofoam cups. "Sorry, I had to wait till it was ready," he said, sitting. "Here's your chocolate. Mine has marshmallows."

Ruth took a cautious sip. It was hot and rich. But the moment of truth had arrived. "I know you made the offer on my property," she said. "You know I don't like to accept charity—"

"It isn't charity, Ruth. I've needed more grazing land for my cattle, and your farm is in a good location. It just made sense to buy it."

"But having the money will make all the difference for me and my children. Now we can buy a home of our own. We can even get a dog for the girls. I'd be ungrateful if I didn't thank you."

"No thanks needed," he said. "I want to talk to you about something else. And I want you to listen until I've finished."

The familiar knot in the pit of her stomach jerked tight. "It's about Skip, isn't it?"

"Yes. All I'm asking is for you to hear me out." He took a deep breath. "I know that I have no right to claim Skip as my son. I accept that. If you want him to believe he's the son of the good man who raised him, I accept that, too. And if you don't want me to associate with him—or with you—after the Christmas parade, that's something I'm prepared to live with. It's no better than I deserve. But here's the thing."

Ruth forced herself to keep still, even though doing so was like waiting for a bomb to explode.

"My parents passed away while I was in

prison," he said. "I was a disappointment even before my arrest. I'll never forgive myself for what my behavior must've done to them—that, and not being around when they needed me in their old age. I was a lousy son and an even worse father. But this isn't about guilt. It's about doing something for somebody besides myself.

"I'm setting up a trust fund for Skip's education. You won't need to tell him it's there or where it came from. But it will be there, and it'll be all he needs. I'll give you the documents when the legal work is done."

She stared at him, stunned, the empty cup dropping from her hand. "This is too much. I can't let you do it."

"You can't stop me, Ruth. And you won't, because you love your son, and you want the best for him."

"Then I've no choice except to thank you. But Skip isn't to know—not until I say so. I don't want him to think he has a free ride. And I don't want to belittle Abner's gift of his wife's Lladró figures, which we're selling to start Skip's college fund."

"That sounds reasonable enough."

"And he's to go to college. No more encouraging him to follow your career path."

"I never did encourage him, Ruth. I only showed him a few things."

She stood, picked up the fallen cup, and tossed it into a nearby trash receptacle. "I need to get back to school."

"Then let's go." His tone was slightly cool as they turned back toward the truck. They said little as he drove her to the school, but Ruth's mind was swarming with questions.

How could he expect her to melt with gratitude when she believed his generosity was a move to claim her son?

And how could she accept special treatment for Skip when her two girls—Ed's daughters—were excluded? That alone was reason to keep Judd at a distance. She and her three children were a package deal. She'd seen no sign that he understood that.

She didn't dare trust him—even though the yearning to be his was still there—to walk hand in hand with him, to lie in his arms and feel his kisses. *Too late.* She repeated the words to herself. *Too late.*

He let her off at the school and helped her out of the truck. She thanked him without any mention of meeting again. As she walked back to the building, she heard him drive away.

Inside, the older students were coming in from second recess. As she walked up the hall to check in at the office, a pretty sixth-grade girl greeted her with a smile and a thumbs-up. "I like your vest, Mrs. McCoy. Where did you buy it?"

Ruth glanced down at Judd's forest-green L.L.Bean vest, which she'd forgotten to return. "Thanks. It's . . . borrowed."

She sighed as the girl hurried to join her friends. Returning the vest shouldn't be a problem. She could give it to Skip tomorrow. He could take it to Judd after school when he went to work on the harness. But she was annoyed with herself for lacking the presence of mind to give it back.

Outside the office, the school Christmas tree shone with the same old-fashioned lights and ornaments Ruth remembered from her own school days as a student here. She checked in with the secretary and picked up a message from Silas, saying her station wagon was ready. Then she walked up the hall to her small office across from the lunchroom.

On her way, she passed colored paper Christmas trees taped to the wall and winter scenes with snowmen made of cotton balls and glue. In the gym, where the piano was kept, a first-grade class was practicing "Here Comes Santa Claus," their song for the program in the park. Janeen would be with them, singing her little heart out.

With Christmas happening all around her, Ruth had every reason to be glowing with holiday spirit. Her children were healthy, she had a steady job, and this Christmas they would celebrate with good food, friends, gifts, and no Ed to spoil the day by getting drunk. So far, her plan to make this the best Christmas ever seemed to be working—not to mention Judd's purchase of her land.

So why did she feel as if she were slinking around under a heavy black cloud?

From the direction of the preschool room, she saw a small figure running toward her. It was Tammy.

"Mommy!" she called as she came within hearing. "Shawn spilled his orange juice all over the story rug. Miss Carson needs you to come quick!"

The call of duty. After slipping off Judd's vest, Ruth grabbed a mop, a bucket, and a roll of paper towels, and followed her daughter back down the hall.

Late that night, Digger rode his motorcycle to the convenience store, stepped into the phone booth, and called the prison. Minutes passed while he fed quarters into the phone and waited for Ed. The big man wasn't going to be happy when he heard what Digger had to say.

"So, did you find the stash?" Ed growled.

"It wasn't there, Ed. Either somebody found it first, or you were lying to me."

"Are you calling me a liar, you little pissant? If you were here, I'd punch your face in for that. The stash was there, I swear it."

Digger had three quarters left in his hand. He deposited two of them. He was running out of time. "You said there was another stash. I need it, Ed. Tell me where it is."

Ed laughed. "Not so fast. First you got to earn it. Bring me something good—or better yet, let me know when you've punished that bastard Judd Rankin so that he'll never touch my wife again. Then it's all yours."

"Give me a clue, at least." Digger put his remaining quarter into the slot. The last sound he heard was Ed laughing before the phone went dead.

*   *   *

Judd was tooling the leather pieces to cover a pair of rawhide stirrups when Skip walked into the workshop alone. His face was ruddy with cold. He was wearing the green, down-filled vest that Judd had lent Ruth the day before.

"Are you on your own today?" Judd asked. "Where are Trevor and Maggie?"

"They'll be along," Skip said. "The bus lets us off at Trevor's house. They wanted to get a snack. I just wanted to get to work, so I walked on ahead." He took off the vest and held it out to Judd. "This is yours. My mom told me to bring it to you."

"You can keep it if you want," Judd said. "It's an extra. I've got others."

"Thanks. It's nice and warm, but Mom would never let me keep it. You know how she is."

"Yes, I do. Proud and stubborn. You can hang the vest on the coat hook. The offer's still open if you change your mind."

Skip hung the vest next to the door and walked over to watch Judd stamp the leather. "What was my mom doing with your vest anyway?"

"I paid her a short visit yesterday morning. We went to the park. She was cold." Judd glanced up from his work. "She was concerned about your keeping up in school—wanted to make sure your time here wasn't interfering with your homework." It was a half-truth, the best Judd could do without saying too much.

"Heck, I get most of my homework done in class."

"But she wants to make sure your grades are good enough to get you into college."

"My grades are fine. But like I told her, I'm not planning to go to college. I want to make saddles, like you do."

"That's what your mother told me. I've seen you work. I know you could learn to make good saddles. But the market for handmade custom saddles is pretty small. Most riders buy their tack ready-made. You've seen those Angus cows in my pasture. It was the livestock, not the saddles, that kept this ranch afloat while I was building my business. They're still my safety net when times get tough. Learn the trade if you want, Skip. Leather tooling can be a great hobby and earn you a little money. But get your education. Get some serious job skills because I guarantee you're going to need them."

Tough talk. Judd could only hope Skip had listened. It was the closest thing to fatherly advice he could give the boy. As his gaze took in Skip's downcast expression, the surge of love he felt was so strong that it almost made him lightheaded. This was his son. Blood of his blood. That was something even Ruth could never change.

"What is it with you and my mom, anyway?" Skip asked. "She doesn't want to come here, not even to let me out or pick me up. She doesn't want me to spend too much time with you. I understand that you two knew each other before you went to prison. But she won't talk about that time or tell me why she feels the way she does."

Judd stalled, taking time to wet down the stirrup leather with a sponge. "We did know each other," he said. "We were friends. But I was a wild boy, and she was a nice girl. She should have done what her parents wanted and stayed away from me."

"So, what happened?"

"About what you'd expect. I got into trouble, got arrested, and broke her heart. I'd hoped she'd wait for me. But she had more sense than that. She married a good man and had you. End of story." Judd picked up a new stamp and positioned it for the first tap of the maul. "You'd do well not to mention this conversation to your mother. It would only bring up painful memories. Do you understand?"

He nodded, as if weighing what he'd heard. "I guess I'd better get to work."

Judd watched his son walk back to where the harness was laid out on the floor. He'd probably told the boy too much. Ruth might not approve. But Skip was growing up. Sooner or later, he would have to come to terms with who he really was.

Trevor and Maggie came into the shop, their faces pink with cold. After taking off their coats, they set to work. Maggie had brought her boom box and left it here last time. Now she switched it on, filling the room with Christmas music from the local station. Christmas songs weren't Judd's favorite, but the music lightened the mood in the room and lent a subtle rhythm to the work.

Time was growing short. The town celebration, with the parade in the morning and the Cowboy Christmas Ball in the evening, was always held on the last Saturday before Christmas. This year, with Christmas on a Friday, the parade would take place on Saturday the 19th. That didn't leave much time.

The youngsters had worked hard, but with the parade just a couple weeks away and school still in session, the repairs to the harness were far from finished. The brass bells had been polished to a gleam. But the new leather bell strips, which the horses would wear like necklaces and belts, would need dozens of holes punched before the bells could be attached. Maggie's small hands weren't strong enough to operate the leather punch, and the boys were busy. Judd would have to do that for her.

Whether he could spare the time or not, Judd was becoming more and more involved in the parade. Alice Wilkins, the parade chairman, had phoned him that morning.

"Mr. Rankin." Her shrill voice and demanding manner were well-known in town. Many people found her annoying, but one had to give her credit for stepping in and getting things done. "I was just checking to make sure you were planning to handle the horses and drive the sleigh in the Christmas parade."

Judd had groaned. Last year, he'd loaded the horses into the trailer, hitched them up, and driven the sleigh because no one else was available. But he'd never meant to make it a permanent job.

"I'm sorry, Mrs. Wilkins, but I hadn't even

thought about it," he'd replied. "I've got work orders to fill. I don't have time. Please ask someone else."

"But you've *got* to do it!" Her voice had risen a full octave. "There'll be children around that sleigh. If something were to go wrong, they could be trampled. We need somebody who can control the team and keep the little ones safe."

Guilt served on a trowel. "There has to be somebody else who can do the job," he'd argued. "What about Buck Winston? He's a farm boy. He can handle a team."

"Sheriff Winston will be busy managing the crowds. He can't possibly do two jobs. Abner has agreed to play Santa again. But we can't have a sleigh without a good driver. Please, Mr. Rankin. Think of the little children."

He was being reeled in. "I'll think about it," he'd said. "But meanwhile, I want you to look for somebody else. Let me know when you find them."

"Certainly. And thank you, Mr. Rankin."

She wouldn't look. He'd known that even as he'd hung up the phone. He could've just said no. But Alice Wilkins had pushed all the right buttons. *Think of the little children,* she'd said. And he was hooked.

Maybe knowing he was actually a father had something to do with it.

When the light began to fade outside, Judd called a halt to the work. Trevor would be going home, but his parents were expecting company, so Skip and Maggie would be walking to Abner's house, where Ruth would pick them up.

Judd wouldn't have minded taking them home himself, but the arrangements had already been made. He stood on the porch and watched them leave, Trevor heading along the road to his house and the other two taking the narrow lane across the pastureland to Abner's. The sky was still light, and they didn't have far to go. Still, he wanted to make sure they were safe.

It grated on him, having Ruth avoid his house. But he told himself it was mostly because of Digger. When the time came, he could only hope his former friend would leave without making a scene.

But Judd's day was far from over. With his young friends gone, he had enough work to keep him busy for hours. Maggie had left her boom box on. He would leave it for now. Maybe the Christmas music would lift his mood.

He'd been working for about twenty minutes when the phone rang. When he answered it, he heard Skip's frantic voice. "We need you, Judd. We're at Abner's. He's fallen down and can't get up."

"Is he conscious?"

"Yes, but we think his back is hurt. We don't dare move him, and Mom isn't here yet."

"I'll be right there." Judd hung up the phone, grabbed his keys, and raced for his truck.

Chapter Ten

As Judd pulled up to Abner's house and climbed out of the truck, Maggie ran to him from the porch. Distress was written all over her face. "Abner's in the kitchen," she said. "Skip's trying to make him feel better, but he's really hurting."

"Has anybody called nine-one-one?" He mounted the porch at a stride.

"Not yet. We wanted you here first. Skip tried to call his mom, but she didn't answer. She's probably driving. Come on."

They rushed into the house. Abner lay face up on the kitchen floor with a cushion under his head. The dog crouched at his side, nuzzling his hand. Skip knelt by his head.

"Howdy, Judd. Sorry you have to see me like this." Abner's eyes were open, his gaze alert. But he was clearly in severe pain.

"What happened, Abner?" Judd leaned over him.

"Damned knee. I turned to get something out of the fridge, and it just gave way. I went down like a sack of rocks."

"Where's the pain?"

"Hell, all over. But mostly my back. Not sure if anything's broken, but if I try to get up, it hurts like blazes."

"Okay, just lie still." Judd glanced at Skip. "Get on the phone and call nine-one-one. We mustn't try to move him without a stretcher. That could do more damage."

Skip went to the wall phone. A moment later, Judd heard him describing Abner's condition. Maggie had gone back outside, probably to wait for Ruth.

The hospital was in Cottonwood Springs, an hour away. But Branding Iron had its own satellite station with a fire engine that doubled as an ambulance and a rotating crew with paramedic training. It shouldn't take them long to get here.

"If I have to go to the hospital, I'll need somebody to take care of Butch, here. He's never been left alone."

"Don't worry, Abner. I'll take care of your dog," Judd said. "I'll watch your property, too. You won't have to worry about a thing except getting better."

"The parade . . ." he muttered. "You'll need to find a new Santa."

"It's too soon to worry about that. Just rest." Abner had been a magical Santa. He'd be hard to replace. But that wasn't Judd's worry. Right now, nothing mattered except getting the old man the best possible care.

Ruth burst in through the front door. Alerted by Maggie, she rushed to the kitchen. "How can I help you, Abner?" She dropped to her knees next to him. "What can I do for you?"

"For starters, you can stop fussing over me," Abner grumbled. "One way or another, I'll get through this."

"We've called an ambulance, Ruth," Judd said. "They should be here soon. Somebody will need to be with him at the hospital. Since you've got your children, that will be me. I'll follow the ambulance in my truck and see that he's taken care of."

She reached for his hand. Her slim, strong fingers gripped his for a moment. "Thank you, Judd. This man is like a father to me and a grandfather to my children."

"Stop it, girl. You're makin' me blubber," Abner muttered.

Ruth caught her son's attention across the room. "Skip, please go out and make sure your sisters stay in the car. With the ambulance coming, we don't need them running around, getting in the way."

"Got it." Skip headed for the door.

"Oh, and Skip—" Judd twisted his house key from the ring. "I left the shop unlocked. When you leave here, could you swing by and lock the doors for me? I've got a spare key, so you can keep this one for now."

"Sure. I'll say a prayer for you, Abner." He

caught the key Judd tossed him. As he headed out the door, the ambulance, its siren fading to a whine, pulled into the yard and backed up to the porch. Skip directed the paramedics to the kitchen before joining his sisters in the station wagon.

Working efficiently, the two husky men checked Abner's vital signs and eased him onto the stretcher. He grimaced with pain as they lifted him.

"You're in good hands, Abner," Judd reassured him. "I'll be driving my truck to meet you at the hospital."

"You'll take care of Butch?" Abner asked to make sure.

"We'll spoil him." Ruth leaned over Abner and kissed his cheek. Then the two men carried the stretcher out the door to the waiting ambulance.

Judd, Ruth, and Maggie stood on the porch watching as the ambulance drove out through the gate. Butch gave a long, mournful whimper as the brake lights vanished down the lane with his master.

"Why don't you let me take Butch?" Maggie suggested. "We've got a fenced yard, and he can be friends with my dog, Banjo. He'll have food and toys and everything."

"That's a great idea, Maggie," Ruth said. "Ask Skip to open the tailgate for you. We'll put him in the back."

As Maggie led Butch out to the wagon, Ruth locked the door with the spare key Abner had given her. Turning to Judd on the porch, she pressed the key into his hand. "You'll need this to check the house. Promise you'll call me the minute you hear how Abner's doing, no matter how late it is."

"I promise."

They stood facing each other. As her warm hazel eyes gazed up into his, Judd was struck by a new truth. All these years, he'd been haunted by the memory of a beautiful, free-spirited girl. But that girl had vanished into the past. Now he was falling in love with a strong, courageous, magnificent woman.

She spoke, "We both need to get going. You go first. Don't worry, I'll remember to have Skip lock your place."

"Thanks. I'll call you." Judd strode down the steps to his truck and roared off down the lane, the way the ambulance had gone.

With Skip in the front seat, Maggie stuffed between the two little girls, and the dog filling up the rear, Ruth drove the graveled lane that led back to Judd's house. With the engine still running, she parked outside the workshop. "Hurry," she told Skip as he opened the passenger door and climbed out. "We need to get Maggie home."

Truth be told, there was no rush to deliver Maggie and the dog to the Delaney house. It was the idea that Digger could be somewhere nearby, watching, that made Ruth's skin crawl. Common sense told her the man wouldn't hurt her. But there was something reptilian about his lurking silence—something in that knowing grin of his that made her feel violated. He was probably watching her right now.

It was getting dark outside. Where was Skip? Why was he taking so long to lock a couple of doors? Ruth's nerves were quivering, but she couldn't drive away and leave her son.

The girls in the back seat were silent, as if they sensed an unseen presence, just as she did.

The dog growled.

Spurred to action, Ruth punched the radio button and turned the volume up. As "Rockin' Around the Christmas Tree" blasted out of the speakers, she reached up and switched on the dome light. Light and noise, that's what would scare the bogeyman away. She'd believed it growing up—but that was before she'd married Ed McCoy. "Hey, let's sing!" she said.

The singing stopped when Skip came around the corner of the house and climbed into the passenger seat. "What took you so long?" Ruth asked. "I was getting worried."

"Nothing to worry about," Skip said. "As long as I was there, I thought it might be a good idea to check the doors and windows in the house, that's all. Everything's fine."

"Good. Let's go." Ruth turned off the inside light, shifted gears, and, with the radio still blaring, headed out of the yard. Glancing in her rearview mirror, she thought she saw a shadow move in the darkness behind her. She couldn't be sure—but never mind, she and the children were safe. She wouldn't think about that now. It was Abner's condition that had her worried. A back injury could mean anything—a quick recovery, chronic pain, major surgery, even paralysis.

As she drove, she said a silent prayer for her friend.

It was after ten o'clock that night when Ruth got the call from Judd. Earlier, when she'd tucked her daughters into bed, they'd both mentioned Abner in their prayers. She could only hope those innocent prayers would be heard.

She'd been waiting by the phone, trying to read, when the call came. Her hand shook as she picked up the receiver.

"Judd? How is he?"

"He's in a lot of pain. They've got him on painkillers and cold packs, but the news is good. It's a strained tendon, along with some muscle spasms. With rest and ice and some physical therapy, he could be doing all right in a couple of weeks."

"In time for the parade?"

"Maybe. But I'm not going to mention that. We want him to take it easy. He's sleeping now. I promised to be here when he wakes up."

"Tomorrow's Saturday. I'll go visit him in the morning. How long will he be in the hospital?"

"A couple of days, until he can get up and use a walker. Then I'll be taking him to my place until it's safe for him to be home."

"Thank you, Judd. I know you have work to do."

"Some things are more important than work." Ruth could hear voices in the background. "Need to go. I'll call you if there's any change."

With a sigh of relief, Ruth sank back into the sofa cushions. She'd been so worried about Abner. Maybe now she could relax and get some sleep before tomorrow.

Or maybe not.

With just two weekends to go before the big Christmas celebration. Skip would want to spend the day working on the harness with Trevor and Maggie. That meant he wouldn't be available to tend his sisters at home while she visited Abner. The hospital was no place to bring young children—and seeing their friend in pain could be distressing to the girls. She'd be better off going tonight while Skip was at home and his sisters were asleep.

After filling the coffeemaker and switching it on, she went down the hall to Skip's room and tapped lightly on the door.

"I'm awake, Mom. You can come in."

She opened the door to find him sitting up in bed, reading. "I couldn't sleep," he said. "Is there any word about Abner?"

"Judd just called." She gave him the news. "If you don't mind babysitting the girls for a few hours, I thought I'd go and visit him now. I'll be back in time for your paper route. Then, if Judd's home, you'll be free to spend the day working on the harness. All right?"

"That sounds great. Let me know how Abner's doing." He closed his book and laid it down. "And Mom, one thing." He paused, swallowed. "I know that you and Judd dated before he got arrested. You're both alone, and I like him a lot. If you ever, you know, wanted to get together again, it would be fine with me. The girls like him, too."

"Oh, Skip!" She wanted to hug him, but the moment was too fragile, too precious. "Judd's a good man, but that was a long time ago. Too much water under the bridge, as they say. Nothing's going to happen. But I love you for telling me. I . . ." She fumbled for words. "I think the coffee's ready. Tell the girls about Abner when they wake up. They've said prayers." She turned away and fled the room to hide the moisture in her eyes.

The coffee was done. She added a dollop of milk and gulped it down before flinging on her coat and dashing out the door. Skip's words had slammed her like a doubled-up fist. *Dating*? Was he really that innocent?

But it was his sweetness that had driven a knife through her heart. As if anything were possible. As if love stories could end like fairy tales, with happily ever after.

Her beloved boy would have some hard lessons to learn.

The nighttime weather was clear, the traffic sparse at this hour. A faint doggy smell lingered inside the wagon. Ruth cracked the window to freshen the air and lowered the volume on the radio.

What if life could be as simple as Skip seemed to think? She could say yes to Judd; they could marry; he would claim Skip and adopt the girls.

She would move her family into his fine home, and they would live happily ever after.

But life wasn't like that. Not for her. Her first love had gone to prison. Her second had been killed. Her third had turned out to be an abusive monster. There would be no fourth try for happiness.

The hospital was at the far end of Cottonwood Springs. Ruth drove up the main street under a dazzle of blinking Christmas lights. Arriving, she parked in the visitors' lot and walked to the main entrance.

She'd been here before but not at Christmastime. The lobby was decorated with a glittering tree in one corner. Traditional Christmas music played whisper soft in the background. Ruth knew that the decorations and the music were meant to put people in a peaceful holiday mood. But all Ruth could feel was an empty hollow in the place where love had come and gone.

After getting the room number, she took the elevator to the fourth floor and followed the numbered doors down the long hallway. Abner's room would be at the far end, past the nurse's station. She could see it now, the door slightly ajar.

Inside, the room was dim, lit by a lamp above the sink. City lights glowed through the slats of the venetian blinds. Judd was nowhere to be seen.

Walking to the bed, she gazed down at Abner. He lay on his side, the faint outline of a brace showing beneath the blanket. His eyes were closed, his breathing deep and even. His resting face looked old and frail. She was tempted to take his hand and wake him, just to make sure he was still the kind, affable man she'd always known. But he was most likely on painkillers and needed to sleep.

An upholstered chair had been placed next to the bed. As she shifted it to sit down, Ruth noticed Judd's coat hanging over the back. He wouldn't have left it behind. He must be somewhere in the hospital.

Bone-tired, she sank into the chair and closed her eyes. She'd been running on nerves and adrenaline since the news of Abner's accident. Now it was as if a plug had been pulled. Only now, as she rested, did Judd's words come back to her.

Some things are more important than work.

He'd been right. Abner's well-being was more important than saddles, more important, even, than being Santa. In the end, friends and family were all that mattered.

When had he become so wise? Clearly, he hadn't yet learned that lesson when he'd left her to ride with his friends. Maybe he'd changed. But she'd changed, too. Life had taught her that she could depend on no one but herself.

Lulled by the warmth in the room, the low light, and the easy cadence of Abner's breathing, she began to drift. She was almost fast asleep when she felt a touch on her shoulder. She flinched and opened her eyes.

"Hey, Ruth." Judd was smiling down at her. "What are you doing here? I thought you were coming tomorrow."

She stifled a yawn. "Tonight was easier. I was able to leave the girls home with Skip. And I was getting anxious about Abner."

"As you can see, he's out like a light." His voice was just above a whisper.

"I promised Skip that I'd be home in time for his Saturday paper route." She followed his cue to keep from waking Abner. "But I can stay until six o'clock. If you need to go—"

"No, I plan to stay until morning, when they'll check him again. I don't want to leave until I know how he's doing and when he can come home."

Ruth stood. "In that case, you can have your chair back. I'll be fine."

"You don't look fine. You look dead on your feet. Go ahead and sit down."

A smile tugged at Ruth's lips. "You really know how to flatter a lady, don't you? Take the chair. See—there's a metal folding chair by the window. That will do me fine."

"Like blazes it will. Come here, you stubborn woman." Clasping her hand, he sat down in the chair and reeled her toward him. Ruth could have pulled away, but something compelled her to follow his lead. She was tired of fighting him—and fighting herself.

Pulling her down, he eased her onto his lap and cradled her in his arms. Unbidden, she laid her head against his shoulder and closed her eyes. As she listened to the steady beating of his heart, her breathing fell into rhythm with his. When was the last time she'd been held like this? It must've been a long time ago.

"Rest," he murmured. "Sleep if you can. You never seem to let go, Ruth. Always pressured, always worried, as if the fate of the world was resting on your shoulders. Even when I try to lighten your load, you fight me over it."

"I know what you think. But there've been so many years when I had no one to depend on but myself. Even with Ed—"

"Hush, I know." His lips grazed her hairline. "You had to be the strong one, the one who was always there for your children. You thought they needed a father—but you were their rock. It was your love and support that helped them become the great kids they are."

She drew back and looked up at him. "Did Skip tell you that?"

He paused, as if hesitant to say too much. "Abner told me a little. I pretty much guessed the rest. Am I wrong?"

"That's an unfair question. I didn't have time to think about how to raise my children. It was all we could do to survive from one day to the next."

His arms tightened around her. "I'm sorry, Ruth. Sorry my bad choice made everything so hard. I would have taken care of you. We could've been a family."

"Don't," she whispered. "We can't go back and change the past. If things had been different, I wouldn't have my girls. They've been worth it all."

"I know we can't change the past. But we can change the future." He lowered his head and found her lips.

For an instant, she went rigid, resisting. Then need took over. She melted against him and caught fire. She had never loved another man the way she'd loved Judd. Not even Tom, for all his goodness, had stirred the heat that had slumbered inside her. It was as if, when Judd was arrested, she'd locked herself in a prison of her own making. Only Judd possessed the touch that could set her free.

For a moment, she let herself spiral back in time. She was seventeen again, and he was two years older, their young bodies warm in the long summer grass, with no desire in their hearts except to give themselves to each other.

What fools they'd been.

Wrenching herself back to the present, she pushed away from him and stood. "This isn't going to work, Judd. We're not the same people we used to be."

His mouth tightened as he rose to face her. "I love you, Ruth. We were good together once. We could be again."

"Think about it. I'm responsible for three children. You've been alone so long, you've no idea what living with a family can be like—the noise, the mess, the responsibility that never lets up. I know you want to claim your son. But what about the girls? They may be Ed McCoy's daughters, but I love them as much as I love Skip. We're a package, Judd. And I can't imagine you're ready for that."

"You could at least let me try."

"We're not talking free trial here. I won't have

my daughters' hearts broken if things don't work out."

The exchange might have become heated, but just then Abner stirred and opened his eyes. He looked up at them and smiled. "Now isn't that a pretty picture." He sounded drowsy. "Just what I wanted to see, the two of you together. Does this mean you've got plans?"

"Whoa, there." Ruth leaned over him and brushed her hand down his cheek. "Don't get ahead of yourself, friend. Nothing's going on."

"How are you feeling?" Judd asked.

"Like crap. But at least I'm alive. How soon can you get me out of this place and home?"

"That'll be up to the doctors. I'd say at least a couple more days until you're able to get around on your own. Until then, you're better off here."

"Can we get you anything?" Ruth asked. "Water, or maybe something to eat?"

"I'll take a sip of water and one of those good pain pills. But I guess you'll have to call the nurse for that."

"I'll go out to the nurse's station and ask," Ruth said.

"No need. I'll just push the call button. Handy little gadget. Too bad I can't take it home with me." He turned his head to look at Ruth. "You look all in. Go home and get some rest. You, too, Judd. I've got good folks taking care of me here. I'll be fine."

"I'm not leaving until you've seen the doctor in the morning," Judd said. "But you might as well go, Ruth. You're tired, and you've left Skip and the girls at home. I'll call you in the morning."

With a sigh, Ruth gave in. Clearly, she wasn't needed here. "All right, I'll go," she said, squeezing Abner's hand. "You take it easy, friend."

"You, too. And get some rest. I mean it, Ruth. You've been taking care of everybody but yourself."

"Abner's right," Judd said. "Listen to him."

She picked up her purse, which she'd left next to the chair. "I'll see you tomorrow, Abner. And promise you'll call me in the morning, Judd. All right?"

"I promise. Now, get going, Ruth. And be careful on the road. There's supposed to be some weather moving in."

"I'll be fine." She walked out the door, passing the nurse who'd been called. The elevator took her back down to the lobby with its shining tree and soothing carols. Taking a moment, she stood in front of the tree, inhaled its fresh scent, and willed the Christmas spirit to flow into her heart. But all she felt was a jumble of confusion. Judd's kiss and her response, concern for Abner, worry over her children, Christmas preparations, fear of Digger and what he might do, tumbled over and over in her mind like clothes trapped in a dryer. And she couldn't seem to make them stop.

"Isn't this lovely, dear?" The silvery voice at her elbow startled her. An elderly woman—white hair, hunched shoulders, a cane in one hand, and her purse over her arm—stood next to Ruth. "That aroma makes you feel Christmasy all over, doesn't it?"

"I wish it did." Something about the woman made Ruth feel the urge to open up. "I've been trying to get in a Christmas mood, but so far it isn't working. I've got too much on my mind."

"Haven't we all, dear?" She smiled up at Ruth, deepening the wrinkles around her eyes. Her hair was perfectly coiffed. Her makeup was in place. She was dressed in gray slacks and a cherry-red cardigan. "Don't worry, it will come. It always did for me, even in the hard times."

"Are you here to visit someone?" Ruth asked.

"Yes. My husband. I always try to look pretty for him when I come."

"You do look pretty."

"Oh, pshaw! I'm an old woman. But as long as I look pretty to Carl, that's all that matters. I'm Vera, by the way."

"And I'm Ruth. If you don't mind my asking, why is your husband here? Will he be going home soon?"

A shadow seemed to pass across the woman's face. Then she rearranged her features into a smile. "He has congestive heart failure, and he's too old for a transplant. But yes, he'll be coming home tomorrow. The house is set up for hospice care. We'll have one last Christmas together— even if we have to celebrate early."

Oh, Vera, Ruth thought. But she sensed that the woman wouldn't welcome pity. "How long have you been married, Vera?" she asked.

"Sixty-six years. And except for when Carl was in Vietnam, we've never missed a Christmas together. We've been blessed that way—and blessed to have one more. The tree is up, the music ready. I'll be cooking food for friends and family to come, so Carl will be able to smell it, even though he can't really eat." She laughed, a brave little sound. "I've even got mistletoe hanging above the bed, because I want to give him lots of kisses." Her voice broke on the last few words. She was strong, but not that strong.

"Carl will be waiting for me. I'd better go. Have a Merry Christmas, Ruth." Vera squeezed Ruth's hand before she hurried off to the elevators.

Ruth watched the elevator doors slide shut behind the woman in the red sweater. She checked the urge to slap herself. Why was she whining when she had so many reasons to celebrate the holiday—three beautiful, healthy children, a decent job, a home, friends, and a man who would love her if she had the courage to let him. What was wrong with her?

But she knew the answer to that question. Over the years, she'd grown accustomed to feeling overburdened. Her joyless attitude had become a habit. Christmas had become just one more source of stress. Even decorating the tree with the children, taking the girls to the park, and shopping for presents had felt like chores to be checked off on her list.

It had taken a woman with a dying husband to show her the true meaning of Christmas.

As she fumbled for her keys, her throat tightened with emotion. She had worried her life away, and her family had paid the price. She had been a dutiful mother. No one could fault her on that. But where was her joy? Her laughter? When was the last time she'd allowed herself to loosen up and have fun?

She had made a promise to give her children the best Christmas ever—the tree, the presents, the food. Only one thing was missing—their mother.

Her problems were not going away. But something needed to change, and that change would have to be genuine.

Buttoning her jacket up to her chin, she walked through the revolving door and stepped out into the night. The lights around the parking lot cast shadows on the gleaming asphalt. Ink-black clouds hid the stars.

The wind that had blown all week was still, the night as quiet as a whisper. As Ruth walked down the row of cars to her station wagon, something cold and wet settled on her cheek. She looked up. Soft, white flakes were falling out of the sky. It was snowing.

Chapter Eleven

On Sunday morning Ruth loaded her children into the station wagon and took the road to Judd's place. Abner would be leaving the hospital today. Judd had gone to Cottonwood Springs to pick him up and bring him to the ranch.

Ruth and her daughters had planned a surprise meal to welcome Abner home. The girls had helped with the cooking. Skip would make the delivery. Everything would be waiting in Judd's kitchen when the two men returned. But they wouldn't know who had left the food. That was the surprise.

Ruth had been unsure about the surprise at first. She'd already made it clear to Judd that she wasn't interested in a serious relationship. She didn't want him thinking she'd changed her mind. But Janeen and Tammy had loved the

idea. They'd been so excited that Ruth had relented. Now she was glad she'd given in. The
girls had had fun, and the experience had given
them a lesson in the joy of service.

Skip sat next to her in the front seat, holding
a Crock-Pot wrapped in a thick towel. Ruth had
put the meat and vegetables in to cook late last
night. By now, the pot roast was done and just
needed to be kept warm. In the back seat, Janeen balanced a pan with the cake the girls had
helped their mother bake and decorate.

"They'll be so surprised," Janeen said. "Do
you think they'll know it was us?"

"They'll probably know," Skip said. "But
they'll still be surprised—and hungry."

"This is fun," Tammy said. "It's lots more fun
than sitting in church."

"The reverend said that doing good deeds is
more important than church," Janeen said. "This
is a good deed, isn't it, Mom?"

Ruth laughed. "I certainly hope so."

The morning sky was clear. Friday night's
snow had melted off the asphalt, but a dusting
of white lay over the fields and glittered on the
dry weeds along the road. A deer, grazing in the
bar ditch, raised its head as they passed.

"Maybe that's one of Santa's reindeer," Tammy said.

"Reindeer have antlers," Janeen said. "That's
just a deer."

A few minutes later, they drove through the
ranch gate and stopped at the house. Ruth
could see Judd's black pickup in the open shed,
but she knew he'd planned to take his spare car,

a vintage sedan, to make the ride more comfortable for Abner.

Digger's Yamaha bike was there as well. A chill crawled up Ruth's spine as she saw it. She gave herself a mental slap. Digger was a creepy little man who enjoyed getting on her nerves. She'd tried not to let him intimidate her. But he knew about her past, and he'd almost certainly guessed the truth about Skip. That gave him power, and he knew it.

Skip had the key Judd had lent him earlier. Juggling the wrapped Crock-Pot and the cake pan, he mounted the steps, opened the front door, and carried everything inside before closing the door behind him.

It would take him a few minutes to plug in the Crock-Pot and set the table. Ruth had settled in to wait when she heard a tap on the side window. Her heart sank. Even before she turned toward the sound, she knew it would be Digger.

His grinning, unshaven face was inches from the glass. Ruth's first impulse was to keep the window closed and ignore him. But that would send the message that she was afraid.

The girls had been chatting. They had fallen silent now. Their eyes were wide and scared, but the rear doors were securely locked to protect them.

"It's all right. Just be still. He won't hurt us," Ruth assured them. Then she lowered the window halfway.

"Hello, Digger," she said. "Is there something you need?"

"Nope. Just came over to say howdy." He rested his forearms on the side of the door. "Beautiful family you've got. I can tell the girls are Ed's. But that good-looking boy, now, he's something else. Spittin' image of his daddy."

Dread tightened Ruth's grip on the steering wheel—not for herself but for her innocent daughters, who could hear every word. They knew nothing about her past and wouldn't understand if they did.

"Skip's father was my first husband," she said.

Digger's tobacco-stained grin widened to show a missing bicuspid. "Sure, lady, I know what you claim. But we know the real story, don't we? What would you give me to keep quiet?"

So that was his game? Blackmail? It sounded like a joke, but Ruth wasn't laughing. "If you're after money, Digger, you're barking up the wrong tree."

"We could negotiate—or I could explain the facts of life to those little girls of yours. I'll bet they don't even know where babies come from."

His words ignited a firestorm of motherly rage. Given a gun, she would have shot him without a moment's hesitation. But she was helpless, and he knew it. If she were to drive off, she'd be leaving Skip. And even that wouldn't stop him. As long as he remained in Branding Iron, there would always be a next time.

She was about to close the window when something flashed in her memory—something Digger had said moments earlier.

I can tell the girls are Ed's.

Ruth pounced on the words like a hungry cat.

"You mentioned Ed, Digger. How do you know him?" she demanded. "You were gone when our family moved to Branding Iron. And by the time you came back here, he was already in prison. Where did you know him? Was it in prison? Is that why you're here?"

Consternation showed in Digger's face. He didn't reply.

Even as she spoke, more pieces of the puzzle fell into place. "The cocaine," she said. "Silas's mechanic found it in my station wagon. Ed's fingerprints were all over it. Is that why you came back here—because Ed told you where he'd stashed it?"

Digger's cocky grin had vanished. "I don't know what you're talking about," he said. "And I sure as hell don't know anything about any cocaine."

"Yes, you do. And before I'm through with you, the sheriff will know, too." Ruth could see Skip coming out of the house. She started the engine, closed the window, and honked the horn, urging her son to hurry.

By the time Skip climbed into the passenger seat, Digger had disappeared. Ruth gunned the engine. The lumbering station wagon roared out of the gate and down the lane.

"Are you all right, Mom?" Skip asked. "I saw Digger. I know you don't like him."

"I'm fine," Ruth answered, and she was. But she needed to decide what to do next. Since Digger hadn't found the cocaine, he probably hadn't broken the law. But the sheriff would want to know about his connection to Ed. Judd

would want to know, too. She would tell him before she spoke to anyone else.

Janeen and Tammy remained silent. They
could still be scared. Ruth would talk to them at
home and make sure they were all right. For
now, everyone could use some Christmas cheer.
She switched on the radio and turned the song
up loud.

Jingle bells, jingle bells, jingle all the way . . .
They sang along, all the way home.

By the time the doctor had checked Abner
and signed his release, it was almost eleven
o'clock. Abner could sit and stand with a back
brace and get around with a walker, but he was
still on pain pills and far from ready to be home
alone. Judd picked him up in the vintage Pontiac Firebird that served as his extra car and set
out for the ranch, where the old man would stay
and recuperate for a few days.

"Boy, am I glad to get out of that hospital,"
Abner said. "It was like being in prison. And I
won't even mention the food."

"I know just what you mean." Judd forced a
chuckle. He hadn't planned on a houseguest at
this busy time, but none of Abner's other
friends had a spare room and an adult who'd be
home to look after him. Yesterday, while Ruth
visited Abner in the hospital, he'd set up a bed
for the old man, made sure he had a comfortable chair in front of the TV, and stocked the
fridge with takeout from Shop Mart. The preparations took a big bite out of his Saturday work

time, but with Abner's family living out of state, somebody had needed to step in.

He'd turned the three youngsters loose in his shop to work on the harness. By now he could trust them to do the job without supervision. But time was growing short. With the parade on Saturday, December 19, school wouldn't be letting out until the day before. That left less than two weeks of after-school work for the harness to be finished, the sleigh to be readied, and the horses groomed for the parade.

And there was no guarantee that Abner, the perfect Santa, would be healed in time. People were getting worried.

"Chester Filson plays Santa for the church party," Grace Delaney had offered when she'd dropped off Skip and Maggie on Saturday morning. "If Abner isn't ready—"

"No!" the three youngsters had chorused.

"He's too skinny," Maggie had said. "And his *ho-ho-ho* sounds like he's got a bad cold. Like this. *Hew-hew-hew.*"

"Maggie, that's not nice," her mother had scolded. "Alice Wilkins called yesterday and asked Sam if he'd be willing to fill in. Sam was Santa two years ago, for the Christmas ball, but he swore that he'd never do it again. Anyway, now that he's mayor, he can't be Santa, too."

"Everybody wants Abner," Trevor had said. "He's like the real Santa."

"You don't believe in Santa, Trevor," Maggie had said.

"Maybe not, but to the little kids who'll be watching the parade, Abner *is* the real Santa."

"Then he'd better get well," Judd had said. "And we'd better help him."

The same thought passed through Judd's mind now as he drove through the ranch gate. He knew Abner didn't want to disappoint the children, but even in the cushiony seat of a smooth-riding car, the old man clenched his jaw with pain. He was going to need rest, good food, and the right kind of movement. The physical therapist at the hospital had given him a print-out of exercises to do, but he wasn't ready to do them alone. He was going to need help.

As he drove past the shed, Judd saw an empty space where Digger usually parked his Yamaha. The issue of Digger called for some attention, too. Judd needed to talk to his former friend and get an understanding of his plans, if he had any. Once Digger had a place to go, maybe Judd could work on getting Ruth back into his life.

Meanwhile, there were saddles waiting to be finished and shipped. At least he'd have a few days after the parade to work, but they wouldn't be enough. He needed more time, but somehow he would have to manage everything.

He parked the car next to the porch and came around to help Abner up the steps. He could tell that every step was painful, but Abner didn't complain.

"I can't tell you how much I appreciate this, Judd," he said. "I know you have work to do. I'll try not to take much of your time."

"We just want you back on your feet."

"And in that sleigh, I know." Abner chuckled. "I'll do my best to be in shape. But you'd better have a Plan B in case I can't make it."

"Plan B is not my job." Judd unlocked the door and opened it for Abner, who paused, sniffing the air.

"Damn, but that smells good!" he exclaimed.

A tantalizing aroma drifted from the kitchen. Handing Abner his walker, Judd followed his nose. On the counter, a warm Crock-Pot filled the room with a savory fragrance. Pot roast. It had to be.

"It looks like you've had a visitor," Abner said.

"But who? And how did they get this in the house? I don't own a Crock-Pot." Judd raised the lid. Pot roast. He was right. It looked and smelled heavenly.

A foil-covered aluminum baking pan rested nearby. Abner raised the foil. "Hot dog, it's chocolate cake! And it's Ruth's. I'd know that old pan anywhere. Judd, if you don't marry that woman, you should have your head examined."

"I won't argue with that idea. But how did she get all this in here?"

Judd had seated Abner at the table and was dishing up the meat and vegetables when he remembered. Before he'd left to follow the ambulance, he'd given Skip a key. He knew, of course, that the food was here because of Abner. Still, it was a nice surprise.

The surprise would have been even nicer if Ruth had been waiting here to welcome him. Judd could almost picture her standing in the doorway with her arms open. For now, that fantasy would have to wait. But he hadn't given up on making it real.

After lunch, Abner was tired enough for a nap. "You're sure you'll be all right by yourself?" Judd asked him. "You could fall getting up and down."

"Blast it, I'm not an invalid, and you're not my nurse," Abner grumbled. "The hospital therapist showed me how to get on and off the bed. It hurts like hell when I do it, but I won't fall. I'll be fine, and you've got saddles to finish. Don't let me keep you from your work."

Resolving to come back later and check on him, Judd went out to his shop. The harness lay spread on the floor. Skip, Trevor, and Maggie wouldn't be coming to work on it until Monday after school. So far, they'd done an amazing job. Most of the larger straps had been replaced. But many smaller pieces needed to be measured, sewn, and threaded through the rings and buckles.

Maggie had been attaching the bells to the leather strips that would go around the horses' necks like jewelry. She'd made a good start, but hours of work lay ahead, threading the base of each bell through a hole punched in the leather, then tying it in place from the back side. Something told Judd that when the kids had decided to fix the harness, they'd had no idea what they were getting into. But he had to give them credit for staying with the job.

Three unfinished saddles waited on their stands. Judd stood back and studied them, organizing the work that remained. The saddle that a wealthy TV producer had ordered for his wife was nearly done. The leather pieces were tooled and needed only to be hand-stitched into place. If he worked steadily, he could finish that one by late tonight, and ship it off tomorrow. That would leave the presentation saddle, which needed the most work, and the one that a breeder of million-dollar performance horses had ordered for a reining competition.

Judd took pride in his craft. He couldn't—and wouldn't—cut corners with materials or workmanship on any of his saddles. Not only were they beautiful pieces of art—they were made to fit the rider's body and rest easily on the horse, so that at the end of a long day's ride, there would be no sore spots. Everything had to be perfect. That was why his work commanded premium prices.

With a plan to follow, he felt more confident about his tight schedule. He would check on Abner once more and make a quick call to Ruth. Then he would get to work.

Back in the house, he found Abner snoring on the bed. The room was chilly, so he laid a light quilt over the old man and stole out again.

He waited until he was back in the workshop before phoning Ruth. His pulse quickened when he heard her pick up.

"Judd? Is everything all right? How's Abner?" There was a note of strain in her voice.

"Everything's fine. Abner's asleep. He's still got some pain, but he's getting around a little better today. I'm really calling to thank you for the delivery. Pot roast and chocolate cake. You know the way to a man's heart—or two men's hearts."

"I'll pass your thanks on to Skip and the girls. How did you know it was us?"

"Abner recognized your cake pan, and I remembered that Skip had a key." He paused. "Are you all right, Ruth? Has anything happened?"

She managed a weak laugh. "You always could read me. But no, everything's fine. When I went to your house this morning, I stayed in the car with the girls while Skip carried the food inside. I'd hoped I wouldn't run into Digger, but there he was, and he came right over." There was a pause. "I won't keep you long, but I learned something. Digger knew Ed—most likely in prison. You already know that the cocaine stashed in my station wagon was Ed's. Digger wouldn't admit to it, but I believe he came here to get his hands on it."

Judd muttered something under his breath. "If that's true, he's more dangerous than I'd thought. Does Digger know you suspect him?"

"Yes. I told him to his face. And I told him I was going to tell the sheriff. It might have been unwise, but I wanted him to stop tormenting me. He denied everything except knowing Ed. I had him dead to rights there."

"Then what did he do? Did he threaten you or your family?"

"Not then. When Skip came out of the house, he disappeared. Is his bike in the shed now?"

"It wasn't when I came home. Let me check the bunkhouse. If he's gone, he could be anywhere. Lock your doors and call the sheriff. Call him now, Ruth. Promise me you'll do it. Have you got a gun?"

"No. Ed had one, but it was seized when he was arrested. Digger's no saint, but I can't believe he would harm me or my children. He just wants to intimidate me."

"I hope you're right, but you can't be too careful. Call the sheriff and tell him what you told me. I'm going outside to check the bunkhouse. I'll get back to you."

Judd ended the call and went outside. The bike was still missing, but when he opened the door of the bunkhouse, he saw the backpack on the rumpled bed, with clothes and gear scattered around the messy room. It appeared, at least, that Digger would be back.

Then what?

Returning to the house, he checked on Abner, who was still asleep, then phoned Ruth and told her what he'd found.

"Did you call the sheriff?" he asked.

"I did. No surprises. The sheriff said that Digger usually hangs out at Rowdy's Roost. He'll send a deputy to pick him up and bring him in for questioning, but without proof that Digger's broken the law, he can't be arrested."

"And Digger will deny even knowing about the cocaine," Judd said. "You're right. No surprises there. What will the sheriff be doing to protect your family?"

"He said he'd warn Digger to leave me alone. But he doesn't have the manpower to post a guard at my house. I told him that was fine.

Hanging around our house would only get Digger in more trouble."

"If you're worried, you're welcome to come to my place," Judd offered. "I'd get you, but I shouldn't leave Abner alone."

"Stop worrying, Judd. We'll be fine," she said. "What about Digger? What will you do if he comes back? Will you throw him out?"

"I've thought about it. But as things stand now, the safest place for Digger is right here where I can keep an eye on him. If I turn him loose, he could be knocking on your door next."

"I understand," she said. "But one thing doesn't make sense. If Digger was after the stash in my wagon, and he didn't get it, why doesn't he just leave town? What's he waiting for?"

"That's a good question." Judd paused, thinking. "What if there's more than one stash—and Ed is making him earn it?"

"Earn it how?"

"The answer to that question might have something to do with you."

"You mean Digger could be spying on me? That sounds so creepy—not that a spy would have much to report. My life is pretty boring."

"Maybe to you. But not to Ed. I could be wrong, but for now, it doesn't hurt to be careful."

She sighed. "I'm not worried about myself. All I want is for my children to be safe."

"They will be safe. I'll make sure of it. I promise on my life."

"Let's hope it doesn't come to that." Judd could feel the emotion in the ragged breath she took. "We'll be in school tomorrow. I suppose the boys will be coming to work on the harness. I may come by after work to see Abner. Let me know how he's doing."

"I'll do that. Be careful." *I love you, Ruth*. He almost said it. But he stopped himself in time. In the next instant, she'd ended the call.

Two nights later, Digger stood in the darkness of the phone booth clutching a handful of quarters. He was still trying to decide what to tell Ed and how much to keep to himself.

He could skip the account of being hauled out of Rowdy's Roost by the deputy and grilled by the sheriff, even though he was proud of the way he'd handled it. True, he couldn't deny that he'd been Ed's cellmate. But there was no evidence to prove he'd been in touch with Ed and none to connect him with the cocaine found in Ruth's wagon. He'd lied through his teeth, and the lawman had had no choice except to let him go.

And he wouldn't bother to tell Ed how Judd had raked him over the coals when he got home. Judd's suspicions about Ed and the drug stash had hit close to home. But again, there was no proof. All that Judd had gained was the promise to leave Ruth and her family alone—a promise that Digger could break anytime he chose.

Deny, deny, deny. It was becoming Digger's favorite word.

He dropped the first quarter into the phone slot. This time he had plenty of dirt on the relationship between Judd and Ruth. He could only hope it was enough to buy him the location of Ed's second cocaine stash.

"This better be good," Ed grumbled when he came on the line.

"It's damned good," Digger said. "There's for sure something going on between those two. Ruth's boy is spending a lot of time over there. And the other day she delivered some food in one of those Crock-Pots. The boy carried it inside. He had a key to the house. It looks like Ruthie might be getting ready to move her family in there. You know what that means. She and Judd will be shackin' up."

Ed mouthed a string of profanity. "You freakin' idiot! You said you had something good. Instead, you tell me something that makes me feel like crap. Let me tell you what good is. It's blood. It's fire. It's something you've done to make Judd Rankin pay for stealin' my family. That's what good is. And you're not gettin' my stash until you can tell me it's done."

Ed slammed down the phone so hard that the sound stung Digger's ear. Pocketing the rest of the quarters, he climbed on the Yamaha and headed back to the ranch in a black mood. He should have known that Ed wouldn't settle for anything but revenge. But how to give him what he wanted—that was the question.

Judd had saved his life years ago. That was water under the bridge now. But killing his former friend would land him on death row. Assault would leave a live witness, as would kidnapping.

Property damage made more sense—easier to carry out, less chance of getting caught, and less of a penalty if he did run afoul of the law. Not that he planned to. All Digger really wanted to do was to sell the stash, hit the road, and be free.

He needed a foolproof plan—one that would damage Judd and impress Ed. That was going to take some thinking.

Chapter Twelve

After the chaos of Abner's accident and Digger's veiled threats, Judd had been braced for more of the same. But the week that followed had been surprisingly calm.

The three youngsters had come after school every weekday to work on the harness. They were making good progress with high hopes of finishing in time for the parade. When Maggie had completed the first string of bells, she'd draped the narrow strap over her shoulders and pranced around the room like a pony, jingling all the way while Judd and the boys applauded.

When Judd had agreed to let the kids work in his shop, he hadn't expected to enjoy having them there. But now he wasn't looking forward to the day when the harness would be finished and the parade over. He could only hope Ruth had changed her mind about his ending the relationship with her and their son. He was coming to realize how empty his life would be without them.

Abner, too, was on the mend. Skip had stepped in to help the old man with extra sessions of physical therapy while he was at the ranch. Abner, though still on pain medication, was getting around with his cane now, instead of the walker. He was looking forward to going home on the weekend and to getting his dog back. Whether he'd be up to playing Santa was still a question.

Even Digger was a surprise. He'd told Judd that he had a temporary job washing dishes and sweeping up at Rowdy's Roost while the regular man recovered from a broken wrist. He'd claimed that he was looking for a better job and a place of his own to live. All good—except that Judd knew better than to trust his former friend. Digger appeared to be working regular hours and keeping his distance from Ruth. But even that wasn't like him. The certainty that something wasn't right kept Judd on edge.

But there had also been good times—like Thursday night when Ruth had come by to pick up Skip and Maggie. She'd brought a pan of lasagna, fresh bakery bread, and some chocolate chip cookies that the girls had helped her make. Ruth, Abner, Judd, and the children had shared dinner on paper plates and eaten every delicious bite. The meal had felt like a big, happy family party—a glimpse of what Judd's bad choices had cost him.

Today was Saturday, and Abner was ready to go home. Judd would be driving him the short distance in his old Pontiac Firebird. Ruth and her girls would be waiting there with lunch and his beloved dog.

Skip and his friends would spend the day working on the harness. Then Skip planned to stay with Abner to help him manage his first night and morning back home.

Judd was proud beyond words of the way Skip handled responsibility—helping his mother, watching over his sisters, and stepping in wherever he was needed. It pained Judd that he couldn't speak of his pride. But at least Ruth had given him the pleasure of seeing what a fine young man his son had become—even though he could take no credit for it.

Maybe someday . . . But that wish could turn out to be a step on the road to heartache.

Now as he backed the car away from the house, with Abner in the passenger seat, he glanced toward the shed and noticed that Digger's bike was gone. Digger had been spending a lot of time away lately, presumably at Rowdy's Roost. And he seemed to have plenty of spending money. Judd hoped he was earning it with honest work. But demanding proof would only borrow trouble.

The distance to Abner's house was less than a mile. They were there in a few minutes. As they stopped next to the porch and Judd opened the door for Abner, a furry brown shape, the size of a half-grown bear, flew out the front door.

Squirming and wagging with joy, the dog hurled himself at his master.

"Butch, you old rascal!" Abner laughed as the dog licked his face. "Did you miss me? Hey, I missed you, too!"

Tammy and Janeen had come out onto the porch. They were giggling and bouncing with excitement. "Welcome home, Abner!" they shouted.

"Let's get you inside. The wind is chilly out here." Keeping the dog at bay, Judd helped Abner out of the car and steadied him going up the steps. The little girls and the dog followed him through the door.

As they came inside, Ruth stepped out of the kitchen. She was wearing a denim apron over her jeans and red sweater. Her face was flushed from the heat of the stove. She looked like an angel, Judd thought. "Welcome home, Abner," she said. "Sit down and rest. We'll be eating in a few minutes."

"What's cooking?" Abner asked. "If it tastes as good as it smells, I'll be in heaven."

"Baked chicken and scalloped potatoes— your favorite. Along with hot rolls and a salad. Judd, we've set a place for you. Please stay and eat with us."

For an instant, Judd was tempted. The food smelled wonderful, and he'd only had coffee for breakfast. But today, sitting at the table with Ruth, devouring her with his eyes, would only heighten the frustration of wanting her.

"Thanks for the invitation, but I need to get home," he said. "I've got work to do, and I want to be there for the kids."

As he spoke, he remembered the night when he hadn't been there for her. Was she remembering it, too?

Before his mood darkened further, it was time to leave.

"Thanks for everything, Judd," Abner said. "You've been a lifesaver."

"Not just me. Everybody helped. We all care about you and want you to get well."

"I'll do my best," Abner said. "Now, Ruth, how soon will that chicken be ready?"

A dry, stinging wind had sprung up, chilling Judd through his jacket as he walked out to the car and drove home. Maybe Ruth had the right idea. If she couldn't forgive him for that night sixteen years ago, it might be better to part company after the parade. Wanting what he couldn't have was getting harder every day.

As Ruth checked the oven, she heard Judd's car start up and drive away. She sighed, feeling a jab of disappointment. She'd been hoping he'd stay for the meal, at least. Despite her resentment, there was something about Judd's presence that made her feel warm and safe. It was almost as if having him at her table filled the empty place in her family. She had to forcibly remind herself what his selfish behavior had done to her life.

She knew that Judd wanted to start over. But how could she? How could she force her children into a new family after the last one had turned out to be a nightmare? Skip would be fine. But what about the girls? And what if things didn't work out? Maybe she could love again. But could she trust again?

"That chicken smells mighty good, Ruth." Abner had taken his seat at the table. "Isn't it about done?"

Ruth gave him a smile as she slid the pan out of the oven. "I believe it is. Girls, stop playing with the dog and go wash up. It's time for our welcome home feast."

Digger slipped a two-liter soda bottle, filled with kerosene, out of the left pannier on his bike. The moon was dark, the wind was gusty and, at this late hour, Judd Rankin's workshop was empty. Tonight was as good as conditions were going to get.

It had been generous of Angelo, the dealer who hung out at Rowdy's Roost, to give him a little weed to sell for a 50-50 share of the profits. It was enough to buy a few essentials like beer, clothes, and food. But selling drugs, even weed, was dangerous for a parolee. Getting caught just once would land him back behind bars.

What Digger really needed was to get his hands on Ed's cocaine stash, sell it to Angelo, and head for the border. But Ed was demanding a high price—a devastating act of revenge against the man he saw as his romantic rival. Digger had thought long and hard before coming up with a plan. Now he was about to carry it out.

From a cautious distance, he'd watched the old man leave for home in Judd's car. He'd seen Judd return alone and go back to the workshop, where Ruth's son and the other two brats were working on the harness for the parade. Several hours later, the kids left, too.

The lights in the high windows of the workshop stayed on until well after midnight. Then they went off as Judd left through the breezeway, locking the door behind him. Moments later, the lights came on in the house. They stayed on for about twenty minutes; then the windows went dark.

Still, Digger kept his distance, his bike silent. He mustn't make a move until he was sure that Judd was asleep.

His plan was a simple one. The exterior walls of the workshop were made of wood. Splashed with kerosene and ignited with a flame from his lighter, the building would go up like a torch. Saddles, tools and machines, valuable tanned hides, and even the harness the kids had worked on so long and hard would be nothing but ashes and charred, twisted leather. Judd would be devastated—and out of business for months, if not for good. And if the house were to catch fire, he would be homeless, as well. If that outcome didn't satisfy Ed, nothing would.

The house had been dark for half an hour. Judd might still be awake, but Digger's nerves were jumping with impatience. Creeping to within a dozen yards of the house, he picked up a small pebble and tossed it at the bedroom window. It struck with a click, loud enough for Judd to hear if he was awake, but too faint to wake him if he was asleep.

Shrinking back into the deep shadows, Digger held his breath, counting the seconds as he waited. No light. No sign of movement. Nothing. The coast was clear.

His pulse was a pounding hammer in his ears. Digger had broken the law more times than he could count—mostly possession, dealing, and petty theft. But he'd never done anything like this.

Too bad he couldn't stay around and watch the spectacle. His bike was parked at a safe distance, the pop and roar of its engine out of Judd's hearing. As soon as the flames caught, Digger would be sprinting across the open fields to the machine that would carry him away. He would show up at the Roost, where he would claim to have been asleep in the storeroom. Plenty of people, including Angelo and his girlfriend, would be willing to give him a solid alibi.

A cold gust blasted his face with grit as he crept closer to the workshop. The wind would spread the fire quickly. But it could also blow out the flame. He would need to stay close long enough to make sure the wood was burning.

A dozen yards, perhaps, separated him from

his target. Hands shaking, he unscrewed the lid of the soda bottle. Should he deliver the kerosene at a run, splashing it the length of the building before using his lighter? Or should he soak one spot, making sure the wood was saturated enough to burn hot and spread? Never mind, he'd figure it out.

Clasping the open bottle in one hand, he charged. He was just a few paces from the wall when the security lights flashed on, blinding him. A roof-mounted siren screamed an alarm into the night.

Cursing God and all His angels, Digger dropped the bottle and fled to the cluster of outbuildings that lay northeast of the house. Behind the hay shed, hidden from view, he paused to catch his breath and ease his burning lungs.

He could no longer hear the siren, but the security lights were still on. Taking a quick look around the side of the shed, he could see Judd with a rifle, peering at the ground. Now he'd found the bottle, which was probably covered with telltale fingerprints. There would be tracks, too, leading right to Digger's hiding place. Time to go.

Keeping to the shadows, he ducked low and headed for the field where tall weeds grew along the ditch banks. On the far side was the spot where he'd left his bike. Crawling much of the way, he reached it, climbed onto the seat, and started the engine. If Judd was following the tracks, he would probably hear the sound and recognize it. But that no longer mattered.

The prints on the bottle would be proof enough that he was here.

He hadn't committed an actual crime, but Judd would never let him on the property again. His pack was still in the bunkhouse. He couldn't go back for it now. But Angelo would probably give him a place to sleep for a couple of nights. By then, with luck, he would have the money from Ed's stash, and his troubles would be over.

But what was he going to tell Ed?

With the cold wind blasting his face, Digger drove the back roads, winding among fields and farms as he struggled to come up with a new plan. The guard who brought Ed to the phone wouldn't be working until tomorrow night. Ed would be expecting the call. But when he asked whether his revenge on Judd had been carried out, there was only one way Digger could get what he so desperately wanted.

He would have to lie.

On Sunday the children would be home with their families. Judd, who hadn't slept since the security alarm went off, was up, dressed, and fueled with coffee before first light. He planned to spend the day working on the two remaining saddles—the presentation model and the competition order. They both needed enough work to keep him busy until Christmas, and he couldn't afford to ship them late. Overdue orders made for unhappy clients, which would hurt his reputation and his business.

Digger was gone. Judd had taken time to check the bunkhouse. The pack lay on the unmade bed, with dirty dishes piled in the sink and smelly clothes scattered on the floor. But no Digger. And after the stunt he'd tried to pull last night, Judd knew he wouldn't be back. Good riddance.

Next week, he would pay one of the hired cowboys to clean up the mess. For now, all he had time for was to lock the door and leave.

Between the familiar boot tracks and the sound of the departing Yamaha, Judd had no doubt that Digger had been his late-night visitor. And the kerosene had made his intent clear. He'd considered calling the sheriff. But that would only take time. For now, he had bagged the soda bottle and cap to save the prints and put them aside.

At least he should call Ruth. If Digger was on the run, she needed to know for her own safety. But it was early yet. He'd give her a little more time to wake up—and give himself more time to anticipate the sound of her voice.

The security system installed on the shop had kept Digger from committing a crime. Judd had told himself to forget the incident and focus on his work. But one question continued to gnaw at him. *Why?*

After he'd given Digger a place to stay, why would the ungrateful bastard try to burn his workshop and everything in it? What did he have to gain?

Forget it. He shoved the question aside. Maybe

he would never know the answer. He could only be grateful that the man he had saved—at the price of his freedom—was gone.

Digger knew better than to use the pay phone at the convenience store. If Judd had reported him, the law could be watching that place. Instead, he'd ridden his bike to a restaurant, twenty miles north of town, on the road to Cottonwood Springs. The phone there was on the side of the building, out of sight from the road.

Even at this late hour, on a Sunday night, the parking lot was crowded. Digger parked the bike next to a van, fished the quarters out of his pocket, and shut himself inside the phone booth.

Tonight, Ed was waiting for his call. "It's about time," he grumbled. "This had better be good news."

A bead of nervous sweat trickled down Digger's spine as he cleared his throat. "The news is the best. I finally got Judd Rankin for you. Got him good."

He paused, licking his dry lips. He could sense Ed's impatience on the other end of the phone. "So, tell me about it," Ed demanded. "Don't make me stand here all night. What did you do?"

"I torched his damned workshop, that's what I did. Burned it to the ground. Splashed the walls with kerosene and used my lighter to start the blaze. By the time Rankin made it outside, the place was an inferno. Saddles, hides, tools, even that fool harness the kids were working on. Everything's gone."

"Fine. What about the house?" Ed asked.

"The firemen showed up in time to save most of it. But Judd Rankin's business is gone. You should've been there to see it, Ed. The flames shootin' up, and Rankin cursing and crying. It would've done you good."

"And where were you all this time? Seems to me you wouldn't have stuck around to watch."

Digger's heart dropped. Had he given himself away?

He scrambled for a reply. "Oh, I lit out, all right. But I stopped in that field and hid in the ditch long enough to make sure I'd done the job. Then I got on my bike, hit the back roads, and hightailed it to Rowdy's. Angelo said he'd cover for me if the law showed up. But nobody did." He took a deep breath. "So how about keeping your promise and telling me where that stash is? I'd say I've earned it."

There was silence on the other end of the line. Was Ed going to come up with another demand?

"I can't keep doing this forever, Ed. Either you play fair with me, or I'm gone." Digger was bluffing, of course. The truth was, he was desperate. His whole future depended on finding and selling that cocaine.

The silence dragged as Digger shifted uneasily in the booth. Someone was waiting outside for him to finish the call. He turned his back and dropped three more quarters into the phone slot.

"All right, I'll tell you," Ed said. "But this is the only stash left. If somebody beats you to it, you're out of luck."

Digger held his breath and waited.

"There's this old man. He used to be my neighbor," Ed said. "Abner Jenkins—lives in that old farmhouse on the east road."

"I know the place."

"He's got an old barn on the property—doesn't use it except for storage. There's some hay bales piled at one end. Probably been there for years. The stash is stuck low, between two bales, almost all the way to the back. Let me know when you've found it. Got it?"

"Got it!" Digger's pulse was bucking like a rodeo bronc. He was about to hang up when Ed spoke again.

"One more thing, Digger. You'd better not be lying to me. If you are, I've got connections on the outside. I'll find a way to make you curse the day you were born."

The call ended with a click as Ed hung up the phone.

Do it now, Digger told himself as he climbed onto the bike, fired it up, and headed back toward Branding Iron. He knew the old man, knew where he lived, and knew the layout of his property. The sooner he got his hands on that stash, the better.

It was a shame that Ed hadn't given him the location before now. A few days earlier, Abner Jenkins had been staying with Judd. It would've been a piece of cake to stroll into the barn, find the stash, and make a safe getaway. But now Abner was home. Getting the cocaine would be more of a challenge, but it could still be done. He would just have to be careful.

With the wind chill numbing his face, he by-passed Branding Iron and took the road to the ranch country south of town. Finding the way to Abner's farm was easy enough, even in the dark. Outside the rickety wooden gate, he turned off the headlamp and cut the engine. The house was dark, but he didn't want any light or noise to wake the old man. Farmers had guns, and he had no doubt that Abner knew how to shoot. Digger's success depended on getting into the barn, finding the stash, and getting out quietly. With luck, the old man would never even know he'd been here.

Leaving the bike outside for a quick getaway, he turned on the pocket flashlight he carried and moved cautiously toward the barn. The memory of blinding lights and a screaming siren was still raw in his mind. An aging farmer wouldn't likely have a high-tech security system, but Digger had learned his lesson. Be prepared.

Keeping to the shadows, he used the flash-light to locate the side door of the barn. If it was unlocked, he'd have it made.

He was edging closer when a sudden sound chilled his blood. It was the deep, fierce barking of what he judged to be a large dog.

An instant later, the beast came barreling around the far side of the barn—a bear-sized bundle of shaggy fur and snapping jaws. As Digger broke into a sprint, a light came on in the farmhouse. A big man stood outlined in the open doorway, a shotgun braced against his shoulder. "Stop, you varmint!" he shouted. "Stop, or I'll fill your carcass full of lead!"

The blast went over Digger's head—probably a deliberate miss. Digger didn't stop. Straddling the bike, he gunned the engine and sped down the road, leaving the dog at the gate.

Damn! Damn! Damn! Why couldn't Ed have let him know sooner? Now, even at night, the dog and the man would be on alert. And next time, the old farmer might lower his aim.

If he wanted to get the stash without being seen, he would have to show up when nobody was home. He'd seen the posters and overheard enough talk to know that his best chance would be during the parade, when Abner was playing Santa. With the whole town turning out to celebrate, the neighbors would be gone as well. There would be no one to see him coming and going or hear the sound of the bike.

The dog might be a problem. If the beast wasn't locked up, he could bring some choice leftovers from Rowdy's, maybe laced with barbituates. As a last resort, he could bring a gun and shoot the thing. Digger didn't like dogs any more than they liked him. But a dead or wounded dog would be a sign that somebody had been here. That could put the law on his trail.

The parade would be on Saturday. That meant six more days of hiding and waiting before he could make his move. Six days—each one a slice of eternity.

Ruth wheeled the floor polisher into the utility closet and locked the door. It was almost five, and the children had long since left the building, laughing and chattering, skipping and racing their way outside. The building was quiet.

Today had been the last Monday of school before the holiday. The students would be supercharged all week. Some of the teachers complained. But Ruth enjoyed the high energy and happy excitement. Sometimes she was even caught up in it herself.

Grateful to be finished with the day's work, she was headed for the faculty room to pick up her girls when she heard an unsettling sound. It was running water, coming from the boys' lavatory. Had she forgotten to turn off a tap when she cleaned the room, or had something sprung a leak?

Pausing, she opened the door and stepped into the room. A fourth-grade boy stood at a low basin, splashing water on his tear-splotched face. His startled blue eyes gazed up at her, as if he knew he'd been caught doing something wrong.

Ruth recognized him at once—the scruffy

blond hair, the ill-fitting plaid coat. "Hello, Robert," she said. "What are you doing here? Why haven't you gone home?"

He dabbed at his eyes with a paper towel, but the tears kept flowing. "I'm sorry, Mrs. McCoy. Please don't get me in trouble. I'll go now."

"You're not in trouble, Robert." Ruth dropped to a crouch, putting her face on a level with his. "But I can see that something's wrong. Do you want to tell me about it?"

"You won't care. Nobody does."

"Try me. Come on," she coaxed gently.

"The fifth-grade boys were teasing me. They said my coat was a girl's coat. They said maybe I ought to wear a dress, too. I tried to hit one of them, but he pushed me down, and they all laughed. I didn't want them to get me on the way home."

"I'm sorry, Robert. Kids can be jerks."

"Mom promised that me and my little brothers could get new coats for Christmas. But she lost her job at the Laundromat. Somebody stole some money. It wasn't her, but she got blamed. Now we won't have any Christmas at all. I told her maybe we'd have another miracle, like we did at Thanksgiving. But she said that miracles only happen once."

"What kind of miracle was it?" *No, it couldn't be. Could it?*

"Mom came home from working the night shift, and she had all this food for Thanksgiving dinner. A big turkey and everything in Shop Mart bags. I asked her where she got it, and she just said it was a miracle."

"Oh, Robert." Ruth blinked away tears as she thought of the desperate young mother, flinging a rock through the rear window of the station wagon. One miracle wouldn't be enough for this little family. They were going to need more.

Chapter Thirteen

R uth had offered Robert a ride, but the boy had insisted that his house wasn't far, and he could walk. Ruth had let him go, but she'd thought about him while driving home with her girls. After her own hard times, she understood the desperate love of a mother who would steal to put food on the table. This little family needed help.

Maybe she couldn't give them a future. But a Christmas miracle would dry a little boy's tears. At least, she could give them that.

After supper, she called her friend Jess, who worked as the youth counselor for the school district. If anybody knew about the family, it would be Jess.

"Yes, I know the boy you mean," Jess responded to Ruth's story. "Robert LaBute. He breaks my heart, but I can only do so much. I've tried to make appointments with the mother, but she won't come in for a conference. I'm guessing she's either ashamed or scared that somebody will try to take her kids. But I'm not Social Services. Unless she asks for help, my hands are tied."

"Well, mine aren't," Ruth said. "I'd like to do something for them. What can you tell me about the family?"

"I'll tell you everything I know. The mother is Marie LaBute. Her husband left her two years ago. She has Robert and three-year-old twin boys. They live in that run-down trailer park on the east side. Space number seventeen. I remember driving by it."

"Yes, I know the place." Ruth sighed. No wonder Robert hadn't wanted her to drive him home—even though the day had been cold and the distance long for a young boy.

"The family gets welfare, but it's barely enough to live on. The mother's tried to get more by working, even though Robert has to tend the twins while she's gone."

Ruth thought of the times she'd been forced to leave Skip alone or watching the girls while she worked. She understood the worry and the guilt. And now, according to Robert, his mother had just lost her job. Maybe she really had stolen the missing money. If so, Ruth could hardly blame her.

"That's all I can tell you," Jess said. "Knowing you, Ruth, I can imagine how you'd sympathize with this family. But you can only do so much. Guard your heart. Don't get too involved, or you might end up sorry."

"Thanks, Jess. I'll remember your wise advice."

And it was wise, Ruth told herself as the call ended. The best way to help Marie LaBute and her boys would be to do it anonymously. That way Marie couldn't refuse what was offered, and she couldn't feel obligated to the giver.

Skip and the girls would enjoy helping the family. And she could afford to be generous. Tomorrow after school, she'd be meeting with the Realtor to finalize the sale of her property to Judd. Most of the money would be set aside for a house, but she could spare enough to give a poor family a happy Christmas.

The next day, Ruth dropped her daughters off at Abner's while she went to sign the paperwork at the Realtor's office. Since she was the seller, the process didn't take long. Judd had already been there to sign his documents and the check. All that remained for her was to sign the quitclaim deed and take the check to the bank.

The plan was to deposit the check in the special account she'd opened, take enough cash for Christmas, pick up the girls, and go shopping for the LaBute family. They would buy coats, hats, socks, and gloves for the boys. Then Ruth would drive the girls back to Abner's to pick up Skip. Sometime after supper, when it was dark enough, they would deliver their early Christmas surprise.

Depositing Judd's generous check left her almost lightheaded. She had never seen, let alone possessed, so much money in her life. But she no longer owned the land that had been in her family for three generations. The money would be gone in time. The land, now Judd's, would remain.

Twenty minutes later, she was picking up the girls. She had told them about the Christmas plan for Robert's family. They knew the boy, and they were excited about playing secret Santa.

Shop Mart had everything they needed. The girls helped choose the styles and colors. Despite the long lines, they were finished in an hour and headed back to Abner's.

As Ruth drove in the gate, she saw Judd's black truck parked in front of the house. She pulled up next to it, let the girls out, and went inside.

The house was cozily warm. Skip was on the couch watching a sportscast on TV. The dog lolled in front of the fireplace. Judd and Abner sat at the kitchen table drinking coffee and talking. But something wasn't right. Ruth recognized the worried expression on Judd's face.

"I take it you cashed the check," he said.

"It's in the bank. But I know that look, Judd. What's going on?"

"You can still read me," Judd said, repeating her words. "Sit down. I'll pour you some coffee."

Taking a seat on the edge of a chair, she shook her head. "Thanks, but I won't be staying long. Just tell me what's going on."

Judd glanced around to make sure the children weren't hanging on his words. "Abner had a visitor in the night. I think it might've been our friend. Tell her what happened, Abner."

"Somebody was sneakin' around the barn," Abner said. "The dog spooked him, and he high-tailed it for the gate. I yelled and fired a blast over his head, but he didn't stop. The next thing I heard was a motorbike starting up and taking off down the road. I know bikes. It wasn't a Harley."

"What would he want in your old barn?" Ruth asked. "There's nothing in there but the Santa sleigh, some old, rusty tools, and a stack of hay."

"I wondered the same thing," Abner said. "Whatever it was, he didn't get it."

"You know that he paid me a visit the other night," Judd said. "Since I found the kerosene bottle he dropped, I'm guessing he meant to set the shop on fire. That alarm system was worth every cent I paid for it. But we're worried about you, Ruth. What if you're next?"

"What do I have that he'd want?"

"What does a terrorist want? To scare you? To control you? Take this seriously, Ruth," Judd said. "I've got a pistol in my truck. I want you to take it and keep it close. If he tries to get into your house, you have the legal right to use it."

Ruth sighed. "All right, Judd. I'll take your gun for the sake of my children. But this isn't why I came here tonight. After supper, we were going to deliver an early Christmas surprise to some people up in the trailer park. It was going to be fun, but now . . ." She shook her head.

A beat of silence passed before Judd spoke. "I could use a good time myself—and I'd be worried about you going up to that place. Let me take all of you to Buckaroo's for supper. Then I'll help you deliver your surprise."

"Yay!" The girls jumped up, cheering, before Ruth could decline the offer. Skip had switched off the remote and was on his feet. "Hey, that sounds cool! Thanks, Judd. I'm starved."

Judd pushed away from the table and stood. "Abner, I'd be glad to bring you something on my way home."

"Don't worry about me," Abner said. "I've had so many food deliveries from kind friends that, if I were to eat everything, I wouldn't be able to fit into that Santa suit."

"Does that mean you're planning to be our Santa?" Skip asked.

Abner laughed. "You're danged right I am. I might need a little help getting in and out of the sleigh, but I can't disappoint the kids. You folks go on now. Have a good time."

Ruth drove her station wagon home with Judd following. Parked in the driveway, she let her children out to climb into Judd's truck and went around to get the shopping bags. In her purse was an envelope with $100 cash in it that she planned to slip into one of the bags before the delivery.

Judd had the back of the truck open. He helped her load, giving them a moment alone.

"Are you going to tell me who these needy people are?" he asked, looking down at her.

"A poor single mom who just lost her job. I was talking with her son at school. Something he said made me realize that she was the one who broke my window and stole my groceries. Can you imagine the desperation it would take to do that? Don't say anything to my children. They don't know."

He nodded. Then his gazed softened. "I love you, Ruth," he said.

The words caught her off guard. Her pulse lurched. "Don't, Judd—"

"Fine. Let's go." He turned away, leaving Ruth to ponder what she'd just done to him. Would she ever hear those three precious, frightening words again? In time, she might be ready. But Judd was a proud man. She might have just thrown away her last chance.

Buckaroo's was busy at this hour, but the round corner booth was free. Judd seated everyone, making sure that Ruth would not be looking directly at him. Once again, he had made a fool of himself. When would he learn to keep his mouth shut?

Ruth's children were happy. For now, that was all that mattered. Buckaroo's holiday decorations had changed little since the 1960s—the string of old-fashioned lights above the counter, the goofy Christmas novelty songs played on aging speakers, and the aroma of food that was always good. At Judd's insistence, they ordered everything they wanted—burgers, fries, and shakes. While they waited for their food, they sang along with "Grandma Got Run Over by a Reindeer."

Ruth had ordered coffee and pie. When her food arrived, she nibbled at it. When Judd gave her a sidelong glance, she didn't meet his eyes. Once more he cursed himself. He needed to remember that Ruth had been brutalized in her previous marriage. She needed time to trust again—but what if she never did?

They finished their meal and left with the children in high spirits. Now all that remained was to deliver the surprise. Ruth gave directions from the back seat, where she kept a firm hold on her daughters. Skip, who would deliver the bags, sat in front on the passenger side.

The trailer park lay along an unpaved street at the eastern edge of town. The lot was weedy, the trailers more of the size for camping than for living. The cars parked next to them were beaters, some with their hoods raised. The place was a hangout for transients and addicts. It definitely didn't look safe.

"There it is, number 17, with the lights on."

Judd parked on the far side of the road. Skip climbed out of the truck. "Wait!" Ruth passed the envelope of cash to him. "This goes in one of the bags."

Judd had gotten out, too. The newly risen

moon was bright enough to see him in the side mirror as he took the envelope from Skip, pulled several bills out of his wallet, slipped them into the envelope with Ruth's money, and sealed the flap.

"Don't tell your mother." With the window down, Ruth could make out the words as he gave the envelope back to Skip. The two of them took the shopping bags, walked across the street to the small yellow trailer, and laid them on the concrete stoop. After Skip knocked on the door, they melted into the shadows and waited.

The metal door opened. Robert stood in the rectangle of light. "Mama!" he shouted. "Something's here! Maybe it's our miracle!"

The woman who appeared beside him was slightly overweight with stringy, dark hair. She was dressed in ragged jeans and a baggy, faded sweatshirt. "Here, out of the way. I'll get those." She swept the bags up in her arms and closed the door. What was happening inside the trailer now could only be imagined.

Judd drove them home and let everyone out of the truck. Skip had a key to open the door for his sisters. The night was cold. Ruth was about to follow her children into the house when Judd said, "Wait, Ruth."

He came around the truck and pressed something cold and heavy into her hand. It was a small pistol. "It's loaded," he said. "I don't have to tell you to be careful. Just keep it handy in case you need it."

Nodding, she slipped the gun into her purse.

"Let's hope I won't have any reason to touch it. Thank you for tonight, Judd. You made my children happy."

"I hope I made you happy, too," he said. "But maybe that's too much to ask. Good night, Ruth."

She swallowed the ache in her throat as she watched him walk out to his truck and drive away.

The next morning, Ruth and her family woke up to snow, tumbling out of the sky in feathery, white flakes. It was the kind of rare storm that would blanket the dry Texas landscape in soft white. But would it last until Christmas? At least it might stay on the ground for the parade.

At school, Ruth hovered by the front door, watching the students come inside. Her eyes searched the crowd for one young boy. Yes, there he was—Robert in his new coat, grinning from ear to ear. "Hi, Mrs. McCoy," he greeted her. "Look at my coat. I knew that we'd get a miracle, and we did!" He took a few steps, then paused, turning his head. "Oh—and my mom got her job back. The boss found the lost money in his desk."

She watched him hurry down the hall to his classroom. Such simple wishes, and so much joy.

She could use a miracle of her own. But she didn't know what to ask for. Maybe what she needed was already inside her, just waiting to be found.

* * *

On Thursday the harness was finished to the last buckle and bell. After high fives and Mexican Cokes all around, Skip, Trevor, and Maggie spent the rest of the afternoon oiling and rubbing the leather, including the collars and bridles, until it gleamed like new.

Judd couldn't have been prouder as the team helped him load the harness into the bed of his pickup. With the kids in the back seat, he drove over to Abner's, where it was laid out in the sleigh to wait for Saturday morning, the day of the parade.

Abner was napping, but they stayed in the chilly barn and spent another half hour polishing the brass on the sleigh and brushing the red velvet upholstery. Then he drove them back to Trevor's house, where they'd be picked up later and taken home.

From there, Judd turned the pickup around in the yard and headed back to his ranch. He had his own work to do.

By now the winter sunset had faded to hues of ash, charcoal, and glowing coals. The truck's headlights gleamed on the snowdrifts that were piled on both sides of the lane. The roadbed shone with packed snow.

The winter storm, rare for this part of Texas, had buried the land in white. The cold spell that followed had slowed the melting. With the parade two days away, snowy ground for the sleigh runners looked like a sure thing.

He should have been in high spirits. But walking into the shop, seeing the empty floor where the harness had been assembled, Judd felt a strange emptiness. Damned if he hadn't enjoyed those youngsters. Maybe he wouldn't have made such a bad father after all.

Maggie had forgotten to take her boom box. Setting it on the workbench, Judd switched it on and turned up the volume. The songs of Christmas filled the silent space as he rolled up his sleeves and went to work.

On Friday, the last day before the break, the students were to be dismissed at noon, following the musical program for the parents. The school was abuzz with Christmas excitement. Most of the teachers abandoned any hope of students learning and showed movies in class or rehearsed the musical numbers for the program.

By eleven, when the parents arrived, the children were as restless as fluttering birds. Lined up by the teachers in the hall, they marched into the lunchroom wearing paper hats they'd made in class—Santa hats, reindeer antlers, angel halos, and elf caps. The songs were performed with enthusiasm and greeted with loud applause.

The outdoor concert by the high school and middle school choirs would be held in the park that evening. Ruth was looking forward to it, even though she didn't expect Judd to be there. He'd been patient, but she couldn't blame him for walking away.

There'd been no sign of Digger during the

week. Ruth had begun to hope he'd left town for good. She'd hidden the gun on the top shelf of her bedroom closet and resolved to forget it was there. Judd had meant well, giving her the weapon. But she'd disliked guns even before Tom was killed. Now, just the sight of one stirred painful memories.

By suppertime, another storm had drifted in. This one was gentler than the last, the wind barely a whisper, the snow falling slowly, in big, airy flakes. Word was out that the concert would be held as scheduled.

Skip left right after the evening meal to walk the few blocks to the park. Ruth waited longer before dressing her girls in warm pants and sweaters under their hooded coats, then adding boots and mittens. The concert wouldn't be long, but the night would be cold, and people would be standing to listen.

By the time they arrived at the park, a crowd had gathered in front of the Christmas tree where the concert would be held. Ruth found a place near the edge and gathered her girls close to keep them warm. Her gaze swept the audience. She spotted Cooper and Jess, and several other people she recognized. But there was no sign of Judd's tall frame and battered Stetson.

But of course, he wouldn't have come. He had work to finish before Christmas. And after their last awkward parting—and her earlier demand that he end his relationship with Skip—why should he make the effort?

She had only wanted to protect her son and to protect herself. Now, if she could, she would take back all the ugly things she'd said to him. But it was too late. Her words would be branded in his memory for all time.

The students were filing onto the risers that had been set up in front of the tree, the girls on one side, the boys on the other. A murmur went through the crowd as people pointed out their sons and daughters. "Can you see Skip, Mommy?" Tammy asked.

"Yes. There he is. Back row, on the end."

"I can see him," Janeen said. "It's easy-peasy."

"I want to see him!" Tammy was stretching on tiptoe and trying to jump. "Pick me up, Mommy!"

Ruth pushed her purse strap to her shoulder, bent her knees, and wrapped her arms around her daughter. But Tammy was old enough to be heavy. That, and the bulk of their slippery, padded coats made for an awkward lift. Ruth struggled as her daughter urged, "Higher, Mommy! Higher!"

"Could you use a boost?" Judd was beside them. Ruth had no idea how long he'd been there. "How about it?" He held out his hands. Tammy reached for him, leaning away from her mother in complete trust. At Ruth's nod of consent, he placed his hands under Tammy's arms and swept her high, onto his shoulder. She giggled as he balanced her in place with one hand.

"So, do you see your brother now?" he asked.

"I can see him. Hi, Skip!" She waved at him. Skip didn't wave back.

"Down you go, okay?"

"Okay! That was fun!" She let Judd lower her to the ground.

"Lift me, too," Janeen said.

"Nope. You said that seeing your brother was easy-peasy. Besides, the program's starting. Let's be still and listen."

A hush fell over the crowd as the prerecorded piano music began the introduction to "Silent Night." Voices joined in the beloved old song. Slowly, the magic began to happen—Christmas lights blurred by falling snowflakes, the sigh of a breeze passing through snowy branches, the fresh scent of pine on the chilly air.

Ruth felt Judd's presence beside her. They stood without touching, hesitant, questioning. Could this be the beginning they'd both wanted to find?

The concert wasn't a long one. The young voices, blending beautifully, sang several more traditional Christmas songs. Ruth waited for the closing number she knew was coming—"Candlelight Carol," by the English composer John Rutter, her favorite.

As the piano introduction began, she felt goose bumps rise on the back of her neck. As the girls' voices began the first verse, she pictured the wind on the water, the stars in the sky, and candlelight shining on a baby's cradle. Her eyes misted as the boys' voices joined in the chorus. Without thinking, she reached for Judd's hand. Her fingers linked with his and felt the pressure of his big, warm palm, closing around them, holding them tight.

Even after the song ended, he held her hand, letting go only as the students broke ranks to go home.

*   *   *

Hunched on a bar stool in Rowdy's Roost, Digger downed the last of his Budweiser and ordered another. Today's appointment with the parole officer had gone fine. He had lied glibly about looking for an apartment and interviewing for jobs—claimed he would bring signed proof next time. And he'd passed the piss test like a boss.

He deserved a small celebration. But his nerves were jumping like crickets on a hot griddle. Tomorrow was the day of the Christmas parade—the day he would carry out his plan to get Ed's cocaine stash.

Earlier today he had scoped out the old man's property. Nothing much had changed, except that there were more people coming and going. Some, like Judd, he recognized. Others were strangers, probably folks involved in tomorrow's parade.

Then there was that damned monster dog, going in and out of the house, wagging its tail and slobbering on everybody who came. If the beast was so freaking friendly, why wasn't it friendly with him?

Sipping the second beer, he went over the mental list he'd made.

The parade was scheduled to start at ten. By then, everybody would be in town. The coast would be clear, but in case anybody drove by, he would hide his bike in the ditch above the road and walk down to the property. There would be plenty of tracks in the snow. One more set wouldn't be noticed.

The dog would be home, but with luck it would be locked in the house. If not, he'd bagged a hunk of leftover steak with a nice bone in it that should keep the stupid animal busy long enough for him to get what he wanted.

Digger had debated taking a gun and decided against it. If he were unlucky enough to be caught, he could be charged with armed robbery. The risk wasn't worth it—not even if he needed to protect himself from the dog. He did have a switchblade, but with luck there'd be no call to use it.

Today he'd seen people going in and out of the barn without having to lock or unlock either of the doors. Maybe there was something inside that was needed for the parade. Just as a backup, he'd carry a small crowbar on the bike. But the less evidence of forced entry he left behind, the better.

What if the stash was already gone? What if somebody had found it, or that bastard Ed had lied to him?

Never mind. He wouldn't think about that now. *Get in, get the goods, and get out.* That would be his focus.

But heaven help anybody who showed up and tried to stop him.

Chapter Fourteen

Thanks mostly to Abner's performance, Santa and his sleigh had become the highlight of the annual Christmas parade. The floats might be tacky, the music sour, the marchers out of step, and the visiting dignitaries a bore, but the Branding Iron Santa was first-rate—simply the best. To the children who waited, watched, and cheered, this Santa was absolutely real—not just because Abner was round and jolly by nature, but because the loving spirit that surrounded him like an aura wasn't an act. It was genuine.

The magic that helped Abner become Santa involved the work of a dedicated behind-the-scenes team. Everything had been carefully planned. Early on the morning of the parade, the sleigh would be mounted on a flatbed trailer and hauled by city employees to the high school athletic field, where the parade would form up. The bed of the sleigh would be padded with quilts and cushions and loaded with bags of wrapped candies for Santa to toss to the children.

The horses—powerful animals of unknown lineage—belonged to Cooper Chapman. With their shaggy coats groomed to shine like polished brass, they would be loaded into Cooper's horse trailer and hauled to the parade ground. Cooper and Judd Rankin would buckle the horses into their new harness, drape them with strings of jingling bells, and hitch them to the sleigh. Judd had agreed to drive the team in the parade.

Because of the snow, the sleigh would be taken off the flatbed to run on the packed surface of the road. The horses would wear special leather boots to protect their hooves.

Ruth and Skip had offered to help get Santa ready for the parade. They arrived at Abner's house with the girls, early enough for Ruth to make him a good breakfast of bacon, eggs, oatmeal, and coffee. While Ruth and her daughters cleaned up, Skip took Abner back to his room to help him dress.

Sitting on the edge of the bed in his underclothes, Abner winced as Skip tightened the brace that would support his back. "A little tighter," he said. "It'll hurt some now, but I need to feel solid."

"Are you sure you'll be all right?" Skip asked him. "The parade's important, but so are you."

"Now, don't go starting that," Abner said. "Get me a couple of those pain pills on the nightstand, and I'll be right as rain."

Skip twisted off the lid of the bottle, spilled two high-dose ibuprofen tablets into his hand, and gave them to Abner with a glass of water. The old man would be going through a lot to make the children happy today. At least he'd been talked out of appearing at the Cowboy Christmas Ball tonight. The children would be writing letters to Santa, which he'd promised to answer personally.

The weather was sunny but cold. Skip found Abner a warm thermal undershirt and a fleece vest for him to wear under the Santa coat. The loose-fitting trousers were held up by suspenders. Next came the socks and boots. The coat and gloves would be put on last, after Ruth had finished doing his makeup and attaching the beard, hair, and cap. Skip watched his mother work, amazed at her skill. The girls played on the rug with the dog.

By the time Abner was ready to go, it was almost nine. Ruth's face wore a thoughtful frown. "With Abner in front, the booster seats in back, and the cushions and blankets for the sleigh filling up the rear, there won't be room for you in the wagon, Skip," she said. "Would you mind if I drop Abner off at the parade and then come back for you? It shouldn't take long. We'll be back in plenty of time for the parade."

"No problem," Skip said. "I'll hang around here, straighten things up, maybe watch a little TV."

"Mom," Janeen said, "I want to stay here with Skip."

"Me, too! We can play with Butch. Please, Mommy," Tammy begged.

Ruth glanced at Skip. "Is that all right with you?"

"Sure," Skip said. "They'll be fine."

"Then let's get going, Abner. Have you got your cane?"

"Right here in my hand."

"Need any help?" Skip asked.

"We can make it." Ruth steadied Abner as they descended the steps and climbed into the station wagon. Skip watched them drive away. Then he went back to Abner's room to pick things up and make the bed. Santa would be ready for a nap by the time he got home.

Digger arrived at his hiding place in time to see the station wagon leave through the gate. Ruth was driving, and her passenger was Santa Claus.

He waited until the wagon was out of sight before he sat all the way up in the ditch to study the house and yard. No dog outside. That was a good sign. With luck, he'd be able to walk into the barn, find the hidden stash, and be on his way to a new life.

For safety's sake, he forced himself to wait a little longer. His canvas army coat was warm enough, but the snow was frigid through his jeans. His feet, in their worn-out boots, had gone numb.

Teeth chattering, he put his bare hands inside his coat to warm them. Moving too soon could ruin everything. He needed to make sure the coast was clear, and no one would be coming by on the road.

But he was freezing and getting impatient. The only vehicle in the yard was a beat-up farm truck, half-buried in snow. Clearly, nobody was down there. It was time to move.

The hunk of meat he'd brought for the dog was wrapped in plastic. As he crossed the road, he fished it out of his pocket. He needed to be ready in case that God-cursed giant mutt appeared.

So far, so good. Keeping low, he followed a set of tire tracks across the yard to the barn. His pulse leaped as he saw that one of the wide double doors in front was ajar. A brief smile tightened his lips. This was going to be a piece of cake!

Skip had finished tidying up. He'd settled onto the sofa to watch TV when the dog, who'd been lying on the rug next to the girls, jumped up and ran to the closed door. With low, whuffing barks, he pawed at the threshold.

Janeen looked up at her brother. "I've never seen him act like that. What's he doing, Skip?"

Skip shrugged. "Maybe there's a cat out there, or even a coyote. When was he last outside?"

"Mom let him out while you were helping

Abner get dressed. Maybe he needs to go out again."

Skip pushed himself off the sagging couch and walked toward the dog. "What's up, Butch?" he asked. "What are you trying to tell us?"

Butch whined urgently, then began to growl, a dark, menacing sound. Something was out there, and Butch's behavior told him that it wasn't a cat. Skip made a move to open the door, then checked himself. If a dangerous intruder was out there—animal or human—the dog could be hurt. Abner would be heartbroken if anything were to happen to his pet.

But Butch was clearly trying to warn him. An animal would eventually go away. But a person? Skip remembered the conversation he'd overheard—how Abner and the dog had scared off a prowler and how, earlier, Digger had tried to set Judd's shop on fire.

If it was Digger, what could he want? Maybe he was here to set the barn, or even the house, on fire. If Ruth came back, she could be in danger, too.

Skip couldn't just stand here and let something terrible happen. It was up to him to protect his family and to guard Abner's property.

Abner kept a shotgun in the back of his closet. Skip had never fired any kind of gun. He didn't know whether the shotgun was loaded or where to find the shells, but maybe that wouldn't matter. With luck, the sight of the big, double-barreled 12-gauge would be enough to scare off the intruder.

He found the heavy gun and brought it back

into the living room. His sisters stared at it with big, frightened eyes. "Don't be scared," he told them. "I'm just going to see what's making Butch growl. Hold on to him, and don't let him outside, understand?"

Still wide-eyed, the girls nodded.

"One more thing. When I go out, lock the door behind me. Whatever happens, don't open it unless you hear me or Mom on the other side. Okay?"

Again, they nodded.

"Good. I'm counting on you to be brave and smart." Ordering the dog to stay, Skip stepped out onto the porch and closed the door. Behind him, he heard the metallic click of the lock.

Digger had reached the barn and opened the door far enough to slip through. At first his snow-dazzled eyes could see only blackness. The air smelled of stale manure, moldering hay, and dust. Overhead, he could hear a trapped bird— or maybe a bat—fluttering against the rafters. The place was freezing cold.

Taking the flashlight out of his pocket, he switched it on. The barn looked as if it hadn't been used for anything but storage in years. Spiderwebs hung in the corners. Four blocks stood in the middle of the floor, where something had been removed—probably the Christmas sleigh. The only other large object looked like an old piece of farm machinery covered with a tarp. Rusty tools leaned against one wall.

At the far end was a ramshackle stack of bales,

the hay tumbling loose from the twine. The hay was probably riddled with mice nests, but that wouldn't matter, as long as he found what he was looking for.

By now his vision had adjusted to the dark. When he switched off the flashlight, he could see well enough to find his way. Getting to the stash would be a matter of reaching into the hay and feeling with his hands.

Ed had told him that the bag would be in the middle, close to the back. Crouching, he thrust his fingers into prickly hay and began pawing it away, onto the floor of the barn.

With the shotgun cold and heavy in his hands, Skip followed the fresh tracks to the barn. From inside, he could hear a rustling sound—like a foraging animal might make, except that the only animal tracks outside were the dog's.

Whoever was in there, they were clearly up to no good. Maybe they were piling hay to start a fire.

Did the intruder have a gun? There was no way to tell, but he had to assume the answer was yes. Storming in through the double front doors could get him shot. The safer approach would be through the smaller side door.

As he sprinted around the side of the barn, Skip forced himself to think. Even with a gun, he was too inexperienced to overcome the intruder and take him prisoner. The sensible thing would be to scare him away.

He stopped at the door, moved to one side,

and shouted, "I know you're in there, mister. I've got a shotgun, and I know how to use it. I'm giving you to the count of three to light out before I step in there and blow your head off."

Digger muttered an obscenity. He recognized that voice. It was Ruth's boy. A skinny kid like that one probably couldn't lick a rooster, but if he really had a gun, and if he meant what he said, Digger would be smart to get out of sight.

One thing was for sure. No matter what he had to do, he wasn't leaving without the cocaine.

Thinking fast, he ducked between the covered piece of machinery and the wall. The shadows were deep there. Maybe the kid would think he'd run off.

In case he was discovered and had to fight, he was going to need a weapon. His hand groped around him for anything he could use—a stick of wood, maybe a tool of some kind.

His fingers closed on a wooden handle attached to a broad, metal blade. A shovel. It was better than nothing. It would have to do.

"One . . . two . . . three!" Skip kicked open the door, silently praying that the invader would be gone.

Light poured through the open doorway. He could see hay pulled loose from the bales and scattered on the floor. Someone had been here, but they didn't appear to be here now.

He took a step inside. Everything was quiet.

He could see the concrete blocks that supported the sleigh and the old combine that was
covered and stored next to the far wall. "Hello,"
he called. "Is anybody here?"

There was no answer. He bent down to exam-
ine the scattered hay. That was when he saw the
melted snow on the floor and the wet boot
tracks—tracks going farther into the barn
rather than out the door.

That was when something hard struck the
back of his head, and the whole world went
black.

Digger picked up the boy's feet and dragged
his unconscious body to the middle of the floor.
The kid was breathing, but otherwise out like a
light. Sooner or later, he'd wake up. By then,
Digger planned to be long gone.

After closing the side door to keep from at-
tracting attention, he attacked the hay again,
digging and clawing until his fingers were raw. A
small mountain of hay dust grew beside him,
and still he hadn't found the stash. What if it
wasn't there? What if Ed had lied to him—just
as he'd lied to Ed?

He glanced back at the unconscious boy. He
wasn't moving. Maybe he shouldn't have swung
that shovel so hard. The shotgun lay a few feet
away. He could take it, Digger thought, but then
decided against it. The heavy weapon would
only slow him down.

Just as Digger's mind had begun to wander,

he felt it—something slick and sharp against his hand, like the corner of a plastic bag. He tugged on it, digging deeper when it didn't come loose on the first pull. As the bag began to move, he felt a sharp prick on the flesh of his middle finger. It hurt, but he forgot about it as the bag tumbled into his hands. He'd found it—enough coke to make him rich!

With no time to waste, he stuffed the bag under his coat and left the barn. Without closing the door or bothering to hide his tracks, he raced across the yard and out the gate to the ditch. Minutes later, on his bike, he was flying along a back road to the far end of town. His finger was beginning to throb—but never mind, he'd tend to that later. Right now, all he needed was a quick stop at Rowdy's for the cash, and he'd be on his way.

Ruth swung the station wagon through the gate and pulled up to the house. She'd delivered Abner to the parade ground in good time, but on the way out of town she'd been caught in a traffic snarl that had delayed her for a good fifteen minutes. Her children were probably getting worried.

Rushing, she climbed out of the wagon, dashed up the steps, and grabbed the knob. The door was locked.

She knocked, but the only answering sound was a faint bark. Using her key, she unlocked the door and opened it. Janeen and Tammy were huddled on the rug with the dog. Skip was nowhere to be seen.

"Mom!" They ran to her, flinging themselves against her legs.

"Where's your brother?"

"Skip went out," Janeen said. "He had Abner's big gun. He told us to lock the door."

"And he hasn't come back?" Worry slammed Ruth like a cold fist.

"No, and it's been a long time. We were scared," Tammy whimpered.

"Where—?" But there was no need for Ruth to finish the question. Butch, taking advantage of the open door, had raced outside. He was headed straight for the barn.

"Stay here! Close the door." She flung the words back at her girls as she sprinted after the dog.

Digger. It had to be Digger. If he'd harmed her boy, she would never forgive herself for leaving her children.

The dog had veered into the barn. Dizzy with fear, Ruth followed him through the wide front doors.

What she saw shattered her heart. Skip lay face down on the concrete floor of the barn. The shotgun lay a few feet away. On the other side of his body lay a rusty shovel.

Fighting back a scream, she dropped to her knees beside her son. She could see that he was breathing, but when she stroked his face, then shook his shoulder, there was no response.

Panic welled inside her. She steeled herself

against it. She couldn't fall apart now. She had to get help. Jumping to her feet, she ordered the dog to stay with him. Then she ran back to the house to call for help.

With the paramedics on the way, she turned to calm her frightened girls. "Skip's been hurt," she said. "An ambulance is coming to take him to the hospital—it will make a lot of noise, but you mustn't be scared. After I phone the sheriff's office, I'll be going back out to wait with Skip. You girls will need to be brave and stay here in the house."

Tammy had started to cry. Janeen shushed her sister. "Can we go to the hospital with Skip?" she asked.

"When the ambulance goes, we'll follow it in the car. Don't worry. I won't leave you."

"What about Butch?"

"He can stay in the house till Abner gets home."

"Mommy, is Skip going to die?" Tammy asked.

Ruth felt the words knife through her heart. "Of course not, dear," she forced herself to say. "The doctors and nurses will take good care of him. Now be still while I call the sheriff."

Hands shaking, she punched in the number. As expected, it was Helen Wilkerson who answered the phone. Struggling to stay calm, Ruth told her what had happened.

"Oh, honey!" Helen said. "The sheriff is at the parade. I'll radio him."

"Ask him to let Judd know—but to keep it from Abner till after the parade—oh, and somebody will need to take Abner home."

"I understand. Don't worry. I'll get word to the right people. You focus on your boy."

After the call, Ruth hugged her girls, pulled a quilt off one of the beds, and rushed back to the barn. She found Skip just as she'd left him, breathing but unconscious. Summoning her courage, she covered him with the quilt and lay down beside him to wait for the sound of sirens.

Judd was seated on the driver's bench, waiting for Abner to come and be helped into the sleigh, when Buck found him. "I've got some news for you, Judd," the sheriff said. "Come over by the cruiser where we can talk."

"Is something wrong?" Judd asked.

Buck nodded. "Helen just passed on a call from Ruth. Skip took a blow to the head at Abner's place. He's unconscious. Ruth is waiting for the ambulance to take him to Cottonwood Springs. She wanted you to know."

It took a few seconds for the words to sink in. When they did, they triggered a sense of urgency that bordered on panic. He glanced toward the empty driver's bench on the sleigh. Right now, all he wanted was to be with Ruth and their son.

Buck seemed to read his mind. "Do what you need to, Judd. I can drive the sleigh and have my deputy handle the crowds. Cooper and Jess can get Abner home. Just go. Be with your boy."

Your boy, he'd said.

"Buck, how long have you known that Skip was my son?" he asked.

"Hell, Judd, this is Branding Iron. Half the town knows. And when word gets out that he's in the hospital, as it will, they'll be sending up prayers. Now get going."

As Judd sprinted for his truck, he heard the wail of distant sirens. Skip and Ruth would be on their way to the hospital by the time he reached Abner's. His best bet was to head straight to Cottonwood Springs and meet them there.

Skip . . . unconscious . . . The words didn't go together. The thought that he might lose his son was almost paralyzing. He started the truck, honking his horn as he roared out of the crowded parking lot. Moments later, he was flying up the road to Cottonwood Springs.

Skip was still unresponsive when they unloaded him at the emergency entrance. That wasn't good, Ruth knew. If his injury had been no more than a slight concussion, he would have opened his eyes by now. The ER nurse shooed Ruth and her daughters through the swinging doors and into the waiting room. They sat in orange plastic chairs, the girls fidgeting, Ruth growing quietly frantic as the minutes crawled past. Just when she felt she was about to break, a tall figure strode in from the entrance.

"I got here as soon as I could," Judd said. "How is he?"

"We don't know. We're waiting to hear." She rose from her chair and walked into his arms. They held each other fiercely tight, drawing comfort from each other's strength. The girls gazed at them as if not knowing what to expect.

Judd opened the space between himself and Ruth. "Come on in, you two," he said, reaching out to them. "What we need right now is a group hug."

With the girls in the middle, the four of them all hugged together. Tears welled in Ruth's eyes. How could she have believed that Judd would never accept her daughters? He had proven her wrong again and again.

A balding man in scrubs walked through the swinging doors. "I take it you're the boy's family."

"What can you tell us?" Fear tightened cold fingers around Ruth's throat, making the words come out as a hoarse whisper.

"His vital signs are normal," the doctor said. "Aside from some bruising, there's no apparent damage to the skull. It's safe to say that he has a concussion, but we don't know how much damage there is. The main concern is that he's still unconscious. I'm going to admit him. If he's not awake by morning, I'll order a CT scan."

"Can we see him now?"

"You can be with him in his room. The nurse will tell you when he's been transferred. It'll take about forty-five minutes. There'll be some paperwork."

"Bring it to me," Ruth said. "I'll fill it out while we wait."

"I'm hungry," Tammy said. "My tummy is growling."

"I could take the girls to the cafeteria," Judd

offered. "Do you want to come, too, Ruth? There should be plenty of time."

She shook her head. "Go ahead. I'll stay here. Maybe there'll be news. Meanwhile, I can fill out the admission papers."

"I'll check back here and hope he's in his room. Come on, ladies. Let's go and find something good to eat."

She watched the three of them walk down the hall, Judd with one of her daughters on either side, holding on to his hands. To her girls, he was already family. She hoped Judd felt that way, too. But what could they make of their shattered family if Skip failed to recover? Cheerful, responsible Skip was the glue that held them all together.

The nurse brought her a clipboard with several pages of forms to fill out. Struggling to concentrate, Ruth pulled her insurance cards out of her purse and began.

She was partway through when she heard a scurrying from behind the swinging doors. Seconds later, the nurse burst through. "Mrs. McCoy, your son's awake. He's asking for you."

Heart pounding, Ruth strode after the nurse, through the doors, and down the hall, past the curtained-off partitions. "We were about to wheel him into the elevator when he opened his eyes and started talking," the nurse said. "The first thing he did was ask for you. You can have a few minutes with him here. Then you can stay with him in his room. We'll let his father know where he is."

We'll let his father know.

As the nurse's words sank in, Ruth knew it was time. She couldn't wait any longer to tell her son the truth.

"How is he?" she asked the nurse.

"Lucid. A bit confused at first, and his head hurts. That's to be expected with this kind of injury."

"But will he know me? Will he be able to understand what I say to him?"

"Find out for yourself." They turned the corner to the elevator bank. A wheeled hospital bed stood in the open space. Skip, wearing a hospital gown and a white bandage around his head, lay against the pillows. An IV was attached to the back of his hand. His eyes were open.

With a little sob, Ruth rushed to his bedside and clasped his free hand. He smiled.

"Hi, Mom," he said.

"Do you know what happened?"

"Kind of. But I don't really remember. I was in the barn. Then nothing."

"How do you feel?"

"Like crap. But they say I'll be all right."

Ruth took a deep breath. "Listen, son, there's something I need to tell you. If you choose to hate me for it, I'll understand. It's about Judd."

"He's my father, isn't he?"

Ruth's heart dropped. "How did you know?"

"It wasn't hard. When I looked in the mirror, I could almost see him looking back at me. All I had to do was check my birth date against his arrest date, and I knew. Why did you wait so long to tell me?"

A lump had risen in Ruth's throat. "I was scared—scared you'd never forgive me for lying."

He squeezed her hand. The bed began to move toward the elevator. "It's okay, Mom. You did what you thought best. We'll talk more upstairs."

Ruth watched the elevator doors close, hiding him from her sight. Only then did she break down and cry.

In the cafeteria, the girls ordered hot dogs with mac and cheese and took their time eating. By the time they'd finished, Judd was getting anxious. He was guiding them back toward the ER when they passed the gift shop. Janeen begged to go inside. "Please. Just for a few minutes, just to look."

How could he refuse? They'd missed the parade, and they'd had a frightening day that could get worse. Judd worried about Ruth and Skip while the girls looked at the toys, flowers, candy, and books. But he drew the line at buying them the teddy bears they wanted. Something told him that Ruth wouldn't approve.

They returned to the ER waiting room to find that Ruth had gone. He got Skip's room number from the nurse. "If you're going to take those children up there, you'll have to keep them quiet," she said.

Judd thanked her and hurried the girls to the

elevator. "Not a peep out of you in the hall, and only whispers in the room," he warned them. "Promise me, or you can't be with your mom and brother."

"We promise." They gripped his hands in the elevator, awed by the unaccustomed sounds and sensations. Judd felt strangely comforted by the clasp of those small, trusting hands. They quieted his own fears. What would he find when he walked into his son's room? Would Skip still be asleep—or awake and impaired? Would the doctor have more news—maybe bad news?

They walked down the hall, following the room numbers. Door number eleven was ajar. Taking a deep breath, Judd nudged it open and walked into the room.

Skip was propped up in the hospital bed. His head was wrapped in a white bandage. A saline drip was attached to his left arm. His eyes were open. He was smiling.

"Hello, Dad," he said.

Judd felt his swollen heart crack open, releasing emotion through his body. He found his voice. "When did you know?"

"Mom just told me. But I'd already figured it out. I've known for a long time. You can hug me if you want to—carefully."

Judd's eyes were wet as he embraced his son.

The girls had run to their mother. "He's not out of the woods yet," Ruth said. "He's got some pain, and he'll be having a CT scan in the morning. Based on what they see, they may be keeping him here a little longer. The doctor says he'll need a lot of rest, but he should make a full recovery."

"So, guess how I'll be spending my Christmas break?" Skip said. "Talk about rotten luck!"

He laughed. The others laughed with him. Ruth's gaze met Judd's. The love in her eyes told him they were already a family.

Epilogue

Christmas, that same year

A fresh storm, two days before Christmas, had blanketed the fields and back roads with thick snow that was perfect for sleigh riding. It was Maggie who'd come up with the idea of hitching up the sleigh again for a Christmas party. "After all that work, we deserve some fun," she'd argued. "Why use the sleigh for just the parade?"

The idea caught on with everyone who'd helped make the Santa sleigh a success. Late in the day, their friends gathered at Abner's, bringing leftover food for a potluck buffet. At twilight, the sleigh, driven by Judd, pulled up to the house. It was packed with warm quilts and cushions, the horses as splendid as ever in their new harness, draped with jingling bells.

"Who wants the first ride?" Judd called out.

"Not me," Abner said. "My back's doing better, but I got my ride as Santa. I think the three who made the harness—Skip, Trevor, and Maggie—should go first!"

Everyone clapped in agreement as Trevor and Maggie helped Skip onto the passenger bench and cushioned him in quilts before they took their places. Skip was healing, but he still needed to rest and be careful.

Judd slapped the reins on the horses, and the sleigh flew off through the snow. The back road circled around the fields and down the lane to Abner's again for a distance of about a mile—far enough on a chilly night.

Cooper and Jess went next, followed by Mayor Sam and Grace. Judd was getting cold, but it was exhilarating, flying along with the horses prancing and the bells jingling. He couldn't remember when he'd had such a good time.

Buck and Wynette had been invited, but they were at a family party. Driving the team, Judd recalled the news he'd gotten from Buck a few days ago. Digger was back behind bars. A highway patrolman had noticed his bike weaving all over the road. Assuming he was drunk, the officer had stopped him, only to discover that he was deathly ill from the bite of a spider—probably a black widow—on his finger. A bag of cocaine was stuffed inside his jacket. A stay in the hospital had saved his life before he was returned to prison for a parole violation. Charges of assault and drug trafficking were pending.

Had saving Digger's life on that long ago

night been worth the cost? That was a question
Judd would never be able to answer.

"Who else wants a ride?" he called out.

"We do!" Tammy and Janeen were dancing
up and down. "And we want to take Butch!"

Ruth, who was standing beside them, shot him
a questioning glance. "Will they be all right? I
could go instead of the dog."

"They'll be fine. I'll go slow," Judd said. "Besides, lady, I'm saving you for last."

The girls climbed into the sleigh. Ruth tucked
the quilts around them, making room for the
dog, who jumped into the middle. Judd drove
smoothly while they laughed and sang, all the
way around the road and back to the house.

"Anybody else?" Judd called as they climbed
out. "Any rerides?"

Nobody answered. It was getting cold. People
were going back into the house. Judd set the
brake, climbed down from the bench, and offered Ruth his hand. "Come sit next to me," he
said. "I'll get you a quilt."

He boosted her onto the high bench and
wrapped her in the down quilt that looked the
warmest. Everyone else had gone inside. No
one was watching as he drove out the gate, taking the horses at an easy pace. He'd come by
her house that morning, bringing little gifts for
her children. But they'd had no chance to talk
privately since Skip left the hospital.

"Did you get your saddles done?" she asked
him.

"I did. Sent the last one express mail two days

ago. I already have new orders. How about you? I don't suppose you've done any house hunting yet, have you?"

"No. There won't be much to look at until after the first of the year. Why are you asking?"

For a long moment he didn't speak. The only sound was the soft wind rippling the surface of the drifts and the gentle padding of booted hooves against packed snow.

"I'm suggesting that you wait. Something better might come along—a better deal on a house, I mean."

"My children can't wait to get into a home where they can have a dog. They'd move tomorrow if we had a place."

"Maybe you do. Not tomorrow, but as soon as you like."

"What are you talking about?" She'd turned to face him.

"I'm talking about my house." He stopped the team. "Marry me, Ruth. Years ago, we did things wrong. Now we have a chance to do things right. We can be a family this time. I love you, and I love your children—all of them. We can do this tomorrow or next summer, or whenever you like. But I never want you out of my life again." He fumbled in his coat, took out a tiny velvet box, and opened it. "I hope you're not going to make me go down on one knee," he said.

She gasped and held out her hand. He slipped the simple but beautiful ring onto her finger. "I take it that's a yes," he said.

"A yes from me, and a yes from my children. Now about that dog . . ."

"Later." He clasped her close. Their kiss went on and on.

Waiting, the horses shook the snow from their shaggy coats, filling the night air with the sound of sleighbells.

Chapter One

December 22

"**O**uch!" The hot cookie sheet slipped out of Kylie Wayne's hand and clattered to the linoleum. Tears flooded her baby blue eyes—not so much for her seared thumb as for the Christmas cookies, which were not only broken and scattered but also burned to a crisp.

"Oh, dear!" Her great-aunt Muriel bustled into the kitchen. "What happened?"

Kylie ran cold water over her thumb to ease the pain. "I smelled the cookies burning and grabbed them with that old brown oven mitt. There must've been a hole in it."

"Heavens, I'm sorry. I've been meaning to mend that hole." Great-Aunt Muriel shook her silvery head. "Those poor cookies! They were so pretty! And you worked so hard on them!"

Kylie sighed in silent agreement. She'd barely had time to unpack the car, but with Christmas less than three days off, and her two children moping like jailbirds, she'd felt the need to create some holiday spirit.

She'd found some old cookie cutters and spent the past hour mixing, rolling, and cutting the dough into Christmas bells, angels, reindeer, and stars. They'd been perfect when she'd slid them into the oven to bake. But she had yet to master the workings of Great-Aunt Muriel's sixty-year-old electric stove.

"I don't understand it," she muttered. "The recipe said fifteen minutes at three hundred seventy-five degrees. When I checked after ten minutes, they were already black and smoking."

"That old oven's always cooked hot," Aunt Muriel said. "I've gotten used to it over the years. You will, too, dearie."

"Yes, I suppose I'd better." Kylie bent to pick up the mess. The offer of a home for herself and her children, in exchange for looking after her grandfather's sister on her small Texas farm, had come as a godsend. At seventy-nine, Great-Aunt Muriel was a sweetheart—a bit absentminded, but pretty much able to do for herself. It was the rest of it—coming home to Branding Iron, Texas, after fifteen years as an army wife—that weighed Kylie down. It was as if she'd come full circle, back to the place she'd been so glad to leave behind after high school. As for her children, she hadn't seen a single smile since their loaded station wagon pulled away from their foreclosed house in San Diego.

She swept the last of the blackened crumbs into the dustpan and dumped them into the trash. "I guess there's nothing to do but start over from scratch. Maybe this time you can help me with the stove."

"The Shop Mart in town has cookies," Aunt Muriel said. "You could just buy some."

"It's not the same. The smell of fresh-baked sugar cookies, and the fun of helping ice them—that's the kind of Christmas we used to have. I want to bring some of that back for Hunter and Amy. After last year . . ."

Her voice trailed off. Last Christmas, the first after her husband Brad's death in Afghanistan, Kylie had been in no mood for celebration. It had been all she could do to toss a few decorations on an artificial tree and wrap a few last-minute gifts for her son and daughter. But this year nothing would stop them from having a *real* Christmas. She would see to it.

"I know it won't be the same without their father," she said. "But they've been through so much. Whatever it takes, I owe them a good Christmas."

"And what do you owe yourself, dear?" Muriel had a knack for asking odd questions—questions Kylie had no idea how to answer.

This time she was saved by the distant *thrum* of a motorcycle speeding down the nearby road. The sound grew closer and louder, its masculine thunder roaring in her ears as it passed the house and faded away toward town. She'd heard it late yesterday afternoon, too, right after they'd arrived here. The sound was so loud and invasive that it seemed to shake the walls of the little farmhouse.

"Good grief, that noise would wake the dead! How do you put up with it?" she asked.

Muriel smiled. "I've rather grown to like it. It makes me feel safe, knowing the cowboy's close by, looking out for me and for Henry."

Henry was Muriel's longtime hired man, who lived in a trailer out back. He appeared to be about the same age as his employer. No doubt both of them could use looking after. But a cowboy on a motorcycle struck Kylie as an unlikely guardian angel.

"I call him 'Cowboy' because I can never remember his name," Muriel said. "It's Sean or maybe Sam . . . something like that. But he says he doesn't mind answering to Cowboy."

"So he lives around here?"

"He owns the ranch to the west. Every few days, or whenever we need him, he drops by to check on us and help Henry with the heavy work. He won't take any money for it, but he never turns down an invitation to a home-cooked supper."

Kylie was already feeling protective of her great-aunt. What if this so-called cowboy was trying to charm Muriel out of her farm, or maybe her life savings?

"So when will I be meeting your cowboy?" she asked.

"Oh, he's bound to show up sometime soon. He's about your age, dear, and—oh, my stars— what a man! Tall and broad shouldered, with dark, curly hair and deep brown eyes . . ." Muriel sighed. "I can't imagine why he's not married. Goodness, if I were fifty years younger, I'd go after him myself!"

"Aunt Muriel!" Kylie was mildly shocked.

"Don't look at me like that, girl! I may be old, but I've got eyes in my head. I appreciate a handsome man as much as the next woman, even if all I can do is look. And, believe me, that cowboy is an eyeful!" Muriel tilted her head, giving Kylie a glimpse of the spritely young woman she'd once been—a woman who'd devoted half a lifetime to caring for her invalid father, passing up any chance she might've had to marry.

"Now, with you it's different," she said. "A pretty thing like you could do a lot more than look if you set your mind to it."

"Forget that." Kylie put the broom back in the corner and began gathering ingredients for a new batch of cookies. "I've got my hands full with two growing children who miss their dad. The last thing I need is a new man in my life—especially some cowboy who goes roaring by on a noisy old motorcycle."

"Well, dear, you won't be hearing that noise much longer. He puts the motorcycle away once it starts snowing—and the weatherman on TV is predicting a big storm this weekend. An honest-to-goodness blue norther!"

"What?" Kylie's gaze flew to the window with its view of dull gray skies and vast sweeps of yellow grass. This part of the high Texas plain didn't get much snow. But storms had been known to happen here—the locals called them "blue northers" because they blew in from the north, and the cold air they left in their wake could turn a body blue. Kylie remembered a few times from her girlhood when blizzards had closed roads and schools and stranded livestock in the fields. This was no time to be low on supplies, especially with children in the house and Christmas around the corner. The cookies would have to wait while she made a run to town.

Brushing a dab of flour off her blouse, she slipped on a fleece jacket and grabbed her purse off the counter. "We'll need to stock up before the storm gets here," she said. "I'll pick up the makings for Christmas dinner. Oh—and we'll be wanting a Christmas tree. Does Hank Miller still sell them in that lot next to his feedstore?"

"He does. But you might have to take leftovers. He'll be out of the nicer trees by now."

"Is there anything else you need?"

"No, dearie. Just get whatever you and the children will like. You know, it's a shame you didn't get here last week. The town had its little Christmas parade, complete with Santa in his sleigh and the high-school marching band. Abner Jenkins is still playing Santa—he's perfect for the job, doesn't even need any padding in his suit. Of course, with no snow, the sleigh had to be pulled on a trailer by those big draft horses of Abner's, but it was still a nice way to get into the holiday spirit."

The old woman turned away, then paused. "Oh, and you would have loved the Cowboy Christmas Ball last Saturday night. It's like something right out of the Old West. The men wear cowboy gear, the ladies wear long skirts.

We always have a live band, and the food . . . oh, my!" She gave Kylie a wink. "There's many a romance that started at that dance. Too bad the next one's a year away."

"I do believe I can wait." Kylie fumbled in her purse for her keys.

Muriel walked into the living room, turned on her favorite soap opera, and settled in the rocker with the gray wool sock she was knitting. The click of her needles blended with the sounds of the TV as Kylie stepped outside and closed the door.

The December air was calm but chilly. The smell and taste of coming snow awakened memories from Kylie's childhood. Her family had lived in town then, and her father had taught math at the high school. Now her parents, like Brad, were gone, lost in a tragic car accident ten years ago. She was alone with no close family except her children and her great-aunt Muriel.

Hunter and Amy had gone outside after lunch. As she rounded the house, Kylie could see them sitting on the corral fence, both of them hunched over their phones, most likely playing games or texting the friends they'd left behind in California.

Kylie waved to catch their attention. "Anybody up for a trip to town?" she called.

Hunter glanced up, shook his head, and returned to his phone. One day the boy would look a lot like his stocky, sandy-haired father. He might even have Brad's easy smile and outgoing charm. But right now, he was going through a rough time, and being thirteen didn't make it

any easier. After Brad's death, Hunter had with-
drawn into a shell. With the move from California, that shell had all but closed around him.

"How about you, Amy?" Kylie asked her
eleven-year-old daughter.

"Get real, Mom! We just spent four days from
hell in that car! Anyway, there's no place to
hang out in town, not even a mall. It's boring,
boring, boring! I hate it here!"

Amy, blond and pretty, was dealing with the
changes in her own way. She'd always been a
thoughtful, tenderhearted child. Was this onset
of brattiness an attempt to hide her feelings, or
was she just moving into her teen years a little
early?

Never mind, Kylie told herself. She needed a
break, and her children would be fine here
without her. She could see Henry over by the
barn, staying close enough to keep an eye on
them without getting in their faces. A good
man, Henry Samuels. He'd been working on
this little farm for as long as Kylie could remember. She knew she could count on him.

Only as she settled into the driver's seat and
started the station wagon did Kylie realize how
tired she was. For the past nineteen months,
since Brad's death, she'd done her best to put a
brave face on things—dealing with her own
grief and the children's, struggling to make
ends meet on her widow's benefit, looking for a
job and failing to find one, packing the station
wagon and driving two grumpy youngsters all
the way from California to Texas.

Right now, all she wanted was to crawl into a

warm, safe bed, burrow under the quilts, and then sleep around the clock. But she couldn't even think about resting—not with Christmas almost here and so much to be done.

At least she wouldn't have to shop for gifts. She'd ordered everything online from a company that guaranteed Christmas delivery. Since she'd used Muriel's address, the packages should be arriving any day now. She had sweaters, computer games, and new phones for the children, as well as a warm cashmere shawl for Muriel and new leather gloves for Henry.

The seven-mile road to town cut a straight line across flat pastureland, dotted here and there with clustered trees and buildings that marked farms or small ranches. Beef cattle, more black Anguses these days than the red-coated Herefords Kylie remembered, grazed in the fields. Aside from that, not much appeared to have changed. Driving down Main Street, on her way to Great-Aunt Muriel's, she'd noticed the new strip mall with a supermarket, a craft shop, and a chain pizza parlor. But the bones of the town—the schools, churches, and modest homes—were much the same as when she'd left for college, where she'd met Brad and married him at nineteen.

But just because she'd come home didn't mean she had to live in the past. Turning on the car radio, she fiddled with the dial until she found the only clear station, which played country-music oldies—one more thing that hadn't changed.

Hank Miller's feedstore was on the way into town. She would buy the Christmas tree first. If it wouldn't fit in the back of the station wagon, maybe Hank could tie it on the top. She'd wanted a nice, fresh bushy pine, but she would settle for whatever she could get. When she'd packed for the move, she'd boxed the precious decorations that went back to the children's babyhood, one for each year of their lives. Putting them on the tree again would make Aunt Muriel's two-story clapboard house seem more like home.

Singing along with Elvis's "Blue Christmas," she pulled up to the tree lot.

The song died in her throat.

The makeshift fence was still rigged around the tree lot. Pine needles and a few broken branches littered the ground. Aside from that, the lot was empty. A sign on one of the posts read, SOLD OUT.

Kylie struggled to ignore the dark knot in her stomach. She couldn't just give up. The tree was too important. Maybe the market would have a few. They might be more expensive, but she was desperate enough to pay any price.

Still hopeful, she pulled into the crowded Shop Mart parking lot. The place was busy this afternoon—most likely with folks stocking up for the storm or buying extra food for Christmas. Kylie drove along the rows of parked cars, SUVs, and pickups, looking for an empty spot. Every space was filled. But on her second time through, she saw a woman loading groceries into the back of a van. With impatient drivers honking behind her, Kylie waited. When the van pulled out, she swung into the parking place. So far, so good. She grabbed her purse and climbed out of the station wagon. Maybe luck would be with her this time.

But she saw no Christmas trees in front of the store. If they'd ever been here, they were gone. As a last resort, Kylie asked a clerk about boxed artificial trees. There were none. For a moment, she weighed the wisdom of driving to the next big town, sixty miles to the north. But there was no guarantee she'd find a tree there, either. And with the sky already darkening, she didn't want to be caught on the road when the storm swept in.

At least the store had plenty of provisions. Kylie found a hickory-smoked ham and some potatoes and carrots to save for Christmas dinner. She also stocked up on the children's favorite cereals and the mac-and-cheese mix they liked. They'd need all the basics—including milk, eggs, butter, sugar, juice, bread, pancake mix, syrup, and bacon, as well as tuna, mayonnaise, lettuce, and pickles for sandwiches. As an afterthought, she slipped some Christmas candy and small trinkets in with the essentials. Aunt Muriel had offered free rent, but that didn't include free groceries. Kylie would provide the food, and she planned to do most of the cooking—if she could figure out that blasted stove.

With her cart piled high, she headed for the checkout. The efficient cashier was too young to remember her. All to the good. Kylie wasn't in the mood to chat about the old days. All she wanted was to get out of here and get home. Maybe Henry or Muriel would have some idea where to get a tree.

By the time she'd loaded the back of the station wagon, a line of cars had formed behind the pickup driver who'd stopped to wait for her parking place. Horns were honking; tempers were flaring. Kylie did her best to hurry as she shut the tailgate and piled into the driver's seat. Only as she shifted into reverse and checked the side mirror did she see the problem. The pickup driver, a flustered-looking old man, had gone a few inches too far before stopping. If she backed straight out, her wagon would hit his front bumper.

With vehicles jammed in close behind him, there was no room for the old man to back up. The sensible thing would have been for him to drive ahead and give the spot to the next car. But either he hadn't thought of that or he wasn't willing to give up. He sat there with his hands on the wheel and his jaw set in a stubborn line.

The honking had risen to a clamoring din. Kylie willed herself to stay calm. Maybe if she swung the wagon's rear end hard to the right, she could back out of the parking space without hitting the truck.

Twisting the steering wheel, she eased down on the gas pedal. Hallelujah, it was working! The wagon inched backward, missing the truck's bumper by a finger's breadth. Sweating beneath her fleece jacket, she pulled out of the parking place. But she was still in trouble. Her vehicle was cross-blocking the way between two rows of parked cars. To get clear, she would need to make a sharp quarter-turn, and there was barely any room.

She steeled her nerves, checked her side mirrors and began a cautious backing-and-filling motion, working the car around in a counterclockwise direction. Some of the waiting cars had begun to honk at her, but she was almost there. One more maneuver should do it. She couldn't wait to get out of this place and back on the road.

But she should have known this wasn't her lucky day. Backing up for the last time, she felt a slight bump of resistance. Then, from behind her wagon, she heard the awful crunch of twisting, folding metal.

Kylie's stomach lurched. She hit the brake and switched off the ignition. Legs shaking, she climbed out of the car. People had turned to look, but nobody was screaming or calling for the paramedics. It couldn't be too bad, she told herself. She'd barely been moving. If she'd caused a fender bender, her insurance would pay for it.

At first, she couldn't see what she'd hit. Then, as she walked around to the back of her vehicle, there it was. Her heart dropped.

Crumpled against the rear of her station wagon was the ruined front end of a vintage Harley-Davidson motorcycle.

Don't miss Janet's newest heartwarming holiday romance, the first of the Frosted Firs Ranch novels!

EVERGREEN CHRISTMAS

Christmas is an especially exciting season in aptly named Noel, North Carolina, host of the annual 12 Competitions of Christmas, not to mention one of the largest producers of Christmas trees in the country—and it's not a bad place for a newcomer to put down roots either. . . .

Barrel racer Jordyn Banks is thrilled to discover affordable land for sale in charming Noel, perfect for breeding her horses. But that's not all. A nomad all her life, with no family—other than her beloved quarter horse, Star—she also hopes to find a home within the close-knit Appalachian Mountains community. Yet Jordyn didn't bargain on inheriting a controversial Fraser fir—or falling for a handsome single dad whose adorable little girl tempts her to dream of being far more than a property owner. . . .

Since losing his wife in childbirth six years ago, Nate Reed has devoted himself to their daughter, Roxanna, and built up their thriving Frosted Firs Ranch. For nine years straight, he's proudly won Noel's contest for the most perfect Christmas tree for the town square. It's a tradition he began with his late wife. But this year, Jordyn Banks is determined to harvest her beautiful

Fraser fir and compete—meaning Nate will finally be challenged—in more ways than one. . . .

Throughout the event, Nate can't help noticing that Roxanna is dazzled by Jordyn's strength, beauty, and quirky sense of humor. Soon enough, Nate is falling for her, too. But can a feisty wanderer ever really settle down? Is Nate ready to open his heart to someone new? And is it possible that sometimes love does grow on (Christmas) trees . . . ?

Visit our website at
KensingtonBooks.com
to sign up for our newsletters, read
more from your favorite authors, see
books by series, view reading group
guides, and more!

BOOK CLUB
BETWEEN THE CHAPTERS

Become a Part of Our
Between the Chapters Book Club
Community and Join the Conversation

Betweenthechapters.net